Maddy Malone

HEARTS OF THE OZARKS
BOOK 2

AVA MacKINNEY

Publishing Coordinator – Sharon Kizziah-Holmes
Cover Design – Jaycee DeLorenzo

Paperback-Press
an imprint of A & S Publishing
Paperback Press, LLC

ISBN -13: 978-1-960499-38-7

DEDICATION

I dedicate this book to my two sisters, Judy Citro and Aleta Burns, who, as kids, not only tolerated my wild imagination, but joined in with their own versions of whatever crazy stories we dreamed up. Our childhood on a sheep farm in the mountains of Vermont was beyond idyllic, with the freedom bestowed on us by our very patient parents, to roam the countryside and let our imaginations flourish.

And now as adults, they continue to love me, encourage me and pursue adventures with me. I am blessed beyond measure. Thank you, Judy and Aleta

ACKNOWLEDGMENTS

So many people deserve to be mentioned as encouragers and professional support as I journeyed down this path. Many friends helped me on my way as beta readers, editors, and with timely kicks in the seat of my pants when needed.

I also want to thank my publishing coordinator, Sharon Kizziah Holmes. She patiently guided me through the publishing path, answering my endless questions and giving her expert advice.

Thanks also to my two editors, Addison Williams and Nanette Sipe whose expertise has helped me craft a novel that is way better than the original.

PROLOGUE

July 1861 – Near Fair Grove, Missouri

Silas MacGregor flicked the reins over the back of his scrawny workhorse and looked back at his two tiny children hunkered down in the wagon-bed. For their sake, he choked back the grief that threatened to tear his very soul out. There was no fighting it any longer. He had to leave his children and farm behind to join the Union forces gathering in Springfield. War was no longer on the horizon. It was here. Here in their backyard.

Almost all of his neighbors under the age of forty had enrolled, some as early as May. Most were leaving their farms in the care of their parents, wives, or able-bodied young'uns. He had no one. Again, he glanced back at his two precious babies; three-year-old Ollie and one-year-old Anabel. He had tried to explain to his wee son what was coming, but how do you get a three-year-old to understand war, much less the length of time his pa would be absent from his life.

Thankfully, both kids knew and loved the Malones. Gertie and Frederick had been like grandparents to them since they had been born. And their daughter, little Maddy, had been a beloved big sister, especially since the day his precious wife Mary died. He gulped back a sob at that memory, still fresh after little more than a year. Ollie still had faint memories of his ma, but Anabel would never know her since Mary had left this world when her baby girl was only a few hours old.

He guided his horse off the dirt road and down the drive that led to the Malones' farm. Off to his right, he spotted Frederick and Gertie lifting buckets of water off their water wagon. By the looks of the small cornfield, it was in serious need of water. The farm's better days had surely been back when Frederick had three strapping sons still working alongside him. Hopefully the two milking cows and three pigs that he had brought over last week would help them through the coming months.

Frederick and Gertie waved then headed toward their house to greet him properly. He had been preparing them for this awful day.

Silas pulled up to a two-story house with a big porch. He lifted Ollie down to the ground and turned to pick up tiny Anabel. Swallowing the lump in his throat, he turned to see Maddy waiting on the porch. She was going to be a looker for sure. Long, wispy, wheat-colored hair. A faint spray of freckles across her perfectly shaped nose. Brilliant green eyes set in a delicate face. She was so thin and small-boned, he doubted she would be of much use on her parents' farm. He guessed her to be about twelve, the surprise baby of a brood of seven children; the older ones long gone, all married and settled on farms of their own.

Ollie ran up the porch steps and threw himself into Maddy's welcoming arms. With his free hand, Silas tipped his hat in greeting. No explanation was necessary. Maddy knew why he was here. Drat it! Were those tears in those eyes of hers? He didn't need her to add to his suffering.

Too brusquely, he handed Anabel over to her and said, "I'll get their things." He grabbed one small satchel that held all their belongings. Before he turned back toward the house, he gripped the side of the wagon and willed himself to get control of his mind-numbing grief. Breathing a prayer of desperation, he turned and followed Maddy and his babies into the house.

CHAPTER ONE

Three and a half years later - February 1865

Maddy Malone slumped down to the ground next to the freshly dug grave. If it weren't for Ollie and Anabel standing next to her, she would have crawled in on top of the coffin. The coffin that held her dear mother. What was she to do? She couldn't go on.

Ollie stepped closer and wrapped his spindly arms around her neck. "It's alright, Ma. I'll love you," he sobbed.

Maddy turned to him and enveloped him in her arms. "Oh, Ollie-boy! I know you will. And I'll love you and Anabel forever and ever!" She reached out and pulled the tiny five-year-old girl into the circle of her arms. The three of them stayed there for what seemed like hours wrapped up in each other's arms, giving what comfort they could before Reverend Frank Richards signaled for the grave to be filled. Maddy stood and gently pulled the two children back a few feet.

Several neighbors stood on the other side of the grave

watching the sad sight. She saw on their faces deep pity. Certainly, they were wondering how this scrawny girl and her two small charges could possibly survive the remainder of the winter. Awkwardly they approached one by one as they paid their respects and expressed condolences. Most had dropped food by the house in the days following Gertie's death.

The Woodwards, whose farm bordered Maddy's on the south, waited until all the others had left, except the reverend and the two Potter brothers. They held back and watched protectively as Sam and Nate Potter sauntered up to Maddy's side. Stella Woodward looked poignantly at her husband, Matt, just before she moved in closer so she could hear what the Potters had to say. Maddy knew that the Woodwards, like everyone else in the area, deeply distrusted the Potters, with good reason.

"So, I guess you might be struggling some, now that both yer parents are gone," Sam said quietly. "We can help, ya know."

Nate chuckled. "Yeah. We'd be happy to do whatever needs to be done around your place, missy."

Maddy tightened her grip on the two little ones at her side and straightened to her full height. "We will be fine, thank you. No need to concern yourselves with us." She turned and moved past them to greet Stella.

Matt, Stella, and Stella's two sisters circled Maddy, only allowing Rev. Richards to join them. Maddy smiled through her tears and whispered, "Thank you." From the corner of her eye, she watched Sam Potter scowl and motion to his brother to leave with him.

"How about we walk you back to your place, Miss Malone?" Matt Woodward asked.

"Yes, please. I would like that very much." Maddy was pleasantly surprised at the Woodwards' friendliness. Without a doubt, they were good people, but in her memory, they had been very distant. Both Matt and Stella were known to be almost hermit-like in their behavior, to the point very few people knew them. Maddy's parents had probably been their closest friends. But the term "friends" was a stretch since they rarely saw them. Recently though, since the death of Maddy's pa in October, Mr. Woodward had dropped by two or three times with freshly shot squirrel and rabbit, leaving them on the porch with a quick wave then retreating.

Stella's two spinster sisters, Rebecca and Naomi, were even more withdrawn from society. It touched Maddy deeply that they had cared enough to break away from their solitude to show up at her mother's funeral. Maddy had seen Rebecca on a couple of occasions, but this was her first time to lay eyes on Naomi, otherwise known as "Boots" to all their neighbors. Seeing her in person, Maddy guessed the nickname came from the big boots the woman wore. Everything about the way she dressed and moved suggested she was a man, not a woman. Known as one of the best hunters and trackers in the region, Boots was respected by everyone that knew her. Respect, in Boots' case, meant leaving her alone to live the life she wanted.

The odd assortment of people made their way down the hill toward the Malones' house. The closer they got, the more Maddy was filled with dread. The grief and deep loneliness she felt at losing her beloved mother was coming to a head. She had been surrounded by women from their church since the moment Gertie took her last breath. They had prepared the body and received callers laden with all manner of food. Maddy and her two little charges had sat in stunned silence for most of the three days leading up to the burial. As she approached the house after the funeral, she was almost choked with terror at having to face the days ahead. Her pa had passed on only four months before of what appeared to be a sudden heart attack. Her ma's health had been failing even before that. Soon after they put her pa in the ground, her ma took to her bed, leaving the running of the house and farm entirely in Maddy's hands. In spite of the toll that took on Maddy, she still had precious moments every day at her ma's bedside. Moments that Gertie seemed to realize would be few.

The Woodwards stopped at the foot of the porch steps and said good-bye. Stella said, "We'll see to it that game gets dropped by now and then. Between Matt and Boots, we usually have plenty. If those nasty Potter boys bother you, just tie a rag or somethin' to this post here as a signal. Matt will deal with them."

"Th-thank you. I'm much obliged," Maddy stammered.

The Woodwards turned and walked away leaving Maddy staring after them, holding the frail hands of her precious Ollie and Anabel. She drew in a deep breath, closed her eyes, and prayed silently. *God help us. I know you're here. I can't feel you, but I know you're here and you love us. Help us, please.*

Her mother had taught her many valuable lessons about life, but nothing was as important as teaching her daughter to rely on God, through good times and through bad times. Lately, it seemed to Maddy to be nothing but bad.

Toward the end of her life, Gertie Malone seemed to sense the urgency of imparting as much Godly wisdom as possible to her youngest child. Maddy choked up at the memory of her mother clinging to her hand each evening before bedtime. She would look deeply into her daughter's eyes and seemed to will her to fully grasp the importance of her words.

"Maddy, dearest, God's Word has so much more to offer us than any of us realize. Every day, honey, every day, I want you to study. Never give up. Even when I'm gone and you no longer have the desire to read His Word; do it anyway! Do you hear me, girl? Will you promise me?"

"Yes, Mama. I promise," she whispered softly as she snuggled close, willing her mother to get better and to never leave her.

And true to her promise, she spent hours poring through the Bible, learning to love it almost as much as her mother did. Every night before bed, she would set Ollie on one side and Anabel on the other and read story after story from both the Old Testament and the New Testament. Often during the day, she would overhear them playacting their favorite stories. Ollie tended toward the more violent scenes, where Good soundly defeated Evil. Anabel was drawn to stories of babies and lost lambs. Her favorite was the birth of Jesus.

One day, Maddy found that Anabel had recreated the nativity scene in one corner of the barn. She found her rocking and singing to Tommy, her rag doll, then placing him in a hay-filled box. Ollie was on the other side of the barn cutting Goliath's head off with a stout stick he had whittled into a sword. After sawing away on a pile of hay for a full two minutes, he triumphantly sheathed his sword into his belt and marched proudly back to face the cowardly army of Israel. Maddy had watched these two precious children, her heart overflowing with love then promptly went back to the house to report their activities to her mother.

Many times, the two of them would laugh at the little ones' antics until tears flowed down their faces. What delight Ollie and Anabel had brought to the three of them during the years of the war. The children had called Frederick and Gertie, Papa and Mama from the beginning because that's what Maddy called her parents.

But it was Maddy that they clung to. Her parents ran the farm. Maddy ran the house and tended to the children. The first time Ollie called Maddy, "Ma," she started to correct him. But she found that she loved it. If he'd had a ma, she would have stopped him, but his ma was dead. A boy needed a ma that was there for him. A ma that could hold him, kiss the top of his sweet head, listen to his stories, laugh with him. And Maddy's very being longed to be that person for her little Ollie and for her tiny baby Anabel.

There were days that she dreaded having Silas return home to get his two children. And then there were days that she longed to see him ride down their long drive. He had come back for a visit the summer of '62, one full year after dropping them off. Anabel didn't know him and Ollie was afraid of him at first. Soon, though, Ollie wouldn't leave his side. Silas took them to his farm for the week he was on leave. Maddy fretted and paced the entire week. She realized with alarm that she had allowed Silas' children to work their way into her heart, so deeply that she knew it would kill her to lose them. They were her very life.

Silas hadn't been back since that day. They knew his regiment had moved east of the Mississippi to fight. Silas had managed to write a few letters but the past six months, they'd heard nothing. They weren't sure if he was dead or alive. Ollie seldom asked about him. Anabel never did. Maddy prayed for him every day. As much as she dreaded losing the children, she knew they needed their father. And, she, too, caught herself longing for him to be there.

Long before Silas' wife Mary died, Maddy and her parents knew the young couple. They had all attended the same church, Hickory Hollow Baptist Church, three miles to the south of their farms. Maddy and her two best friends couldn't help but admire the good-looking couple; Mary with her ready smile and beautiful brown curls and Silas with his handsome face, tall height, and rugged build. He, too, had a quick smile for the three slightly besotted teens. All three girls knew their boundaries and only occasionally mentioned him to each other while quickly smothering their giggles. At the time, Silas and Mary had seemed a generation older than the three girls. When Ollie was born, Maddy was just thirteen but looked much younger. Her two friends were only a couple of years older. Silas and Mary were a decade older than Maddy.

Mary's death hit the community hard. The church

family, led by Reverend Richards, surrounded the grief-stricken husband. Frederick and Gertie took the children in so Silas could grieve and tend to his wife's burial. After Mary was put in the ground, Maddy's family continued to tend to the two babies during the day so Silas could take care of his farm. Eventually Silas joined them for evening meals. The two children were as much at home on the Malones' farm as they were on their pa's. So, when Silas reached the horrifying realization that it was inevitable that he join the ranks of the fighting, the choice of who to leave his babies with was unquestionably the Malones. And particularly Maddy, who had already won the hearts of his children.

Maddy cleared her head, looked down at the two tiny people pressed against her side, turned them gently around, and guided them into their empty house.

CHAPTER TWO

Three months later, May 1865

Maddy felt a gentle nudge in her side. Then the bed rocked as five-year-old Anabel crawled up onto the bed and pulled the blankets back. With shame, Maddy realized, this had become the morning routine. She should be waking Ollie and Anabel up every morning, not the other way around. And that, after having milked their cow and after having fixed a hearty breakfast and after having swept the kitchen and porch. Lazy! That's what she was! Simply lazy! There was no other word for it.

She sat up, pulled Anabel into an embrace with one arm and pulled Ollie up onto the bed with the other. She buried her nose into Ollie's hair then Anabel's, and inhaled their sweetness. Both kids giggled and wrapped their arms around her.

"What was last nights' story? Do you remember?" she asked.

"Of course we remember," Ollie answered. "It was about Joseph."

"And where in the Bible did we read that story?"

"Genesis!" Anabel answered quickly before her brother could beat her to it.

"What happened to Joseph, Anabel?"

"His really mean brothers sold him to some bad people."

"That's right. And what happened next, Ollie?"

"Those bad people traveled a long, long way away from Joseph's home and then they sold him to someone else so he could be their slave."

"That's right. Some pretty horrible stuff happened to Joseph, right? Do you think God was still watching out for Joseph?"

"Yeah," both kids answered, with shrugs.

"As hard as it is to believe sometimes, God never, ever forgets His people. He is always at work. Even when we can't see what He's doing. And every day He wants us to thank Him for what He's doing. Let's pray."

As always, Maddy started then nudged Anabel, who offered her sweet, little girl prayers., Then Ollie prayed and Maddy finished. They hugged, bounced out of bed, and started their day. Maddy smiled as the two enthusiastically ran from her room to do their morning chores, Ollie to feed the pig and Anabel to feed the five chickens and gather the eggs.

Maddy sighed, pushed her dirty hair out of her face, walked over to her wash basin and looked in the mirror. Her face had grown thinner over the past year and especially so in the months since her ma had passed away. Food was scarce and she had seen to it that Ollie and Anabel got what their growing bodies needed. If it hadn't been for the occasional attention of the Woodwards, she was certain they wouldn't have survived. Both the pig and the chickens were gifts from Matt and Stella. Her pa had butchered their last pig in the fall of '63. That meat was long gone. Between the birds, squirrels, and rabbits Ollie shot or trapped and a few offerings of venison from Boots, they managed through the past winter.

Maddy splashed her face with water and dried it with the rag of a towel that hung on a nail in the wall. She walked over to her window to check on the children. From her second-story bedroom she had a good view of her little farm. More than once she, had spied either Sam or Nate Potter lurking about. She'd told Ollie and Anabel whenever they saw her white handkerchief sticking out her window, they were to get in the house as quickly as possible. And they were trained to look up at her window often. Many times, one or both of the Potters knocked at her door. If Ollie was close by, he would run to get the shotgun then stand in the middle of the hallway. Only once did one of the Potters manage to worm his way past Maddy's objections. One look at the feisty seven-year-old heaving the gun to his shoulder was enough to make the unwanted visitor end his call and be on his way.

Maddy quickly got dressed and took one final look in the mirror. The sight of dark circles beneath her eyes and strings of hair out of place increased her despondency. She shook her head and forced herself to move down the stairs. The war was over. She should be overjoyed. But, no matter how hard she tried, she couldn't seem to shake her deep sadness and lethargy. Every day for the past month, she simply managed to put one foot in front of the other. She knew what must be done to survive, what must be done for the children to be healthy and happy. And that's what she did, day in and day out. If it weren't for Ollie and Anabel, she'd have nothing to live for. She knew that wasn't true, but it's how she felt. Oh, how she longed to be able to unburden herself to her dear mother. Those precious conversations had somehow been able to work miracles in her.

Again, she walked to a window to see if the children were alright. Ollie was hanging on the outside of the stout pigpen scratching their scrawny sow behind her ears.

Anabel was just emerging from the hen house with eggs clutched in her apron. Thankfully the chickens had started laying again. Eggs were nonexistent during the cold winter months.

No sign of the Potters. Maddy turned and walked over to the stove and stirred the embers. Reaching into the wood box, she grabbed a handful of small bits of wood and bark, threw them on the embers then went to the sink to pump water into a pan for boiling. After adding a few more sticks to the fire, she rushed out the door to the outhouse.

The sun was already streaming through the branches of the oaks that lined their drive. The air was warm and filled with the scent of dirt and trees and flowers. Maddy lifted her head and breathed deeply. "Lord, I need you," she whispered. Birds seemed to sing from every tree as if they were bursting with excitement that a new day had begun. Maddy stood still, and listened. "I remember being that happy. I miss it. Oh God, how I miss it. Help me."

"Ma! The water's about to boil! Ya want me to throw in some meal?" Ollie hollered from the porch.

"No, Ollie. I'll do it. But I need you to bring in some more wood. The woodbox is almost empty."

Ollie jumped off the porch with a whoop. "Can I chop some more?"

"Only if you need to. And make sure Anabel's not near you while you chop."

Back inside, Maddy found her little girl sitting at the table looking at her favorite book, a very worn copy of *A little Pretty Pocket Book* by John Newbery. The children's fascination with this book led them both to quickly learn first the alphabet then to read. Even five-year-old Anabel could read. Maddy checked the fire, added cornmeal to the boiling water and set it to the side to simmer.

"Check the porridge in a few minutes, Anabel, while I milk Daisy. Don't touch the pan though. Let Ollie do that."

"Alright, Ma. I will," Anabel answered as she turned a

page.

Maddy walked to the table and wrapped her arms around Anabel. "I love you, little girl."

Anabel quickly stood in her chair and returned the hug. "I love you, too, Ma."

Maddy heard Daisy moo as soon as she opened the door. She walked the short distance to the barn and breathed a prayer of thanks for their cow, as she did every morning. Several times in the past few years, she thought the cow was about to be stolen, but for whatever reason, the men who showed up to forage off their property chose to leave Daisy alone. Both cows that Silas had left with them had been stolen, though, as well as the three pigs. Thankfully, although her production was dwindling, Daisy was still giving them milk after birthing a calf more than a year ago. The calf went to the Woodwards in payment for the use of their bull. Maddy realized she needed to use their bull again if she expected to continue to use Daisy for milk. But the milk kept coming. One more thing to be grateful for.

When she was done milking, she carried the bucket into the house where she found Ollie standing on his stool stirring the porridge. She divided the milk into two smaller metal containers and took one out to the springhouse. The springhouse... another blessing she thanked God for every day. Also, the root cellar, a stone-walled room under the kitchen, accessible through two slanting doors on the side of the house.

Maddy remembered when she was a toddler, watching her pa and older brothers dig the root cellar then line it with rock, before they ever started building the two-story house they lived in now. At the time, they were living in the family's first house, nothing but a two-room cabin. That cabin was the smaller of their two barns, being used for the chickens. In the floor of that old cabin was a hidden trap-door that opened into a tiny cellar, a space that Maddy and her parents had found necessary to hide in twice during the last two years of the war. Both times, a warning came from Matt Woodward to take cover. Marauding gangs of bushwhackers were passing through. At those times, Maddy's pa would quickly gather his wife, Maddy, Ollie, and Anabel, and run to the small barn where they disappeared down the trap door hidden in a corner. The trap door was covered with an old pile of boxes conveniently nailed in place. They fared better than some families in Southwest Missouri, whose farms were often burned to the ground.

Maddy walked from the springhouse to the doors of the root cellar. After making her way down the solid rock steps and over to the vegetable bin, she selected two wilted potatoes to slice up for their breakfast. A month earlier, she had taken most of the potatoes and planted them in furrows that she and Ollie had dug in the garden. It would be several weeks before they could harvest those. In the meantime, their measly pile in the root cellar was dwindling. As was their pile of turnips. The carrots were long gone.

Thankfully, wild edible plants were in abundance this time of year, between when the root cellar emptied and when their garden started to produce. So, every day after breakfast, Maddy and the kids took long walks through the fields and forest, gathering what they could find; winter cress, dandelions, and plantain in the fields. Bellwort and cattail shoots along the creek and beaver dam. And spiderwort, wood sorrel, and bellflowers in the woods.

As abundant as their food sources seemed, it was barely enough for three meals a day every day for three people. And Maddy was tired. Bone-deep tired. She had never felt this way in her life. It frightened her. After watching both her parents weaken and die before her very eyes in just a few months' time, she was filled with fear. But she hid it well. Ollie and Anabel were thriving; body, mind, and spirit. And that is what Maddy lived for. What she prayed throughout every day for, that God would enable her to stay healthy for the kids. To keep them both healthy and happy until their pa came to the rescue.

CHAPTER THREE

The next morning, Maddy disciplined herself to roll over and crawl out of her bed before either of the children were awake. Again, she splashed water on her face and quickly dried it with a towel. Out of habit, she walked to her window and looked down on her farm looking so peaceful in the predawn light. She scanned every bush, tree, and building for signs of her unwelcome neighbors. Thankfully, she saw nothing, but just as she turned away, something unfamiliar caught her eye. Peering down through the branches of the big oak in the front yard, she thought she could see someone on horseback, slowly making his way down her drive.

Heart pounding, she eased her way into the hall, opened the closet door, and pulled out the shotgun. Ollie opened his door and came out, rubbing his eyes.

"Are the Potters here?" he asked, eyes opening wide when he saw the gun.

"Shh. No. Someone on a horse. Probably just a peddler. Stay up here with your sister."

"Shouldn't you get dressed first?" Ollie asked.

Maddy looked down at her nightgown, sighed then grabbed her father's coat from the closet. With her heart pounding, she slipped into the coat and crept down the stairs. She got a glimpse through the sitting room window of the man's horse tied just in front of the porch, but no sign of the man. Then she heard the creaking boards of the front steps. Heart pounding, she quietly made her way over to the window and peeked between the curtains. A heavy knock sounded at the door. At her angle, she could tell it was a large man but couldn't see his face. He took his hat off and knocked again.

Maddy cracked the window and said in a high, shaky voice, "Go away. We don't need anything."

He turned toward her voice. "Maddy? Is that you?"

Maddy dropped the curtains and fell backward, sitting hard on the worn rug. She would know that voice anywhere. Silas came back! He's alive! She sat in stunned silence until a loud knocking shook her out of her stupor. Quickly she scrambled to her feet, ran to the front door, and flung it open. When she saw his kind, strong face and knew without a doubt he truly was Silas, she covered her face and sank to the floor in a mixed-up puddle of nightgown and oversized coat. Then she started bawling uncontrollably.

Silas stood and watched, not sure what to think. Dread gripped his heart as he reached down to help her to her feet. He was shocked at how skinny she was. Gently steadying her, he held her shoulders and noticed her gaunt face. His dread grew.

"Maddy? Are you all right?" He swallowed. "Are...are Ollie and Anabel st-still here?"

Maddy nodded and wiped her face. She didn't speak. Just then, he heard a small voice from the top of the stairs.

"Ma? Ma? Can I come down?"

Silas' hands gripped Maddy's shoulders as a sob escaped. "Is that my boy?" he stammered.

Maddy nodded. She held up a finger and whispered, "Wait. Let me tell him. H-he needs a little time to...to get used to the news that you're back."

Silas gripped his hat and nodded, tears blurring his vision as she walked toward the stairway. She turned before she ascended and said, "Please sit down. I...I need to change clothes and talk to both of them. It might take a little while."

Again, he nodded then found a chair in the sitting room that had a clear view of the stairway.

After long, anxious moments of listening to creaking floorboards and muffled conversation, Silas finally heard several sets of footsteps making their way down the stairs. He stood just as his beautiful Ollie and Anabel came into sight. While frightened little Anabel clung to Maddy's skirt, Ollie, precious boy, stood tall and looked expectantly into his father's eyes. That look drove Silas to his knees. He opened his arms wide and Ollie ran straight to him without hesitation. Both father and boy clung to each other and wept. Silas pulled his head back to gaze into his son's eyes. He gently held Ollie's face in his big hands and stroked his cheeks with his thumbs, wiping tears away.

"Ollie, Ollie, my boy! How I've longed for this moment."

He pulled him into his arms again as Ollie answered with a smothered cry of, "Pa!"

When Silas looked up, he saw that Maddy had eased Anabel over to him. He reached out to stroke her soft blonde hair. "My baby girl," he whispered. Anabel yanked away and clung even more tightly to Maddy.

"It will take time, Silas," Maddy said with soft tenderness. "She was only two when she saw you last."

Silas merely nodded then hid his tears in Ollie's neck.

"C-can I get you some breakfast?" Maddy asked awkwardly.

Silas stood with Ollie still in his arms. "Yes, please, if it's not too much trouble."

Ollie wriggled free and slid to the floor. He grabbed his pa's hand and turned to Maddy. "Can Pa help me with my chores, Ma?"

Maddy smiled and answered, "Yes, of course he can, Ollie." She reached down to pick Anabel up. "Maybe your pa could help Anabel, too."

Anabel's response to that was a grunt and arms that clung tightly to Maddy's neck, almost strangling her. Maddy mouthed an, "I'm sorry," to Silas. He put his hat on and gently ran his hand down Anabel's back.

"That's alright. Maybe Ollie and I can do all the chores today. Although," he said, looking down at Ollie, "he'll have to show me what to do."

Ollie whooped with enthusiasm, ran through the door, and jumped off the front porch with a grin as wide as his face. "I'll show you, Pa! Come on!" He waved his arm in invitation.

Maddy watched from the window, her heart overflowing with a mix of emotions. Most of all, she felt relief and deep gratitude that Silas was alive. She chose at that moment to pour her emotions into welcoming their soldier home, come what may. Whispering comforting words into Anabel's ear, she disentangled her arms from around her neck and stood her on one of the dining room chairs. She smoothed Anabel's wavy hair into place and stooped to talk to her face-to-face.

"Anabel, that's your pa. Remember? We've talked about him a lot. He's a good, good man and he loves you, sweetheart." Maddy picked her up again and carried her to the window. "Can you see him out there?"

Anabel nodded and watched intently as Silas and Ollie walked hand-in-hand to the barn. "He's going to help Ollie milk the cow and feed the pigs and even gather the eggs. Would you like to help me fix a delicious breakfast for him?"

Anabel stuck her finger in her mouth and nodded.

"Good! Let's get started." So, with help from her tiny companion, she bustled quickly about, building the fire, getting water to boil, making porridge, mixing up a batch of biscuits, frying eggs, and making coffee.

The chores took longer than usual because Ollie delighted in explaining every detail to Silas as if Silas had never stepped foot on a farm. Silas, in turn, delighted in every word that came from his son's mouth. Finally, they finished and walked up the porch steps, bearing a bucket of milk and a basket of eggs.

Maddy met them on the porch and said, "Breakfast is ready. But would you please put the milk and eggs in the springhouse for me? I'll tend to them after we eat."

When the two were finished, they entered the kitchen and sat at the small table in the center of the room. Anabel waited expectantly in her chair, but as soon as she saw Silas, she made a dive for Maddy. Maddy kissed her head and gently turned her to face the table.

"Silas, would you please say grace?"

"Of course," he answered and reached out to take the hands of those on either side of him, Maddy's on his left and Ollie's on his right, a tradition he had learned at that very table. Anabel scowled, took Ollie's and Maddy's hands, but refused to look at him.

Silas suppressed a grin, bowed his head, and began, "Father, God, we bow before you with great reverence and with gratitude. Thank you for your abundant blessings. Thank you that I made it back to my precious"—he choked on a sob—"to my precious children. Thank you for Maddy and her parents for taking care of them while I was gone." Overcome with emotion, he stopped.

Maddy finished the prayer with a whisper. "Thank you, Father, for this food and all your blessings. Amen."

"Amen," both children echoed.

Silas looked up and blinked away tears. Then he looked at his food and dug in.

"Why's he cryin', Ma?" Anabel whispered.

Silas froze. He looked at Maddy. "Ma?" he repeated.

Maddy looked down.

"It's alright," Silas said. "We can talk about it later. In private."

"Why, Ma? Why's he cryin?" Anabel persisted.

Maddy kissed her head. "Because, sweet girl, he's so happy. Sometimes people cry when they're happy. I know I do."

"Why's he happy?"

"Why don't you ask him, Anabel?"

Anabel dared to look directly at Silas then quickly turned to hide her face against Maddy.

Silas chuckled and answered her question. "Why am I so happy, Anabel? Because I'm here with you and Ollie. Because you and Ollie are both doing great. You're strong and healthy and most important of all, I can see that you're both happy." With these last words, he looked into Maddy's eyes and smiled. "And for that, I have Maddy and her parents to thank."

Anabel smiled at him and looked quickly away. Silas looked longingly at his daughter then took a bite of his eggs followed by a buttery biscuit.

"Mmmm... so good. It looks like you've learned your

ma's amazing skills with food. I don't think I've ever met anyone who can cook like her."

Maddy dipped her head. "Thank you, Silas," she whispered.

"Speaking of your ma, where is she?"

Both Ollie and Anabel stopped eating and stared at him. Silently he looked from face to face and then realized the awful truth.

"Mama died, Pa," Ollie said. "We buried her." Tears came to his eyes as he choked out the last words. Maddy and Anabel teared up as well.

"I'm so sorry. I didn't know." He reached out to capture Ollie and Maddy's hands in his.

Maddy squeezed his hand. "Pa, too. Ma this past February. Pa just four months before her."

Silas stared in shock, still clinging to their hands. "How...how have you managed all alone, Maddy?"

Maddy pulled her hand free and wiped her eyes with her apron. "We've managed... Our neighbors have helped."

"Surely not the Potters?" Silas asked with concern.

"No, Pa! Not the Potters!" Ollie exclaimed. "I'd shoot those varmints before they could step one foot in this place!"

Silas' eyebrows lifted. "Have they tried?"

"Yep! Lots of times! But I had my gun and scared 'em off every time!" Ollie bragged.

"Is that right?" he asked, looking pointedly at Maddy.

She again lowered her head.

Silas grabbed her hand again, and said, "It's alright, Maddy. You have nothing to fear. It's obvious to me you've done a fine job. We just need to have a long talk. Soon. If that's alright with you, that is."

Maddy nodded, wiped her tears and said, "Of course it is. And it was the Woodwards that helped us. Not the Potters." She smiled through her tears. "It's truly good to have you back home, Silas." She looked quickly away, covered her face with her apron, and stood. "I'm sorry," she choked on a loud sob as she ran from the room. Anabel scowled at her pa and followed Maddy out of the room and up the stairs.

CHAPTER FOUR

Silas paced back and forth in the front yard, Ollie on his heels every step of the way. Several times, he stopped and looked up at the second-story windows, hoping to get a glimpse of Maddy possibly peering down from her room. He had already sent Ollie up to check on her. Ollie had come back to report that, "Ma's just layin' in her bed with the covers over her head."

"And what's Anabel doing?" he had asked.

"Sittin' next to her lookin' at her books." After a moment he said, "She stuck her tongue out at me."

Silas chuckled. "Now, why would she do that?"

"I dunno. I think she's mad at me. I think she thinks I made Ma cry."

Silas rested his big hand on Ollie's head. "You didn't make her cry, son."

"I know I didn't. You did. Why'd you do that, Pa?"

Silas was silent for a while then knelt down to look Ollie in the eyes. "I don't know, son. I sure didn't mean to. Do you think she was just sad thinking about her folks dying?"

Ollie shoved his hands into his pockets and stared down

at his toe drawing circles in the dirt. "I guess. I just don't want her to be sad anymore."

"Is she sad a lot?"

"Yeah. I think so anyway. She smiles at us all the time though. And hugs us." He wiped a tear trickling down his cheek.

"Well, I can certainly understand why she's sad. Both her pa and ma died not that long ago. And this war has made pretty much everyone sad. It's going to take a long time to feel normal again."

He stood and took Ollie's hand. "Show me around the farm, Ollie. It looks like you and Maddy have been working mighty hard to keep this place running."

Ollie beamed with pleasure at his father's words. "Sure, Pa!" He dragged Silas to visit the barn for the second time that day. "You already met Daisy, but you haven't seen the whole barn yet. It's huge. Anabel and I play in here all the time, especially when it's raining. The loft is our favorite." Together, they climbed the ladder to the second floor.

"Looks like you've run out of hay. Did you have enough for Daisy through the winter?"

"Naw. We always stake her out in the back field. Unless it's snowin' real bad. Then we take her some of our potatoes and stuff from the root cellar."

"I brought a couple of cows and three pigs over here just before I left. Are they still here?" Silas asked as they stood at the second-story window and looked toward the field.

"No. Them bushwhackers took 'em."

"Bushwhackers? They came here?" Silas asked, a burning pain growing in his gut.

"Yep," Ollie answered then turned to strut over to the ladder where he continued his answer as he climbed down. "Came a couple of times, actually," he said when his feet hit the floor.

Silas climbed down behind him and stared at his small son. "Tell me about it, Ollie, boy."

Ollie grinned up at him. "Yeah, Papa and I rounded up Mama, Ma, and Anabel real quick and made 'em hide in the cellar. Those crazy bushwhackers never found us." His chest puffed out with manly pride.

Thoroughly stricken, Silas could barely get his words out. "H...how long ago was this, son?"

"Oh, I dunno. A year or two ago."

Silas quickly calculated that if Ollie were correct, he would have only been five or six years old at the time. "That must have been pretty scary for all of you, Ollie."

Ollie shrugged and looked down. "Well, Anabel sure was scared."

He forced a smile. "You did a good job, son. I'm proud of you."

Ollie blinked back tears and merely answered, "Yep."

Silas knelt down and opened his arms. "Come here, Ollie," he whispered.

Ollie slowly walked into his father's embrace. Silas stroked his head and whispered into his hair, "I'm so sorry I wasn't here to help you, son. But you did good. Real good."

Ollie's skinny arms came up and encircled his pa's neck and he started weeping. "It's okay, Pa. You couldn't help it."

"I'm here, now, boy. And if I can help it, I'll never leave again."

Ollie nodded and squeezed more tightly.

They parted and looked into each other's tear-streaked faces. "I've been dreaming of this day for years, of holding you and Anabel in my arms again and taking you back home with me. Of the three of us being a family again. I can't begin to describe how full my heart is, Ollie. You and Anabel are medicine for my wounded soul."

Ollie smiled through his tears and nodded. "I'm happy, too, Pa. Sorry about Anabel." He shrugged his narrow shoulders.

Silas laughed. "Anabel will come around in time, Ollie. We won't rush her." He stood to his feet and said, "How about let's finish our farm tour?"

From the barn, they went outside to the pigpen then across the yard to the henhouse, where Ollie showed Silas the cleverly hidden trap door to the cellar. "This is where we hid from them bushwhackers, Pa. See? When it's shut you can't even tell there's a door here."

Silas was amazed at the ingenuity of the design. He then followed his boy down a narrow ladder into a dark, damp space. He tried to imagine five frightened people hiding here while listening to the pillaging taking place outside.

"Let's get going. I hate it down here," Ollie whispered as he led the way back up the ladder and out to the springhouse then down a path past the old cornfield to the creek on the north side of the property.

"This path keeps going. Where does it lead?" Silas asked.

"To the Potter's farm I think," Ollie answered. "I'm not sure. Ma won't let me follow it. I'm 'strictly forbidden.'"

"Well, it sure looks like someone uses it a lot."

"Them Potters. I told you. They come here all the time."

"Why? What business do they have here?"

"They keep tellin' Ma that they want to help her. But she keeps tellin' 'em, 'no thank you. We're doin' just fine.'"

The two continued walking through the cornfield down toward the creek that ran along the north side of the property. "What do the Potters do when your ma, er, when Maddy tells them no thanks?"

"Sometimes they leave. Sometimes they just stand at the door and beg her to let them in."

At this, Silas stopped dead in his tracks and turned to face his son. "They try to get in the house? Have they ever succeeded?"

Again, little Ollie's chest swelled with pride. "Once or

twice, they stepped into the hallway, but the first thing they saw was me aiming the shotgun right between their blasted eyes!"

Not sure whether to be alarmed, amused, or proud, Silas chose the latter for the sake of his son. These were trying times to be sure and there had been no man present in the home for months.

"Was that enough to stop them, Ollie?"

"Yep. They're both cowards to the core. I'm not afraid of them. As long as I have my gun."

Silas sighed and ran his hand through Ollie's thatch of uncombed hair. He raised his eyes to heaven and prayed for wisdom. "I think, now that I'm here, you won't have to worry about the Potters any more, son."

The two slowly made their way back to the house to find the downstairs still silent and empty. Ollie ran to the hutch in the dining room, pulled out a box, and took it to the table. He looked Silas in the eye and asked, "Do you know how to play chess, Pa? If you don't, I'll teach you."

"It's been a long time, but I'll play if you go easy on me." He sat and watched with fascination as his seven-year-old expertly set the game up then looked at him with a twinkle of challenge in his hazel eyes.

Maddy watched from her window as Silas and Ollie walked back to the house. Anabel continued to play happily on the bed behind her, oblivious to the turmoil stirring in Maddy's heart.

Silas. Silas was finally home. Maddy wiped the tears away again, trying to regain control so she could go downstairs and face him. What must he think of her? She wasn't even sure what she thought of herself. She washed her face with cold water and took a deep breath to steady her nerves.

She should be ecstatic. And she was. But woven tightly through her joy was fear and panic. What would the next few days and weeks bring? Would she lose her babies? Of course she would. They weren't truly hers. She'd tried to remind herself of that fact a thousand times in the past few months. But in her heart, they were every bit as much hers as if she'd given birth to them. Nothing could ever change that. If she were to lose them, it would tear her very soul out.

On the other hand, she would rather die than separate them from their pa again. She couldn't do that to them. Or to him. There had never been any doubt of Silas' deep love for his offspring. Seeing him with them this morning had verified that fact to her a hundredfold. She went to the window again and looked up through the branches of their massive oaks.

God, I'm not sure what Your plan is but I know Your plan is good. I surrender all of this to You. She clenched her fists under her chin. *At least I'm trying to surrender it all to You, but it's so, so hard.* Unwelcome tears burst from her eyes again and trailed down her cheeks. *Help me to trust You, Lord. Help me to surrender. My future is in your hands.*

CHAPTER FIVE

Maddy crept quietly down the stairs to start the noontime meal. She nodded a greeting toward Silas and Ollie playing chess at the dining room table and turned to the kitchen. Anabel followed a minute later and also turned to join Maddy in the kitchen. But when she saw Silas and Ollie with the chess set between them, she walked slowly to the table and quietly climbed up into the chair next to Ollie, as far from Silas as she could get. Silas smiled at her but she wouldn't make eye contact. When Silas glanced up at Maddy, she gave him a quick nod and smile then turned back to her work.

Only a few embers remained from the fire she had built for breakfast. She added kindling, blew on it until a flame came to life then added more wood from the wood box beside the stove. In no time, she had a roaring fire and a pot of water about to boil. She cut some venison jerky into small pieces, added them to the water then went to the cellar to get a potato and a turnip to cut up and add to the stew. Finally, she took a short walk to the creek to gather wild onions growing along the path.

When she returned, she was surprised to hear Anabel and Ollie both laughing. "No, Pa! You don't eat 'em when you capture them! You just set them on the table, silly!" Ollie said.

She glanced over to see Silas with one of Ollie's bishops between his teeth. Anabel's eyes danced with glee. Finally, the five-year-old dared to look directly at her pa. Relief coursed through Maddy at the beautiful sight. She laid the onions on the kitchen table and walked through the dining room to join in the fun.

"Ma, he's eating the bishop!" Anabel squealed.

"I can see that," she answered. "What should we do? If he eats it, we won't have a complete set to play with!" she exclaimed, her hands on her cheeks.

"I'll get it!" Ollie hollered. With that, he jumped from his chair and lunged for his pa. Silas stood to his feet with the bishop clenched between his teeth and wrestled Ollie to the floor. Anabel climbed down and ran to Maddy who swooped her up in her arms. Together, they circled the two fighting males, laughing and cheering for Ollie to win. Which he did when Silas rolled to his back. Ollie straddled his pa's chest and yanked the chess piece from between his teeth. He ran to the table and loudly announced, "I win! I get my bishop back!"

"What?" Silas laughed. "I captured him, fair and square!"

"Yeah, but you didn't put him in your prison, where he belongs. So, I won him back!" Ollie declared. "Fair and square!" he added with a triumphant tone.

Silas sat up and laughed. He put both hands in the air. "Alright! Alright. You win. This time. And where's this prison of mine?"

Ollie laughed and pointed at the pile of chess pieces that Silas had already captured and set neatly next to the chessboard.

"That's my prison? I think I might need to build a wall

around it."

"Naw. I won't touch them if they're there where they belong."

Silas looked up at Maddy, smiled, and shook his head. She smiled back at him.

"Well that's it, then. I'll never, ever try to eat another chess piece." He looked at Anabel and winked.

To everyone's delight, she giggled and said, "No! Never!"

Maddy twirled Anabel around then put her back in her chair to continue watching the game. She returned to the kitchen to chop onions for the stew, her heart feeling much lighter even though her circumstances hadn't changed.

Soon the game was finished, Ollie the victor again. Maddy set steaming bowls of stew before them. After praying, Silas announced that he planned to go check on his farm when he was done with his meal. "I'm not sure what I'll find. The place has been abandoned for four years. It was in pretty bad shape when I saw it three years ago, after just a year of neglect."

"Can I go with you, Pa?" Ollie asked with excitement.

"Not this time, son. Maybe tomorrow though. No telling what kind of varmints have moved in. Possums, raccoons, a bear or two. Possibly poisonous snakes, wasps, bees, hornets. I don't know yet. I'd rather you not be with me when I find out."

Ollie's and Anabel's eyes grew big at this news. "Are you serious, Pa?" Ollie asked.

"Yes, I'm serious," Silas answered between bites. "All except the bear." He turned to Maddy. "I haven't had food this good in years! You, dear Madeline, are an amazing cook!"

Maddy dipped her head. "Thank you," she answered quietly.

Silas covered her hand with his own, oblivious to the effect it had on her. "I hate to continue to be a burden,

Maddy, but might I ask to board here until my place is fit to sleep in? Both me and the children? I could sleep in the loft in the barn, of course. Not the house."

Maddy looked at his big, warm hand, still covering hers. Then up at his face, looking expectantly at her. "Of course, Silas! As long as you need to," she whispered.

He gave her hand a squeeze and smiled. "Thank you so much, Maddy. I know food is scarce, so in a couple of days, I plan to take a wagon to Springfield and load up on supplies, including food to replenish your pantry."

Unbidden tears came to her eyes. "You don't need to do that, Silas. I can manage."

"It's pretty obvious to me that you can manage, Maddy. But don't ever refuse to accept anything from me. It would take more than a lifetime to repay you for what you've done for me."

For the second time that day, she saw tears in his eyes. Choking on a sob, she again stood, covered her face, and wept. This time, Silas jumped to his feet and caught her by the arm before she could get to the stairway.

"Madeline, don't run from me. I know it's been hard, but let's talk about it." He pulled her into his arms as if she were a child and held her.

Maddy struggled to stop the flow of tears. "I'm so embarrassed," she choked.

"Embarrassed? By what?" he asked, still holding her tightly.

"This. Me. All this ridiculous crying!"

Silas gently chuckled. "It's not ridiculous. It's probably necessary."

"It's weak," she snuffled.

"A weak person could not have done what you've done."

"Ma, why are you crying?" Anabel asked as she tried to pull her free from Silas' embrace. Soon, Ollie joined them by trying his best to wrap his skinny arms around all three of them. Maddy looked down and in spite of herself started laughing through her tears. She dropped to her knees and engulfed both of her little ones in a hug.

"How about I head on over to my place and you and I can sit down and have a long talk after the kids are in bed?"

Maddy looked up at him and nodded. Silas ruffled the hair of both Ollie and Anabel then turned to leave.

Maddy and the children watched Silas ride down the winding drive. Had it been a dream, this sudden appearance of a man she thought they might never see again?

"I hope he comes back," Ollie blurted out with a faint sob.

Maddy pulled him to her side. "Of course, he will, Ollie! If he can make it back after four years of fighting in a war, I don't think he'll have any trouble getting back here after an afternoon fighting whatever varmints he finds on his farm."

That evening around the supper table, Silas filled them in on his war with the varmints. "Snakes, wasps, spiders, you name it. They all seemed to think it was their right to move in and take over. I got stung twice by those blasted wasps, too," he said and pulled his sleeve up to prove it. "I think I might have to burn the place down to get rid of them all!"

Maddy covered her mouth with her hand. "Surely not, Silas," she exclaimed.

Silas chuckled. "Not the house or the main barn but I'm seriously thinking about tearing everything else down and rebuilding. Most of the out-buildings are rotting and falling apart. You should see the outhouse!" He laughed and slapped his knee. "Let's just say I'm happy there's plenty of thick brush all over the place."

He took a few more bites of potatoes and venison jerky. "Mmmm... You certainly do have a way with food, Maddy. I...I feel bad for asking, but in addition to sleeping in the barn, would it be too much for you to feed me, too?"

"Of course not, Silas. I'd be delighted," she answered with a faint blush.

"I know there's not enough food, but one trip into Springfield should take care of that. Do you have enough for tomorrow?"

"Yes. Plenty of eggs, milk, and jerky. A couple of potatoes and of course some delicious turnips," she answered with a teasing smile. "The kids and I can gather up some poke greens and I think I have enough ingredients to make another batch of biscuits."

"If I buy some livestock, may I keep them here until my place is ready?" He wiped his mouth with his napkin and smiled at her.

Maddy smiled a shy smile and looked quickly down. "Yes, Silas. Of course."

"Livestock, Pa?" Ollie almost shouted in his excitement. "What are you going to buy?" He jumped up from his chair and fairly danced around the kitchen.

Silas threw his head back and laughed. He grabbed Ollie and pulled him into his lap. "What do you think we need, son?"

"Everything!" Ollie answered with unbridled enthusiasm.

"Sheep! Sheep! Sheep!" Anabel stood in her chair and shouted, surprising everyone. "I've always wanted sheep! They're so cute and cuddly and they're everywhere in the Bible!"

Silas looked at Maddy and without intending to, they both burst into gales of sweet laughter. Maddy quickly stood and swept a slightly offended little girl into her arms. "Oh, Anabel! I think that's a splendid idea!" she said as she shot a teasing smile toward Silas.

"Well, now, sheep weren't on my list but perhaps you can convince me, Anabel. Come here, sweetheart," he said ever so gently as he held out his big hands.

Maddy carried her over to her pa and watched as the tiny girl leaned into his arms. Silas settled her on his lap and asked, "What do you like best, white sheep or black sheep?"

This question seemed to shock her out of her shyness. She looked into her pa's face and answered with firm conviction, "Oh, white sheep of course! Didn't you know that black sheep are trouble makers? We can't have any troublemakers here on our farm! Didn't you know that, Pa?"

When Silas heard the sweet sound of "Pa" uttered by this beautiful, little daughter of his, he knew he was in trouble. At that moment, he would have given her anything she asked of him. He cleared his throat so he could speak. "Well then, I'll have to admit sheep weren't on my list, but now that you mention it, I suppose we could get a couple."

Anabel sucked her breath in and turned her blue eyes up at her Pa's face. "Really, Pa? Really? When? Today?"

Silas tapped her on her tiny nose. "Not today, Sweet-pea. I'm not sure. First, I have to find someone who has sheep. Are you willing to care of them? I think you're big enough."

Anabel jumped out of his lap and stood next to him, as if to prove that, yes indeed, she was big enough. "Yes, Pa! I know I can take care of them. That is if you will build a special pen just for them. Daisy might step on them and the pig will make their wool dirty. We have to keep them clean so we can have nice wool, you know."

Before Silas could respond, Ollie started jumping up and down. "What about me, Pa? Can't I have some animals to take of?"

"Well, Ollie, that goes without saying. You're a big strapping boy of seven. Of course, you'll have animals to take care of."

Ollie jumped higher. "My very own, Pa? My very own? Anabel gets her very own."

Silas reached his hand out and grabbed Ollie's so he could pull him in for a hug. "Yes, son. Your very own. Although, I want you to take some time to think about it. Farm animals are not for our pleasure. They're for our needs. Sheep will give us wool. What animal do you want that will give us food or something of value?"

Ollie's finger stroked his chin as he thought, "Hmmm...maybe a couple of cows for meat and a horse." With this last word, he looked at his pa with longing. "A horse won't give us milk or meat or wool, but I'll need one to take care of my cattle. Pa," he said with conviction, "I want to be a cowboy! It's my life's ambition!"

Taken aback by his son's intensity, Silas swallowed and stroked Ollie's head. "A horse is a lot of responsibility, son. I'll need to give it some thought."

Clearly disappointed, Ollie looked down and replied softly, "Yes, sir."

Silas lifted Ollie's face with a finger. "Look at me, son. If you prove to me that you're as good and as responsible as I think you are, then you'll have your horse someday."

Ollie's face lit up with joy.

"And if you really work toward it, you can be a cowboy someday. But in the meantime, can you just work alongside me and be the best farmer you can be?"

Ollie's head bobbed up and down with his enthusiastic answer. "Yes, Pa! Absolutely! I never want to stop being a farmer. Just like you, Pa! I just want to be a cowboy farmer. I want to wear a cowboy hat and do my work from a horse, that's all."

Silas tousled the boy's hair. "That's good to hear, son. Now, how about you and me get out there and do the evening chores so the ladies can clean up the dishes?"

CHAPTER SIX

That evening, Silas stood with Maddy outside the children's bedroom, chuckling as they watched the two little ones giggle and toss pillows at each other. Silas insisted that she follow her normal bedtime routine. "I want to reacquaint myself with my children. It helps if I become familiar with what they've been doing for the past few years."

Maddy looked into his sincere eyes and declared, "You, Silas MacGregor, are a good, good father."

He whispered his response so his children wouldn't hear. "No, Maddy. A good father wouldn't leave his children for four whole years. For the rest of my life, I will do everything in my power to make it up to them."

Maddy looked at him with kindness and didn't say a word.

"The longing for home and for family was mighty powerful among us soldiers. It was what drove us; the hope that maybe someday again we could have what we'd walked away from. Some of the men couldn't bear the huge load of guilt and sorrow that they carried. They went loco, got careless, and lost their lives because of it."

They were interrupted by two noisy children. Maddy hushed them and crawled into Anabel's bed with her well-worn Bible. "We take turns with the beds. Last night, I read to them in Ollie's bed, so tonight, we'll read in Anabel's bed."

"Come sit with us, Pa," Ollie entreated, throwing the blankets back to include him.

Silas shifted his feet and stammered, "Not tonight, Ollie. I want you to do things like you've done them without me. I just want to watch."

He caught Maddy's eye just before a blush crept up her neck and onto those pretty cheeks of hers. Both of them were well aware of the impropriety of this moment. How tongues would wag if people knew he was upstairs, just outside the bedrooms of the home of a young, unrelated female. Desperate times call for desperate measures, he tried to reason. He'd just been through the most desperate of times and he was beyond desperate to share in the lives of his offspring.

After Maddy helped the children review last night's reading, she took up where they had left off, in Genesis, chapter 39, verses 6-23. Maddy read with such expression that he was drawn into the story of how Potiphar's wife unsuccessfully seduced Joseph, followed by Joseph eventually being thrown into prison, where in spite of everything, he trusted God and thrived. Silas noted with a trace of admiration and humor that Maddy quickly read through the seduction scene and moved on to emphasize Joseph's extraordinary life in prison. Then all three of them joined together in a heartfelt prayer. Maddy snuggled them some more, kissed the tops of their sweet heads, and blew out the candle. Ollie jumped down and reluctantly walked to his bed.

After Maddy left the room, Silas walked in and placed his hand on each of the kids' heads, prayed a silent prayer over them, gave hugs, and followed Maddy. He found her pacing on the porch. When she saw him, she lifted her big, sorrowful eyes to his and talked rapidly and nervously. "I...I cleared out a spot in the hayloft and put a pillow and extra blankets up there. I don't think you'll be cold. The nights are warming up considerably."

Bothered yet slightly amused at her skittish ways, he walked slowly over to the porch swing and made himself comfortable. She stood and stared at him.

"Thank you, Madeline, for everything that you've done," he said in his deep, husky voice.

"Oh, you're most welcome, Silas. It was my pleasure. Those two are nothing but a delight."

Her words seemed forced to Silas' ears. Whatever was going on, he meant to get to the bottom of it.

After awkward moments of Silas' perusal, Maddy blurted, "Well, tomorrow's a big day. I best be off to bed." She turned and opened the door.

Silas jumped to his feet. "No, Maddy. Don't go. Please."

Maddy paused and turned cautious, almost frightened, eyes toward him.

Silas gently turned her away from the door and led her over to the swing. "Sit down. We need to talk." When he noticed her trembling, he chose to sit in a chair a few feet away.

"Maddy, what is it? Do I frighten you?"

"Oh, no! Of course not!" she answered then looked down. "Well, maybe a little," she said, almost too quietly to hear.

"But why? We've known each other for years."

She dabbed at her eyes and tried to compose herself. "I know. I shouldn't have said that. I'm really not afraid of you. It's something else entirely."

"What is it? I need to know."

"No...no, you really don't need to know this, Silas. I'm just being silly."

"Is it the Potter boys?"

"No."

"Your food supplies? Clothing for the kids? The livestock?"

"No, Silas. Really. It's nothing. Let's drop it." She got to her feet.

Silas also stood. "Maddy, if it concerns you, then it concerns the children, and therefore it's very much my business."

Maddy sighed and threw her hands up. "It was simply some unnecessary fretting of mine that needs to be put to rest. And I really don't want to talk about it." She sat back down and looked boldly at him. "You wanted to discuss something with me. What is it?"

Silas slowly lowered himself into the rocking chair and cleared his throat. "I wanted you to tell me about my children. How have they been? How are they doing now? What significant events have touched them, such as hiding from bushwhackers? Why do they call you 'Ma?' Insignificant details like those for a starter," he said in a challenging tone, which he regretted as soon as he saw her face.

"Oh," she said, looking down at her feet and fidgeting with her apron.

"I'm sorry, Maddy. It's just that I've worried and grieved over them for years and now here I am, and I find out that they've had to hide in a cellar from a ruthless enemy and...and now they've shifted so easily away from Mary to you. It's a lot to take in in one day."

Maddy hung her head, seemingly in shame. "I'm so sorry, Silas. I really, really tried my hardest every day to do what was best for them. Everything, *everything* I've done was for them!" She dropped her face into her hands. "Oh, Silas, if you only knew what those two mean to me. I would die for them! I'm sorry if I've displeased you in any way."

"Displeased me?" He reached over and grabbed her hand. "Dear Maddy! You haven't displeased me in the least! Under these circumstances, no one could have possibly pleased me more. I'm just puzzled about some things and I want answers."

Maddy nodded.

Very gently, Silas pried, "Can you tell me when they first started calling you Ma?"

With her face averted she tried her best to answer a very delicate question. "Very early. Ollie started calling me that before Anabel could talk, so it's the only name she's known me by. When Ollie first called me Ma, I started to correct him, then I looked into those sweet, trusting eyes and couldn't do it. He told me his first ma died and he needed a new one. He declared me to be his new one. The poor little tyke didn't have a pa or a ma and he needed one. So, I very happily stepped into that role." She dropped her head again. "I'm sorry. Y...you can explain to him that it's time to stop."

Silas ran his hand through his thick, dark hair and sat back. "That might be tough." He stared out into the evening dusk, filled with the sweet sound of spring peepers. "Maybe it would be wise to wait awhile."

Maddy silently nodded. In spite of her worst fears, she found herself relaxing. She glanced at Silas' profile and allowed herself the comfort of the moment; sitting in the presence of a good man that cared for her babies as much as she did. She, too, looked out over her yard, took a deep breath, and listened to the music of nature. At that moment of stillness, she sensed the sweet Presence of the Holy Spirit. The tension drained out of her. No matter what came, she knew she was His child and He was at work.

Silas leaned forward and clasped his hands together. "Wow. It's so peaceful, isn't it? Last night, I was curled up in my bedroll in a field east of Fair Grove, filled with such fear I could barely take a breath."

"Fear? Why?" Maddy asked.

"I knew I would be able to get here in the morning, but I had no idea what I might find." His voice choked. "I didn't even know if my babies were alive. Or if they were still here. And if they were, would they welcome me?"

Maddy reached for his hand. "Oh, Silas. I can't imagine."

"What I found when I got here is far beyond my dearest dreams. And for that, I have you to thank, Maddy." He held her hand firmly in his and looked her squarely in the eye. "Again, I can't thank you enough. I promise, I'll spend the rest of my life making it up to you." He pulled her to her feet and gave her a big, smothering, brotherly hug.

Maddy laughed then pulled away and wiped her tears. Silas held her shoulders and looked down at her with a troubled expression.

"What's the matter, Silas?" she asked.

"Maddy. You're nothing but a skeleton! I noticed that you'd lost weight, but I had no idea it was this bad. Do you feel alright?"

"Y...yes. I'm fine."

"I think you need to see a doctor."

"Nonsense! I think food is all I need."

Silas didn't seem to be convinced. "We'll talk some more tomorrow. For now, I think we both need sleep." He cupped her face with his big hand, winked then turned to head to the barn.

Maddy stood alone on the porch for a long time after that, looking up at the stars. In spite of her pounding heart, she tried to drink in the beauty and stillness of the night.

After breakfast the next morning, Silas went back to his farm. Ollie sulked because he wasn't invited. Anabel ran to the window several times to see if her pa was coming down the drive. In between her chores, Maddy paced. She wasn't sure what to expect. She knew Silas would eventually take the children to his home. When, was the question on her mind. And after they were gone, how often would he let her see them? When she looked around her house, she couldn't fathom the place without their presence.

CHAPTER SEVEN

Silas stood and surveyed his abandoned wreck of a farm. The work required to restore it was immense. He wasn't sure if he was up to the task. His dream had been that he'd bring the children back here to live after a couple of days of sweeping cobwebs out. But four years of neglect had produced far more than cobwebs. He stood in his front yard almost paralyzed. Where should he start? From years of training and practice, he did what he knew he must. He knelt down in the midst of the weeds and prayed a simple prayer. A prayer for strength and wisdom, and a pure, simple call for help.

When he stood, he knew that his first step was to make a list. He walked up the steps of his porch, scooting around the rotten, broken boards, and into the kitchen where he had a small desk. In the drawer, he found a brown-stained notebook where he had years of notes about planting times and locations, when the bull had been let loose with the cows, calving times, names of people that he had hired for harvest, their hours and wages, cost of lumber and fencing, amount of wool and what it sold for each year, on and on;

filling almost the entire notebook. But there were several unused pages in the back. In the back of the drawer, he found a stubby pencil. He pulled out his small pocket knife and whittled a sharp point on the end. Then he divided the pages into three categories; house, fields, and barns.

Silas, like any true farmer, knew that the crops had to take top priority. It was May; late for planting in Missouri, but the season was long enough that he had a chance if he started right away. So, he went outside to focus on the fields and whatever was needed to get seed in the ground. Southwest Missouri was beautiful, but southwest Missouri was a thick, fast-growing jungle of weeds, brush, small trees, and vines if it wasn't constantly beat back. The sight of his fields was daunting. It was as if he were starting from scratch. But, he reminded himself, as he stood to his full height and squared his shoulders, he owned this land, free and clear. And he had enough money to buy the needed supplies. At least he thought he did. He had been quickly promoted to second lieutenant which earned him a little over $100 per month, most of which he had saved.

He had given some of it to Maddy when he had returned for his visit in '62, but carefully hid the rest on his farm. The wages for the next three years were paid in paper greenbacks which Silas kept in a pouch securely strapped to his body at all times. When he rode down Maddy's drive a few days before, he had $2,500 in his possession. He also had $500 buried in a corner of one of his sheds, which was, at present, inaccessible because the shed had rotted and caved in. Three thousand dollars would go a long way toward restoring his farm, he realized with relief. He needed help and a farmhand would cost him about ten cents an hour or $250 per year. Realizing that hiring a man was an absolute necessity if he wanted his farm to thrive, actually gave him renewed hope.

Silas jotted notes as he thought.

Hire strong, honest, hardworking, young man

Clear field west of garden to plant to oats
Clear field behind barn to plant to wheat
Clear the two east fields to plant to corn
Clear garden plot
Plow and harrow above fields
Buy seed and plant oats, wheat, corn, and garden, in that order
Rebuild fences beginning with oat field
Prune apple trees in orchard

Next, Silas jotted down quick notes concerning barns and sheds then last, the house. The house could wait. He was counting on Maddy to continue caring for Ollie and Anabel at her place. The fields and barns were necessary to having a productive farm. He decided to ride to some neighboring farms to inquire about able-bodied men in need of work. First stop should be the home of Reverend Frank Richards who lived next to the Baptist church he had attended years ago. The reverend and his wife knew everyone in the area and might have suggestions for him. He hoped the reverend was still there. Because of time, he fought the urge to stop at Maddy's on the way to pick Ollie up. He would have been overjoyed at joining his pa for the rest of the day.

Silas pulled a biscuit and jerky from his pocket and munched as his horse trotted down the road. When he arrived, he was relieved to see healthy signs of life about the place. A dog howled at his approach and a plump, smiling lady walked through the open door of the church.

"Sister Richards? Is that you?" he asked as he slid off his horse and walked toward her.

"It sure is, Silas MacGregor! Why, I'd know you anywhere! Good to have you back home, boy!" She enveloped him in a motherly embrace. "Reverend Frank!" she hollered over her shoulder. "Come on out and see who dropped in!"

Soon a tall, skinny, white-haired man joined them. His

ice-blue eyes danced with merriment. "Praise be to the God of Glory!" he exclaimed. "Those sweet babies have got their pa back! God of mercy!" He slapped Silas on the back. "How have you been, boy?"

Silas laughed a hearty laugh and replied, "None the worse for wear, Reverend. In spite of that nasty war, I'm doin' mighty fine, sir."

"How are those young'uns of yours? I haven't seen them in a few weeks. I've been meaning to drop in for another visit but we've both been under the weather."

"Pshaw! *You've* been under the weather. And I've been occupied taking care of you, old man," Sister Richards said with a twinkle in her bright blue eyes. The reverend dropped his long arm down around her ample shoulders and squeezed.

"She's right. I don't know what I'd do without my Martha. I'd be dead. I'm sure of it," he said, laughing.

Being in their presence was like having his heart drenched in the balm of Gilead. Silas had forgotten how much he had missed them, what comfort they gave him.

"Speaking of, Martha, when are you going to get yourself a helpmeet, Silas? Mary has been gone five years, right?"

All comfort came to a screeching halt at the reverend's words. Silas stammered, "What are you talking about? I just got back."

"But surely, you've been giving it some thought all these years?" the reverend persisted, not seeming to care at all that Silas looked like he regretted coming to see them. It was the reverend's job, after all, to spur people on to better living and apparently Rev. Richards thought Silas couldn't go on with his life without a wife by his side.

Silas stared at them, befuddled by the drastic turn in where he intended to take this conversation. Sister Martha was no help. By the look of her, she was enjoying his discomfort far too much. Silas cleared his throat. "I came here to ask you if you knew any young men that need employment. I need a full-time farmhand."

Drat it! Neither of them seemed inclined to drop the touchy subject they had brought up. They simply stared and smiled. He stared back. If this was a game they were playing, and it probably was, he thought he could win. He smiled. They laughed. He was outnumbered and they knew it. He put his hat back on and turned to mount his horse.

Giving a loud sigh, he turned back to face them. "I declare! I forgot what busybodies you two were!"

Both of the Richards laughed heartily. "I guess we did kinda spring that on you, didn't we?" the reverend said with merriment dancing in his eyes.

"I'll say! You don't exactly play fair, you know. I was just beginning to think I needed to get back to going to church on Sundays, but now I'm not so sure."

The reverend laughed again. "Back to your question, Silas. I can think of two qualified boys for you to hire. Their fathers have returned from fighting but their families need the extra income. Luke Owens lives close enough you wouldn't have to board him. James lives a good five or six miles south of here."

"Is Luke Pete and Lori's boy? He's kinda young for this kind of work."

"He's four years older than the boy you remember. And big! Like an ox. If he's available, he's exactly what you need. He has a younger brother that can help their pa on his farm. Plus, a few little sisters."

"Thanks. I'll head on over there."

"Silas, please come back to church," Martha said before he could leave. "And bring those kids with you. Maddy, too, of course. She hasn't been here but two times since we buried her ma. I'm worried about her."

Silas paused and looked into Martha's kind face. "Me, too, Sister. She's so skinny and..." He shrugged his shoulders. "And... sad. Still grieving, I would imagine. Her pa and ma were everything to her."

"Well, maybe not everything. I think your two young'uns have worked their way into her heart in the past four years."

"She's but a child herself, much too young to be left alone," Silas said.

The reverend and Martha glanced at each other. "She's not a child anymore, Silas," Martha said.

Silas went on, "And those Potter boys won't leave her alone. She needs protection from them. I wish I could get her away from there for a while. She needs someone to take care of her, at least until she can get her strength back."

"Don't forget, Silas, that farm is hers," Reverend Richards said. "Who would take care of it if she leaves?"

"I would, of course," Silas answered. "I'm staying there, so it would be easy for me."

"You're staying there?" Martha asked, slightly aghast.

"In the barn, not the house," Silas explained. "My place is not fit for beast, much less a man and his two little ones."

"Are you taking your meals there as well?" Martha asked.

Silas shifted his feet and looked down. "Well yeah. Of course."

"So..." the reverend said as he put his hand on Silas' shoulder, "basically, other than sharing her bed, you're living like you're married to her."

Silas' head snapped up. "No! Not at all!"

"Silas," Martha said gently. "We trust you and Maddy to be circumspect, but what concerns me is how this will look to others. If Maddy's parents were still alive, this would be different. But she's a young, single woman. Her reputation is at stake."

"Surely people realize Maddy's but a child. She can't be more than sixteen. I'm thirty, almost old enough to be her father."

"Why don't you just marry her?" the reverend asked.

"That would solve a lot of problems. For both you and her."

"Marry Maddy?" Silas was shocked. "Don't even put such a thought into my head, Reverend! With all due respect, didn't you hear me just now? She's not more than sixteen!"

"We have women in our congregation that married when they were fifteen," Martha said.

"And their husbands were probably fifteen as well. I'm thirty. Almost twice her age! When, and if, I marry, it will be to someone my own age." Silas held up his hand when he saw the reverend about to contradict him. "Please, Reverend. No more about marriage."

"Suit yourself, Silas," the reverend said. "I forgot what a stubborn man you were."

Silas snorted. "Reasonable, not stubborn."

"I think I might have an idea about what to do for Maddy," Martha said.

Both men turned to her.

"Do you remember Daniel Long and his daughter, Eliza? Eliza was one of Maddy's best friends."

"Of course, I do. Didn't they move to Springfield just before the war?"

"Yes. Daniel became an officer under General Lyon. He was killed at the Battle of Wilson's Creek."

Silas bowed his head for an instant. "I'm so sorry. I hadn't heard. What happened to Eliza?"

"She married an old friend from northern Missouri, Jonathan Monroe. I think he'd reached the rank of Captain. I ran into her at the mercantile on the square in Springfield last time I was there. They have a baby boy and live in a big house not far from the square, on Elm Street, I believe. Take Maddy there for a visit. Ollie and Anabel, too. Knowing Eliza like I do, I'm sure she'll insist they stay with them for a while. They are well off. It won't be a burden to them."

Silas smiled and thanked her. The men shook hands amiably and with a promise to come to church on Sunday, Silas mounted and began the ride to the Owens' farm two miles to the east.

Luke and his parents were thrilled for Luke to get the job as Silas' farmhand and Silas had made good use of him already. The day after he hired him, he sent him to Springfield with a message for Jonathan and Eliza Monroe, asking if Maddy and the children could come for a visit. Eliza's enthusiastic answer was all he needed to convince Maddy to pack a few things and set out.

Since Luke didn't have a horse of his own, he had told Silas he preferred to sleep at the farm and go home on Sundays. "I can sleep anywhere," he told Silas when Silas tried to describe the poor conditions at his farm. "I'm sleepin' in the shed at home anyway. We've outgrown our house. And besides, it's noisy at my place. Too many sisters. I wouldn't mind at all getting me some peace and quiet for a change."

"How about the barn at Maddy's until we can fix things up a bit?" Silas asked. It dawned on him that it might help with appearances if someone else besides just himself stayed in the barn.

"Stay at Maddy's?" Luke said a mite too eagerly. "Yes, sir. I'd like that. I'd like that a lot. She's a right purty little thing."

Unexpectedly annoyed, Silas questioned his choice in a farmhand. "You will refer to her as Miss Malone and at all times treat her with the utmost respect. Do you understand?"

"Uh...yes, sir. I sure didn't mean any disrespect. She and I went to school together and I've always called her Maddy. I'm sorry about her folks. They were good people."

"Yes, they were," Silas answered. "Luke, I declare, if

you work as much as you talk, I think you'll be fine." He laughed. "If not, I'll be sending you back to your sisters."

CHAPTER EIGHT

Two days later, Maddy and two excited children were in a buckboard on their way to Springfield with Silas at the reins.

At about ten in the morning, Silas pulled the wagon up in front of a big blue house on Elm Street a few blocks from the Square. Maddy's eyes hungrily scanned the front, longing to see her old friend. Silas helped her down first then little Anabel. Ollie jumped to the ground with a loud whoop.

"You go on, Maddy. I'll get your bags," he said with tenderness. Just then, the door burst open and Eliza ran down the steps in a flurry of blue calico.

"Madeline Malone!" she almost shrieked. "Maddy! You've come!" Eliza enveloped Maddy in a long, tearful hug and kissed both of her cheeks. Maddy laughed through her tears. "Let me look at you." She held her at arm's length and exclaimed, "Oh, Maddy! You've always been skinny but this is scary!"

"Why, thank you," Maddy answered.

"I'm sorry. That was indelicate of me, wasn't it?" Eliza

tucked Maddy's arm in hers and started for the house. "But it's true. Have you been sick?"

"No...just working hard and skimping on food," she answered, too happy to be in the least bit offended.

"Well, we can take care of that while you're here," Eliza said. "For the past couple of years, food hasn't been an issue for us. We have a farm south of here that my husband and a couple of others have brought back to life."

They stepped through the front door and Maddy's eyes traveled over the beautifully ornate interior. "Eliza, this is beautiful! Is it yours?"

"No. This house belongs to Elin Johnson. Wait until you hear how I met her. You will never, never in a thousand years believe the story I have to tell you, my dear friend. And I can't wait to get started!" She squeezed Maddy's arm. "But first, let me introduce you to the amazing lady that owns this place and of course reacquaint myself with these two little ones of yours." She turned to Ollie and Anabel and lowered herself to their level. True to form, Anabel stuck her finger in her mouth and Ollie stuck his hand out for a handshake.

Maddy chuckled and put her hand on their heads just as Silas walked in with their baggage. "This is Anabel. She's five. And this big gentleman is Oliver MacGregor. He's seven." She turned to Silas. "And of course, you remember Silas."

Eliza greeted the children then turned to Silas. "Silas, it seems like it's been a lifetime since I saw you last. How have you been?"

Silas removed his hat and gave a small nod of his head. "Very well, Mrs. Monroe. You have changed very little since the last time I saw you. Congratulations on your marriage. Where's Mr. Monroe?"

"He's at our farm trying to get it ready for us to move into. And please call me Eliza and my husband, Jon. Something tells me we'll all be close friends."

"I'm so sorry to hear about your pa. He was a man I looked up to."

"Thank you, Silas," Eliza answered. "It's been almost four years and I still miss him."

"I understand that. It's been five years since I lost Mary and not a day goes by that I don't think about her." He looked down for a moment and cleared his throat. "When would you like me to come back to get you, Maddy?"

Maddy glanced at Eliza and answered quickly, "Day after tomorrow, if you don't mind. I don't want us to become a burden."

At this Eliza gasped. "A burden? Dear girl! You are a gift to my starving soul. A month and no less!"

Maddy laughed. "Surely you jest, Eliza! I forgot how funny you were! At the end of a month, you'd be begging Silas to come back to get us. Besides, he's been away from them for four years. I don't think he could handle one more month."

"I'm not at all exaggerating when I suggest a month. I'd like it to be several months."

"But, the cost of feeding three extra people, Eliza! We can't impose like this. Besides, I have a farm to take care of."

"Maddy," Silas said quietly, "I'll be more than happy to take care of your farm. And as far as the children are concerned, I'll ride in every Sunday and spend the day with them."

"But, Silas..."

He interrupted, "I'll not be able to see much of them for the next month anyway. Even with Luke's help, I'll be working from sunup to sundown. I'll have time for a quick supper then I'll have to hit the sack."

"Who will cook for you?" Maddy protested.

"We'll manage. I'm heading over to the Square to stock up on food supplies. Whatever nuts, beans, flour, and jerky I buy, we can supplement with what we hunt down. Plus, milk and eggs. I think we'll survive. I also learned to make halfway decent biscuits while I was on the trail," he said with a wink. "I might even pick up a few more chickens."

"Silas, are you sure?" she asked, trying not to worry.

With a wink at Eliza, Silas stepped toward Maddy and gently led her out to the porch. "Yes, I'm sure." He turned her to look at him and lowered his voice. "Maddy, you're not well and I'm worried about you."

She stared at him a moment and then to his surprise, she looked down and wiped tears from her eyes.

He pulled her into his arms then released her when he remembered Sister Martha's words about appearances. "Maddy, honey, I'm sorry, but it's true. Surely you, yourself, know this."

Maddy nodded. "I suppose you're right. I haven't been myself since Pa died in October. And then losing Ma, I thought…I thought…" She hid her face as she cried some more. "I'm sorry. I've tried to be strong for Ollie and Anabel. But I…I'm just so tired, Silas. So tired and I can't seem to shake it. Sometimes I feel like I'm sinking into a dark hole."

"Oh, believe me. I understand that dark hole. I've been there. And, understand this, Maddy Malone. You *have* been strong for my children. In no way have you failed them or me. I'm amazed at your fortitude. Never, never be ashamed. I will never regret my choice of who I left my children with." He found himself holding her face in his hands and stroking the tears away. Then again, he stepped quickly back. Confound appearances.

Maddy finally agreed to stay for a month after she talked to Eliza again and met the lady of the house, Elin Johnson, who joined Eliza in expressing what a delight their company would be. Silas and all three women were taken aback at the reaction Ollie and Anabel had toward Elin. They both melted into her arms as if they had known her forever. The tenderness in their eyes and their reluctance to leave her embrace warmed the hearts of all who were watching. Silas stood in awe. It seemed as if something magical had just happened.

Silas wrapped his two babies up in his big arms and said his good-byes with promises of many fun-filled visits. They took off squealing in the direction of the backyard when Elin invited them to visit her gardens and her secret passageway.

After Silas left, Eliza showed Maddy to their rooms at the top of the stairs. Maddy unpacked her few belongings and those of Ollie's and Anabel's. She freshened up at the washstand and went down the stairs to find Eliza, who was busy in the kitchen with a sweet-faced, young black woman.

"Maddy, I'd like you to meet Jessica. She and her children lived with us during part of the war."

Maddy happily greeted Jessica who, it appeared, was in the middle of baking several loaves of bread. Eliza was busily putting together the noon meal. "May I help?" Maddy asked.

"Actually, I'm almost done. You could go call Elin and the children and meet me in the dining room."

Maddy stepped out into the beautiful gardens in the backyard. She walked down the garden paths in search of the happy voices she could hear a distance away. Her heart was warmed at the sight that greeted her. Elin sat on a bench cuddling Anabel while Ollie did cartwheels in the grass.

"It's time to eat, my little ones. Are you having fun?"

They both ran to her. "Oh, Ma!" Ollie exclaimed. "You should see this place! There's even a secret passageway to another house. Miss Elin promised to take us there if it's alright with you."

Maddy smiled. "Of course, it is. After our meal though."

After a delicious and filling meal, Elin took a walk with the kids and Eliza took Maddy to the parlor. Jessica served them both tea and cake. Eliza's eyes danced with her eagerness to share her story, but first, she expressed her sorrow over the loss of Maddy's parents and asked how she had fared over the past four years.

"It's...it's been difficult but we've managed. Thank God it's over. I'm not sure I would have survived the months after my ma passed if it hadn't been for Ollie and Anabel. They gave me a reason to get up every morning."

"Maddy," Eliza said as she put a comforting hand on her arm, "they are thriving. You've done more than well, concerning them. Anybody can see that."

"As difficult as it's been, I will have to say, it's been filled with sweetness and love," Maddy said with a sweet smile. Unbidden tears sprang to her eyes. "I'm sorry, Eliza. I can't seem to get control of my crying lately."

Eliza squeezed her arm and waited. "How long ago did Silas come back?"

Maddy wiped away the tears that had run down her face. "Less than a week ago."

"Has he taken the kids to his place yet?"

Maddy gulped down a sob just as a baby's cries came from upstairs.

"Excuse me, dear. My Daniel calls. I'll be back."

Maddy paced the room and tried desperately to compose herself before Eliza returned. She was being such a ninny! To think that she ever entertained the idea that Ollie and Anabel might belong to her. Pure foolishness!

Eliza swept in with one of the most beautiful babies

Maddy had ever laid eyes on. "This is our precious Daniel," she announced with apparent pride as she put him down to toddle across the room.

Maddy dropped to the floor to welcome the cherub into her arms. "Eliza, he's adorable!"

Just then Jessica entered. "Does the little master need to be fed, 'Liza?"

"Yes, please, Jessica. And could you take him for a spell? Maddy and I need to talk."

"Of course! With pleasure, ma'am."

When they left the room, Eliza turned sympathetic eyes onto her friend. "I can think of many reasons for your tears, dear girl, but I want you to tell me." She led Maddy to sit again.

Maddy shook her head. "I'm afraid I'm being a fool, Eliza."

"A fool? I think not! You've lost both of your parents in the past few months." Maddy hid her face and nodded. "And you're about to lose your babies," Eliza added softly.

Maddy sucked in a torturous breath.

"Aha. My suspicions have been confirmed."

A strangled sob burst unbidden from Maddy. "I should have known," she wailed. "I *did* know, but I still let it happen!"

"Maddy, dear, of course you did. I'm sure I would have done the same. I'm not at all surprised by this. I saw you with them four years ago."

"So...so you know what I'm talking about?"

"That they've become your children?"

"Yes. It's not what I planned." She wrung her hands. "It...it just happened. The poor little tykes don't have a mother and...and well, I so, so badly wanted that role, so when Ollie started calling me 'Ma' I didn't correct him."

"Well, I can certainly understand you doing that, Maddy."

"I don't think Silas was at all pleased when he found

out. He...he wasn't angry. You know Silas. He's too kind to show his anger to me. But he was not happy about it. I'm sure of that."

"Oh, I see." Eliza stroked Maddy's arm. "He's very fond of you, Maddy."

"Who?"

"Silas, of course."

"Well, we've been neighbors for years. He and the kids came to our house almost every night after Mary died."

"If you two got married, it would solve your problem, you know."

Maddy's head jerked up. "Eliza! For shame!"

Eliza merely laughed. "I'm surprised you hadn't already thought about it."

Maddy looked away in shame.

Eliza laughed again. "I knew it! You have thought about it!" She reached up and cupped the face of her friend. "You have the most delightful, little, freckled, elfin face. I do think our Silas is a bit taken with you."

"Hush!" Maddy felt absolutely mortified.

"Come on, admit it, Maddy. You used to dream about him back before the war. You weren't alone, remember? Megan O'Mally and I were pretty infatuated with him as well."

"I might admit to some attraction way back when I was a child. That was a very, very long time ago. And he was a much older, happily married man. We should have all been ashamed of ourselves."

"We were schoolgirls and didn't know any better."

"I'd prefer to put those silly days way, way behind me and never bring them up again. His poor wife. She probably wanted to slap all three of us."

"Mary knew and Mary adored us."

Maddy shook her head to rid herself of unwanted memories.

Eliza softly added, "He's not married now, Maddy."

"Eliza Long! You are shameless! I'm sure if Silas is even considering marriage, which I sincerely doubt he is, then it won't be me he's drawn to."

"And why would you say that?"

Maddy couldn't believe the audacity of her meddling friend. "Silas is extremely handsome, in case you hadn't noticed. And I'm a mousy little nobody."

"Maddy! Surely you don't believe that about yourself. You are one of the most beautiful women I know. Maybe even the most beautiful. And Silas is not blind!"

"You are out of your mind, Eliza!"

At this, Eliza threw herself back in her chair and roared with laughter. "You've never seen yourself the way others see you, Maddy, and that makes you so endearing to everyone that knows you."

CHAPTER NINE

Maddy realized that she, Ollie, and Anabel were thriving under the care of Elin and Eliza. Elin sat down with Maddy in the parlor on her second day there and demanded that she get proper rest and nutrition. Eliza could have suggested the same thing, but Maddy would have rejected her advice outright. Sixty-eight-year-old Elin, on the other hand, had years of practice getting people to bend to her will. "Madeline," she started out gently, "I've seen this condition in people in the past and unless you follow my orders, I'm afraid you won't heal."

"What condition?" Maddy asked somewhat alarmed.

"Oh, some doctors might call it melancholia. Others call it depression. Whatever you want to call it, in your case, it's simply a deep sadness that's very understandable but very difficult to recover from. Both Eliza and I have suffered from it and understand you completely. This is nothing to be ashamed of."

"Eliza suffered from this?"

Elin chuckled. "Oh yes. After her father was killed. She

displayed it as anger and bitterness and handled it through revenge."

"Dear, sweet, happy Eliza?"

"I take it she hasn't told you her story yet?"

"Story? What story?"

"I'll save that for her to tell. I know she's dying to fill you in on her first two years of the war. Now that the war's over and we won, we both feel safe sharing this with others."

"Safe? What were you and Eliza up to?" Maddy asked with suspicion. "Oh, wait! Does this have anything to do with those bundles Eliza hid on my farm?"

Elin held up her hand. "Say no more. I know nothing of any bundles hidden at your place. Apparently, Eliza had more going on than I realized, the sneak! Let's get back to your health, missy. What you need, and what I intend to see that you get, is lots of rest, good food, fresh air, laughter, and friendship. I think you'll get all of those here. If you follow my orders, that is."

"I can't let you and Eliza and Jessica do all the work. I'm responsible for Silas' two children. I'm not some invalid he dropped off to be coddled."

"Actually, the reason Silas brought you here was to give you an opportunity to heal. And unless you, too, see the need for healing, I'm afraid you will be a very difficult case to deal with."

"No disrespect intended, Elin, but I'm not a 'case.' I'm your guest."

"Exactly. A guest in *my* house. And I expect my guests to follow my rules." Elin reached out and gently took Maddy's hand. "Maddy, I've watched you. You never relax. You're always finding work to do. I have some training in nursing and I insist that you put yourself in my care while you're in my house."

Maddy gazed into Elin's eyes and started to tear up. "You insist?"

"Yes, Maddy. And I will not budge. So please let me do my job. I'll take great pleasure in seeing the difference this month will make if you'll cooperate."

"And the children?"

"You can still cuddle them and read to them and tuck them into bed. Just no more kitchen work or housework. I want you to sleep as late as your body requires and I want you to take at least one nap per day."

"Oh my! I'm to become a lady of leisure. Is that it?"

"Exactly. For one month. Take strolls through the neighborhood, read books, knit, spend lots of time with Eliza pouring your soul out, laugh, pick flowers. Whatever strikes your fancy. But no work. And you must eat! Child, you're a scarecrow! I intend to fatten you up, Maddy, dearest."

Maddy sat back and looked into Elin's kind eyes. "I think this might be fun," she said slowly. "If I can get used to it."

"Why don't you start your healing process with a nice leisurely stroll through the neighborhood with Eliza so she can tell you the beginning of her story. I will be delighted to watch the children. They bring me joy, Maddy."

Thirty minutes later, the two bosom friends walked down Elm Street then turned right on South Avenue toward the Square. "I have a gift for you, Maddy. I guess you can say it's a thank-you gift because you allowed me to hide something precious on your property four years ago."

"Eliza, I was happy to help. Surely you know that."

"I know. But quite possibly I was putting you and your parents in danger, and for that I'll always be sorry and always be grateful."

"Danger? Why? What did you hide?"

Eliza looked around to make sure no one was listening. "For now, let me buy your gift. When we're back home, I'll tell you more about that day."

When they reached the mercantile, Eliza led Maddy over to the fabric. "Let's pick out colors to suit you. One for an everyday dress and one for church."

"Eliza, the cost! Please, no," Maddy protested.

"This is just part of the amazing story I have to tell you. I now have scads of money."

Maddy just stared and grinned.

"You don't believe me, do you?" Eliza's eyes twinkled. "I, dear Maddy, am an heiress."

"Your pa?" Maddy asked.

"Yes. And another completely unexpected gentleman who died at the beginning of the war. When we get back, I'll explain everything. For now, choose your fabric. Jessica is dying to get started. She sells the bread she bakes, she takes in laundry, and she sews for people. That's how she feeds her children. So, we're helping her."

Together, they chose a beautiful green calico for Maddy's everyday dress and shiny, brown satin fabric for a church dress. Maddy was so excited she could barely take a breath as she watched Eliza pay for the fabric and instruct the storekeeper where to send the package. Next, Eliza led the way to a shoe store where she insisted Maddy select a new pair of serviceable boots. Again, Maddy protested, but Eliza argued back. "I've seen your boots, Maddy. There are holes in the soles and your toes are about to burst through the ends. The time has come for you to get new ones."

When Maddy hesitated at the door, Eliza whispered in her ear, "Those sacks I hid at your place were filled with gold and it's all mine."

Maddy staggered back at such outlandish news. Eliza merely held her finger to her lips and nodded. "I'm paying you for being my bank during a very dangerous time."

"Is...is it still there?"

"I sure hope so. I haven't looked yet. One of these days soon, Jon and I plan to ride out there with a wagon and claim what's ours."

"You're so...so nonchalant about all this. It's too incredible to take in."

"You should have seen me when I found out. I was anything but nonchalant."

"Did you know what you were hiding?"

"I knew it was gold but I had no idea it was mine. Actually, it wasn't mine yet."

"The gold was part of your inheritance?" Maddy asked as they entered the store.

Eliza put her hand on Maddy's arm and shook her head to silence her. "We'll talk later," she whispered. Maddy found the perfect boots, and at Eliza's insistence added a pair of high-heeled, dainty boots for church.

On the way home, Eliza started her story. "When I learned of my father's death after the Battle of Wilson's Creek, I thought I'd suffocate in my grief. That grief very quickly turned to anger then a blind rage. I wanted to kill anyone and everyone associated with the South, so I dressed like a boy and tried to enlist." She went on with one of the most fascinating, unbelievable stories Maddy had ever heard. But it was true. This old friend of hers had become a spy operating out of two houses in Springfield, Missouri; one of those was Elin's house, who was also engaged in the Springfield spy ring. Eliza had been captured by the enemy, beat, almost hung then rescued by Union soldiers. Eliza told part of the story on their walk home and finished it while they sat alone in Elin's parlor. Maddy's mouth hung open through most of it. Eliza told of how she and Captain Jonathan Monroe, an old friend from her childhood, fell in love then married. Then she added the surprise of Abe Goodman's will which left all of his belongings to her. He was a wealthy banker, landowner, and best friend of her pa.

"Abe actually left all of his belongings to my father, who in turn left it all to me. And my father surprised me. He had sold our Fair Grove property, the farm near you, and used the money to buy a farm south of here, land adjoining Abe's place. Between the two pieces of property, I inherited 600 acres. My father also had a sizable amount of gold stashed at Abe's bank."

"So, you inherited both your pa's gold and Abe Goodman's gold?" Maddy asked.

"Yes. Although it could still be contested by Abe's nephew, Henry Goodman. He's the worst scoundrel this earth has ever seen and more than once, he's tried to force me to reveal the location of the gold. Thankfully he ran off just before the war ended." Eliza shuddered then continued with her unbelievable tale.

"A few minutes before the lawyer gave me the good news, I thought I was penniless. Except for what Jonathan was offering me, of course. He had proposed to me by then. We planned to get married and live at his place, but he quickly decided Abe's place was the better choice. It's bigger and more developed."

"Has he sold his place?"

"Not yet. Now that the war is over, we expect the price of land to soar. We'll wait."

"Unbelievable, Eliza. Every bit of it. You must be charmed."

Eliza's smile faded. "I'd give it all up to have my pa back. Not Jonathan and little Daniel, of course," she quickly added. "But I'd happily live in poverty if I could just have Pa back."

Maddy sat next to her and wrapped her up in a tight, warm hug. "I know, Eliza. Believe me, I know. I want my pa and ma so badly I can barely swallow sometimes. That house is so, so empty without them." They sat for several minutes and wept healing tears. When Maddy sat back she asked, "Who hasn't been touched by death recently? It's so heartbreaking. I feel like I'm being such a baby."

Eliza reached out and wiped Maddy's tears. "Your loss is so recent, honey. I desperately miss my pa, but the deep, gut-wrenching grieving is over. I'm truly happy now. You're still adjusting to your loss. And the possibility of more loss when Silas takes his little ones home."

Maddy's throat constricted.

"Not to mention your fatigue and starvation."

Maddy chuckled sadly and shook her head. "Fatigue and hunger, we can fix. Losing my babies is another matter."

CHAPTER TEN

Silas pounded one more nail into the top step and looked around with satisfaction at the finished porch. He had torn the old, rotten one down and built a new one from lumber he had picked up in Fair Grove. He could see Luke out in the cornfield checking on the new sprouts. Luke had turned out to be better at working than at talking and that was saying a lot. He was quite the talker, for sure. Silas found himself liking the boy more each day. At first, he tried to tune him out, but then he realized he was actually quite entertaining. To Silas' great surprise, Luke was a veritable workhorse, definitely worth every cent he paid him and more. Perhaps he should stop thinking of him as "the boy." He was certainly doing the work of a man. More like two men.

An unfamiliar noise drew his attention toward the driveway. A small buggy approached with a woman at the reins. Silas took the nails from between his lips and stood to his full height. He couldn't identify the woman, although there was a vague familiarity about her. She pulled up and stopped a few feet from the bottom step.

"Hello, Silas! I heard you were back. It's so good to see you again," a tall, slightly plump lady exclaimed in a smooth, almost purring voice.

Silas wracked his brain in a desperate attempt to conjure her up in his foggy memory. Nothing. The woman never skipped a beat as she held out her hand to be helped down from the buggy. Silas recovered quickly enough to wipe his dirty hands on his pants and reach out just in time.

"I figured you two hard-working men might need some sustenance so I brought a meal for you." She proceeded to reach into the back of her buggy to pull out a basket. Then brushing past him, she went up the steps and into his house.

"I'm surprised I haven't seen you in church," she said loudly over her shoulder. "Reverend announced you were home."

Silas walked uncertainly into his disaster of a kitchen to find her wiping the table off.

"There! That should do. For now anyway." She looked around at the rest of the room with distaste. "My! This place needs work. How can you eat in here?"

"We don't," he answered with a touch of annoyance in his tone.

She brushed off a chair and sat down. "You eat outside, then?"

"Sometimes. We eat most of our meals at..." He was about to say *at Maddy's*, but quickly decided against it. *Who is this woman?* "I'll go call Luke."

"No, no, no. Sit," she commanded as she patted the only other chair at the table. "Luke is busy. We don't need to bother him. Besides, you and I have a lot of catching up to do."

"Catching up?" he asked dumbly.

"Yes, you silly man." She again patted the chair next to her. "Sit."

Silas sat numbly as he watched her unload the contents

of the basket. She rattled on about the old days before the war while she set before him thick, fragrant, beef stew and steaming, flaky biscuits. He said a quick prayer and dug in to his meal, nodding at her rambling. Nodding, but not paying attention to anything she said.

"Weren't those the sweetest of times though?" she asked.

With his mouth full of buttery biscuit, all he could do was nod.

"Oh, Silas, I'm so glad that you think so, too," she gushed as she laid a hand on his arm.

At that, Silas was abruptly awakened from his dreamy gluttony. He shifted his arm away from her and said as politely as he could muster, "I'm really sorry, ma'am, but I'll have to admit that my mind has been on your delicious food and not at all on what you were saying. I guess I was hungrier than I realized." When he saw the annoyance in her eyes, he quickly added, "I can't thank you enough for this meal. What a kind, neighborly thing for you to do."

She softened and reached for his hand. "It's nothing, Silas, considering our connections."

Silas gently removed his hand on the pretense of needing to wipe his mouth. There was certainly something very familiar about this woman, but for the life of him, he could not bring up a name or even a face that he knew. Had he been more injured than he realized? He stood. "Thank you again, but I must get back to work. I'm sure Luke would welcome you dropping his portion off when you pass him on your way out." He saw slight irritation cross her countenance again as she quickly packed the basket.

"Shall I bring a meal by this evening as well?" she asked.

"Oh, no. No thanks. We already have our meal waiting for us," he lied as he escorted her out the door. "We're actually eating with the reverend and his wife." That was the truth because Silas had just decided they needed to drop in and take Sister Martha up on her offer to drop by anytime. He needed some answers about this woman before she showed up again, which he was quite certain she would.

The buggy creaked under her considerable weight. Silas fought his unkind thoughts of how nice it would have been for her to share her apparent abundance of food with poor Maddy and his children during their years of need.

"Tomorrow, then," she said in farewell. She flicked the reins and was gone before he could protest. He watched her trot down the drive, stop at the edge of the cornfield, and wave at Luke. Luke approached her wagon, received the bundle she handed him then stepped back as she quickly drove away. Luke walked toward the house, his big strapping frame looking as if he could work for several more hours.

"Who was that?" he asked when he got to the porch. "She didn't introduce herself."

"I don't know, but I think I'm supposed to know her. I think she goes to our church."

"Really? I've never seen her before, but I'm not always there," Luke said between bites. That's when Silas noticed Luke's meal, a small slice of ham and a hard, cold biscuit.

That evening at Sister Martha's table, Silas asked a few questions about their mystery visitor. Both the reverend and Martha racked their brains for possibilities. Even with a description from both Silas and Luke, they weren't coming up with any answers.

"She said she heard you announce in the service that I had returned," Silas said.

Martha looked with puzzlement at her husband. "I don't remember you making any such announcement."

The reverend scratched his beard. "I didn't. I talked to people after the service about your return. Hmmm..."

Just then, they heard the dog bark and a clatter as a wagon pulled up in their yard. Reverend Richards rose to greet his visitor while the others lingered at the table. A very familiar, female voice drifted through the door.

"That's her," Silas said quietly to Martha.

Martha stood, laid a restraining hand on his arm as he started to get up, and said, "Stay here, Silas. I'm going to get to the bottom of this."

He and Luke watched her leave and strained to hear the conversation out in front of the house. The only words they could make out were from the visitor whose voice was louder than even the reverend's. It carried in snatches to their curious ears. "Oh, yes! Such a lovely day... I thought you might appreciate some dessert...oh! I see you have company...yes, I live not far from...yes, now that the war's over...I've missed your sermons..." On and on she went, apparently slow in taking the hint that, yes indeed, they had company and they weren't going to invite her to join them.

Finally, to his relief, she drove off. Both the Richards walked back into the house with eyes full of laughter and mischief.

"Oh no," Silas said, shaking his head. He pinned them both with a challenging look. "You two have the answer I'm looking for, don't you? Out with it! And please try to control your laughter while you're at it."

"Well, I'm obviously missing something, aren't I?" Luke said.

Martha plopped the dessert down on the table. "Apple pie, anyone?" she asked as she and her husband sat.

"Yes, please," Luke exclaimed as he held out his plate. "Was that the same lady that brought a meal to us today, Silas? I like her. That's mighty sweet of her."

Silas grimaced, refused the pie, and asked, "So? Who is she?"

Frank answered first, "I can see why you didn't recognize her, Silas. I didn't until Martha came out and greeted her by name. She's changed a little since we last saw her." His eyes twinkled.

"I don't think I would have known her, either. It was her voice that gave her away," Martha said. "She was in Mary's class at school. Bonnie Adams. Remember?"

Silas scratched his head. "No. No memory at all. Mary was younger than me and other than Mary, I never paid attention to the younger girls."

"Back then, she was very, very skinny. Tall and skinny."

"Sorry, I'm drawing a blank."

"Does the nickname 'Scrawny Bonnie' ring a bell?"

It finally dawned on Silas. "No! She was a quiet, little scarecrow! There's no, absolutely no resemblance to Scrawny Bonnie!" Silas stood and paced the floor.

He stopped and looked at the reverend with sadness. "I...I wasn't the kindest boy back when I was 12, 13, 14." He shrugged. "I might have been one of the boys that called her Scrawny Bonnie."

The reverend chuckled, "Might have been?"

Silas shook his head. "I'm sure I did. I'm not proud of it. But I don't remember being mean to her. Like I said, I didn't pay attention to the younger girls. Mary had my heart, even way back then."

"Well, whatever you did to Bonnie back in your school days, apparently all is forgiven," Martha said with a smile. Silas shook his head at her.

Martha continued with a little too much mirth in her tone. "And now, you have a chance to make it up to her, Silas."

Silas ran his fingers through his hair and sat back down at the table. "All I want to do right now is fix my place up so my children can come home and live with me." He looked with pleading eyes at Frank and Martha. "Can I at least hope that the two of you could offer a little advice?"

Martha's eyes softened. She put a comforting hand on Silas' arm. "Always, Silas. This is just too much fun to ignore."

"Believe me when I say today was not fun for me."

"What do you mean, Silas?" Luke asked. "A pretty lady drops delicious food off for us. I, for one, enjoyed it."

Reverend Richards asked in his very serious reverend tone, "What happened today, son?"

Silas glanced at young Luke and answered carefully, "Let's just say, she made her intentions known."

"Where was Luke?"

"In the field."

"Do you expect her back?"

"Yes, sir. I do."

Frank turned to Luke. "Luke, I think Silas might have another job for you."

Silas nodded his agreement and leaned toward Luke. "I want you to schedule your time so that you are near the house at noon and every time you see Miss Adams come down the drive, you are to drop what you're doing and come to the house to join me for our meal. Understand?"

Luke nodded.

Silas put his hand on Luke's shoulder and squeezed. "Every time."

"And," the reverend added, "stay by his side until Miss Adams is gone."

CHAPTER ELEVEN

Silas was true to his word in traveling the twenty miles to Springfield each Sunday to be with his children. The last two weekends, he left on Saturday evening so he could spend more time with them. And each weekend, he was pleased to see the remarkable changes in Maddy. She had gained weight and energy and had lost the chronically fretful look in her eyes. She laughed more and cried less.

Ollie danced in excited circles when Silas arrived to pick his family up. On every visit, he had filled them in on the progress he had made on his farm. The house was far from being finished, but his old bedroom was fixed up enough that he and his children now had a place to sleep. Luke had fixed up a corner of Silas' barn for his bedroom, so neither of the men needed to use Maddy's barn.

Maddy listened to all of Silas' news with a sweet smile, but Silas noticed it didn't quite reach her eyes.

When Silas put the last of their luggage in his wagon, he reached his hand out to Maddy to help her step up to the seat. Both Elin and Eliza had tears in their eyes as they said their good-byes. "Please come back often, Maddy," Elin said. "And bring those children with you. I feel like I'm losing my grandchildren." She dabbed at her eyes with a white hankie.

"I'll bring them, if Silas lets me," Maddy answered.

Silas smiled warmly. "Of course, I will," he answered. "I've seen you with them, Elin. I think they both need a grandmother in their lives and I can't think of anyone better."

"Bless you, Silas. You've made a happy woman out of me with that promise. I'm making it a promise, if you don't mind."

Silas chuckled and held his hand out to her. "I don't mind. Let's shake on it, dear lady. Then you'll know I'm in earnest."

Elin took his big hand and held on. She quietly said, "I'll be the best grandmother possible. But they need a mother, too, you know, Silas."

He chuckled indulgently and winked at her. "Everything in its time, ma'am." He straightened, waved, and flicked the reins over his horse. The little farm wagon creaked as it turned and made its way down Elm Street and around the corner. Both Anabel and Ollie waved until they could no longer see Elin and Eliza.

Silas couldn't wipe the smile off his face. He had dreamed for years about this day, the day he could finally take his children home. He talked about the crops he and Luke had planted and the work he had managed to get done on the house and barn. "It's still a mess but it's home and I think you're gonna love it."

He glanced back to see Ollie grinning and Anabel scowling.

"Did I tell you I bought a horse?" Silas asked.

"A horse? For me?" Ollie almost shouted.

"No, son. That will come later. I bought a big work horse from the Donaldsons. Her name is Maud."

"Oh. Can I ride her?"

"We'll see. Don't try it without me though. She's awful big and I'm not sure she'll know what to do with you. You might get stepped on."

Silas glanced at Maddy, who seemed awfully quiet. "I tried to not make too much of a mess of your house, Maddy. I had to use your kitchen for our meals most of the month. I managed to clean my stove out last week to the point it's useable now."

Maddy gave him a weak smile and a nod. Silas flicked the reins and grew silent. After two hours of plodding along the road, Silas pulled over to a creek to water his horse.

"Jump down, youngsters. Let's stretch our legs and eat that picnic that Jessica packed for us." He reached up to help Maddy down. The children ran down to the creek to look for frogs and crawdads. Maddy spread a blanket and unloaded the basket of food. When Silas backed his horse away from the creek, he looked at the downcast face of Maddy. He took a moment to loosen the harness and rub the horse down. Then he walked over to the blanket and lowered himself down.

"You're quiet today," he said. Maddy looked at him briefly and smiled.

"I don't think I've heard one word from you since we left. Are you alright?"

"I'm fine," she said in a soft voice as she continued to set the meal out.

"You're sad to say good-bye to Eliza and Elin, aren't you?"

Maddy nodded and turned away. "Would you call the children?" she managed to say. "The food is ready." He obliged and the two little ones came running with delighted squeals. Ollie grabbed at the food as soon as his bottom hit the blanket, and Anabel almost threw herself into Maddy's lap. Silas reprimanded his son and watched his tiny daughter cling to Maddy. It was a beautiful sight to his battle-hardened soul.

Three hours later, they passed the lane to Maddy's house. "It won't be dark for a while and I want all of you to see what we've done," Silas said. In a short distance, they turned down the drive to his farm. He pointed out the corn and wheat fields on either side then stopped in front of the house to show them the repaired porch and roof. Inside the house, he proudly showed them the kitchen, dining room, and one bedroom with three pallets.

"It doesn't look like much, but if you had seen the mess it was a month ago, you would be amazed at the changes," Silas said with deep satisfaction in a job well done.

"Silas, it's lovely," Maddy said. "I truly am amazed." She turned to take it all in. "And so clean! I wouldn't have expected that from two men."

"Why thank you, Maddy." He didn't want to mention that a certain unwelcome guest had insisted on cleaning every time she dropped her meals by. And he hated to admit to himself how much he enjoyed the cleanliness.

"I got a lot more done in these past few weeks than I thought I could, thanks to Luke. He's better than two men," Silas said as he took Maddy's hand and led her out to the porch.

Maddy was ashamed at the effect his strong, warm hand had on her. Heat washed over her face and she tried to avoid his eyes. But Silas' mind was thankfully elsewhere. She enjoyed watching him show off his newly restored farm. All he and Luke had accomplished in such a short time was all consuming to him at the moment.

"Look, Maddy! Look at what we've done. I never dreamed we'd accomplish all this in such a short time. I figured we'd get all the seed in the ground and the fences repaired. Maybe repairs on the barn." He pulled her down the steps with both Ollie and Anabel skipping happily around them. He led them past the neat garden and out to the barn. "Look at the barn and corral. It's ready for animals." Silas dropped Maddy's hand and squatted down next to his kids.

"I want you two to go with me when I buy our animals. How does that sound to you?"

Ollie whooped and jumped in the air. "Yes, Pa! When? Today?"

"Not today, son, but sometime this week."

Anabel stuck her finger in her mouth and moved next to Maddy. "I want to stay wif Ma," she declared around her wet finger as Maddy stroked Anabel's messy curls.

"Of course, you can stay with Maddy, little one," Silas said. "If that's alright with her."

"Always, Silas," she answered as she pulled Anabel closer.

Silas stood with a happy sigh. "Come on. I want to show you the inside of the barn." He opened a newly constructed door and held it for them as they entered. The intoxicating smell of new lumber and fresh hay filled her nostrils. He showed them three new stanchions for milk cows and three new stalls for horses. He had also built two new enclosures in the corner, each of which opened up to their own outdoor pens within the bigger corral. "One for pigs, the other for sheep."

Maddy finally caught his enthusiasm. She was truly amazed and delighted at his work. "Silas, this is wonderful! I can't believe you did all this!" she gushed as she twirled around, taking it all in. "Oh, I can hardly wait to see it filled with animals!" She turned to look at him and saw tears in his eyes. "Silas! You did it! What you've been dreaming of all these years!" She wanted to throw herself into his arms but turned awkwardly instead to run her hand along the half doors of the horse stalls and inspect more closely the finely made stanchions.

Silas seemed to speak past a lump in his throat, "There's more, Maddy."

She turned to see him pointing to a ladder that led up to the hayloft where Ollie had already climbed. Silas set Anabel on the rungs and climbed right behind her, followed by Maddy. The hayloft was open from end to end with a railing around the ladder opening.

"I had this little one in mind when I added the railing," Silas said, resting a protective hand on Anabel's head.

At the west end of the barn, opposite the corral, was a large opening for hay to be loaded in. Blankets and a makeshift shelf filled with books were in one corner.

"Is this where Luke's been sleeping?" Maddy asked, walking over to look at the books.

"Yes. I'm surprised he has energy to read at the end of our workdays."

Maddy noticed a kerosene lantern in the corner. The hay had been cleared away but she was still concerned. She exchanged an understanding look with Silas.

"I'll have a talk with him," he said. "There are more layers to that boy than I'd realized. Maybe I'll invite him to add his books to my collection and read at the house before he turns in." He chuckled. "I'm liking that boy more all the time."

They left the barn and walked past the garden and house to the newly built chicken house, tool shed, and well house. "I hid a good amount of money in a hole under the tool shed but couldn't get to it for days because the shed had rotted and fallen in. To my great relief, all of it was still there." He turned to look at Maddy. "God has blessed me, Maddy. More than I deserve."

She reached out and quickly squeezed his hand. "Silas, you deserve every bit of it."

Silas cleared his throat and said, "I need to get you home so we can eat and get out of your hair before it gets dark." He stepped to the side and whistled for Luke who was watering the corn seedlings in the northeast field. Turning again to Maddy, he said, "I know you won't have time to fix us much of a supper, but I brought a ham from town and there are quite a few eggs and some milk and bread at your place."

"Thank you, Silas. That should be plenty. Is there any cheese?"

"Yes. Lots."

"I'll make ham and cheese sandwiches, then. Do you like them warmed up in the skillet?"

Silas grinned from ear to ear. "My mouth is already watering, dear girl. I think you've for sure inherited your ma's cooking genes."

Maddy laughed. "If warming up a sandwich makes for a good cook, then I'd imagine even Luke will qualify."

"Luke will qualify for what?" Luke said as he reached them, out of breath from running all the way from the field. Just then, he remembered his manners. "Good evenin', Maddy, uh, Miss Malone," he said with a nod and a quick removal of his hat.

"Miss Malone?" Maddy asked with hands on her hips. "Do I look that old, Luke?"

"Oh, no, ma'am! It's just..."

"Ma'am? Since when have I been a ma'am to an old school chum?"

Luke glanced at Silas. "Well. I...I..."

"I've always been Maddy to you, Luke, and I'll always be Maddy to you! Nothing else. Understand?"

"Yes, ma'am. Uh...Maddy! Thank you, Maddy. Maddy, it will be from now on." He looked at Silas and shrugged.

Maddy looked at Silas and winked.

CHAPTER TWELVE

As expected, Anabel refused to go with her pa when the meal was done and it was time for Silas to finally take his kids home. Both he and Maddy tried to be firm, but Anabel only clung to Maddy's legs and sobbed.

"I wanna stay with Ma," she wailed.

Maddy dropped to Anabel's level and pried her hands loose from her eyes. "Sweetheart, your pa has worked so hard to fix up his place for you. It's your place, too."

"No. This is my place. My room is up there." She pointed to the steps. "Next to you, Ma."

Maddy started to say more, but Silas put a hand on Anabel's head and interrupted. "It's fine, Maddy. She can take more time if she needs to."

Maddy saw sadness in his eyes and she wanted to cry for him. At the same time, she gathered the tiny girl up in her arms and battled with the rising relief she felt as she hugged her baby girl. She didn't have to lose her yet.

Ollie was oblivious to the entire exchange as he ran around the yard chasing a stray cat that had made itself at home while they were away. Suddenly he stopped and ran into the house. "Pa! Pa! Can we get a cat? And a dog? We need a dog. Every farm needs a dog. Maddy needs a dog. One that will chase off the Potters whenever they come around."

Silas put a restraining hand on his enthusiastic son as he sent a look of concern Maddy's direction. "Will you be safe, here?"

"Oh, yes. Remember, I have a shotgun. I've managed for four years." Her smile was just a little too forced.

"Actually, less than a year as the only adult here. Maybe a dog's a good idea, Ollie," he said as he ruffled his hair. "Let's work on that. Alright, son?" He turned back to Maddy. "If it's fine with you, we'll all drop by for breakfast in the morning, then help with your chores."

Maddy agreed happily, hugged Ollie good-bye, and watched the two MacGregor males ride off down the drive. Anabel still clung to her. "I don't want Ollie to go," she sobbed.

Maddy stroked her back. "Neither do I, Anabel. But he's only going around the corner. And he's coming back in the morning. Why, it's almost as if he's just sleeping in the next room."

"I don't care," she cried. "We've always slept in the same room. I want him to come back."

"Well sometimes we don't always get what we want, do we?" Maddy said as she carried her into the house and set her at the table. She took a seat around the corner. "Your pa is a really good man and he has made such a nice, new home for you and Ollie."

"And for you, too, Maddy," Anabel declared.

"No, honey. Not for me. But I'll always be right here and you can come visit me anytime you want."

"Visit? No! I'm gonna live here!" She jumped down and ran to the bottom of the stairs where she turned, stomped her foot, and hollered, "This is my home and you are my ma! Forever! I'm never leaving you, Ma!" With that, she ran up the stairs, sobbing all the way.

The next day, she refused to leave the house, certain they would trick her into going to her pa's. After breakfast and chores, Silas sat with Maddy at the table and talked.

Silas lowered his head to his hands. "This is not going at all how I'd expected," he said.

"We could force her to go," Maddy suggested weakly. "We are bigger than she is, after all," she chuckled.

Silas looked at her. "Do you think that's wise?"

"No," was her simple answer.

"Then what?"

"Time and patience. Remember what it took for her to even look at you when you first came home?"

"She was pretty frightened, wasn't she?"

"If we can somehow make the changes in small steps, I think she'll adjust."

"I thought we were already doing it in small steps."

She smiled at him. "Smaller."

Silas sat back and thought for a while. "Hmmm…" He ran his thumb over the stubble on his chin. "How about if both of you come over and spend the day tomorrow? I'll need help keeping an eye on Ollie, also. We can pack up enough food for both meals and when evening comes, I'll drive you both back here."

"Good idea. That way, she can get used to being there. We can even take some of her dolls and books. I think it might work if we promise that at the end of the day, she gets to come back here with me."

"Yes. And over time, the change won't seem so scary."

"Maybe we can start with her spending one night a week with you and then more as she decides."

"And," Silas added, "if she can see some sort of a schedule on a calendar, she might be less afraid of losing you."

Maddy laughed. "We're going to a lot of trouble for a five-year-old."

"We could just force her," Silas said with a shrug. "No, seriously. I don't want her in my home if she has to be forced. I want her to come because she loves me and wants to be with me. So, we'll take it moment by moment, day by day."

He reached over and took Maddy's hands. "Kind of reminds me of how God invites us into relationship with Him. He won't force us. He's already done His part, hasn't He?"

Maddy nodded, tears in her eyes. "And just like you, He's already prepared a place for us."

So, beginning the following day, they did just as they had discussed. Day by day, Silas, Ollie, and Luke had their breakfasts at Maddy's. After doing chores together, they loaded up in Silas' wagon and headed for the MacGregor farm. The first day, Anabel refused to leave the front porch. They had gotten no more than five feet down the drive before she shrieked for them to stop. She clamored aboard and spent the day glued to Maddy's side.

The following day was much the same but with Anabel daring to wander around the house, porch, and yard, dragging her favorite doll behind her. On day three, she ventured forth to go play in the barn loft with Ollie. But when Maddy dared ask if she wanted to spend the night, she answered with an emphatic "No!"

Day three also brought a surprise to Maddy. A strange woman appeared at the door with a basket of food for the men. Maddy had already prepared and set food out for the noon meal so when the woman walked into the kitchen, she stopped as if in shock.

"What's the meaning of this?" she sputtered.

"Of what?"

"Of this." She swept her hand toward the meal laid out on the table. "Who are you? And what are you doing in this kitchen?"

Dumbfounded, Maddy watched as the stranger cleared the table and replaced Maddy's meal with the contents of her basket.

"Has poor Silas come to this? That he needs to hire a little servant girl to feed him. Poor, poor man. It's worse than I thought." She bustled about getting plates and arranging a meal for two. "You may leave to attend to your other duties, whatever those may be. Silas and I would like to eat in private like we usually do."

Maddy quietly gathered up the food for her and the children, loaded it in a basket, and carried it quietly to the porch, where she met Silas hurrying up the steps.

"Late for an appointment, are you?" she couldn't help ask with a touch of humor and challenge in her tone.

Silas blushed and stammered, "Is she here? Did she bring…? What's in your basket? Why are you out here on the…?" He stopped and rubbed his hand over his face. "I'm sorry, Maddy. I should have warned you."

"Who *is* she?"

"I'll tell you later. Right now, let's get this over with." He turned to go into the house then stopped and looked at the basket. "Did she send you away?"

Maddy grinned and nodded. "Quite rudely in fact."

His face turned red with anger as he grabbed the basket. "I will not have this in my house! Ring the bell for the meal. We're all eating together!"

Maddy rang the bell and waited for Ollie, Anabel, and Luke to show up before she went inside. They found Silas placing food on the table and talking a blue streak.

"I sure do appreciate your food, Miss Adams. It will go perfectly with what Maddy already fixed. What a blessing you two are. Luke and I have never eaten so good. Sit down, children, and meet Miss Adams. Miss Adams, I'd like you to meet my two children, Ollie and Anabel."

Bonnie nodded politely. "Ollie, Anabel, nice to meet you. I've heard so much about you from your pa in the past several weeks." She purred. "Your pa and I go way back." At this, she reached over to stroke Silas' arm.

"And," Silas said as he shifted away from her, "it is my privilege to introduce this wonderful woman, Maddy Malone, the woman who took care of my children while I was at war. Let's pray."

The tension was so thick, it was difficult for Maddy to take a breath. Conversation after the prayer was brief and stilted. When Ollie and Anabel finished, they politely asked, as always, "Ma, may we be excused?"

After they left, Bonnie delicately dabbed at her lips and looked directly at Maddy. "Ma?"

Maddy merely dabbed at her lips, smiled the sweetest smile, and answered, "yes." Then she stood to gather the food and clean the kitchen.

"May I have a word with you, Silas, dear?" Bonnie said as she stood. "In private, please?"

As Maddy worked, she could hear snatches of conversation coming from the porch. Silas' voice was only a quiet rumble, but Bonnie's voice was a high-pitched, agitated whine. "What right... She's but a child herself...I won't allow it... Those children deserve... You know I'm only thinking of your best when I..."

Maddy heard her buggy leave just as Silas reentered the house. He stood silently in the kitchen watching her. "I honestly don't know how to get rid of that woman," he finally said.

Maddy laughed. "She wants to marry you, you know!"

Silas slapped his hat on the table. "I know! What do I do?"

Maddy couldn't help the peals of laughter that spilled forth. She wiped her eyes on her apron and choked out, "I'm sorry, Silas. Really, I am. You just look so pitiful right now and I've never in my life seen you look pitiful."

"Well, could you possibly stop laughing and give this pitiful man some advice?"

"Tell her to stop coming. You don't need her anymore."

"That sounds mean, after all she's done for us."

"All she's done for you?"

Silas sheepishly answered, "Yeah. She brings meals several times a week and she...she's been cleaning for us."

"Oh! That's why everything is so clean and tidy around here? And I thought it was you two men. No wonder she hates me. I'm her replacement."

"She doesn't hate you, Maddy."

"If that wasn't hatred, then it was very strong dislike. I'm a threat to her, Silas."

"Nonsense. In fact, maybe you two can become friends. That would solve everything."

She stared at him a moment in disbelief. "Friendship is the last thing she wants. If you had seen her in here, kicking me out, then you would understand. Since you can't tell her to stop coming, then I'll simply make myself scarce whenever she's here. I'll take a walk. That's what I'll do. I love taking walks, but I've been too busy. Now I can." She took her apron off and threw it on the table. "In fact, I think I need one now."

"Maddy," Silas said as she breezed by him. He took a step and caught her arm. "Please try to understand, Maddy. You need to know that...that it's difficult to send her away because apparently, I was very mean to her in school and...well frankly, I'm ashamed. I'm doing everything I can to be kind without encouraging her advances."

"Is it working?" Maddy asked before pulling free and walking out the door.

Bonnie Adams continued to come with a meal every Monday, Wednesday, and Friday. Only because Silas begged her did Maddy stay for those meals. Then she gathered the children and left for a walk, not returning until

Miss Adams's buggy was gone. She tried to form a friendship, but it was clear that Miss Adams wanted her out of the house. She seemed more determined than ever to stake her claim on poor Silas.

In the meantime, Anabel was warming to her pa and her pa's home. On week three, Maddy asked if she'd like to spend just one night a week with her pa and six nights with Maddy. Anabel agreed only after she secured a promise from Maddy that she'd truly let her stay with her for six nights every week. Silas told her that Anabel cried herself to sleep that first night, with he and Ollie both cuddling her through her tears.

After that first night, she was able to stay overnight with Silas without fear of losing her "ma." She worked up to two then three nights every week. By the end of July, she only stayed with Maddy two nights a week. But only if Silas agreed to continue having breakfasts at Maddy's and allowing her and Ollie to spend their days with her.

All was going according to the plan, and Maddy knew it was only a matter of time before both children made the transition away from her. Her heart was filled with dread.

CHAPTER THIRTEEN

One hot evening in early August, Maddy walked home from Silas's farm and found a horse tied to a tree and a strange man standing on her porch. He was quick to reassure her that he meant no harm.

"Hello, Miss Malone? I have a note for you from Eliza Monroe."

Maddy put her hand to her chest. "Oh, I hope it's not bad news."

"Oh no, ma'am. I think you'll be quite pleased with its contents," he said as he handed it to her with a grin.

She tore into the envelope and read.

Dear Maddy, I hope this short note finds you well. I wanted to let you know than Jonathan and I plan to drive out soon to get our "belongings." I hope that's fine with you. We'll be bringing Daniel and hope to spend a night with you. Would you please send an answer home with Todd so we can begin our preparations?

"I'm Todd, by the way." Todd dipped his head.

"Hello, Todd. It's good to meet you. My answer is 'yes' of course!" she said with great enthusiasm. "Should I write a note? Of course. What am I thinking?" She made a beeline for her front door while Todd stood and waited. Soon, she emerged with not only a note but a glass of cold lemonade as well.

"Thank you, ma'am. You are kind."

"Pshaw! It's the least I could do after getting such good news than leaving you standing out in this heat. How long have you been here?"

"Oh, I'd say an hour or two."

"I am so sorry. In the future, if you ever come bearing a note again and I'm not here, just go down the road to the first farm to the north. I'm often there taking care of Silas MacGregor's two children while he works in the fields."

"Will do, ma'am. Well, I better be on my way before it gets dark." With that, he mounted his horse and took off at a trot, Maddy watching him with renewed enthusiasm.

The evenings and nights without the children had become very long, boring, and often filled with sounds she couldn't identify. She often took walks with her sketchbook and box of watercolors, doing simple paintings of flowers and the farm animals. As satisfying as that was, her heart still ached for her children. Being alone, she was discovering, was wearing to her soul. She longed for the nights with both children snuggled into bed with her, listening to Bible stories. Then tucking them in with bedtime prayers. The mornings, kissing their tousled, sweet heads. Listening to the sweetness of their voices as they sleepily greeted her.

She hugged herself with pleasure and turned to go back into the house. There was work to be done! In her note, she had begged them to stay for a week. That it would be balm for her soul. Quickly she stripped her parents' bed and started two big kettles of water boiling. She took all the blankets out to the porch for a good shaking. Then she grabbed a rag, dampened it, and wiped down every surface downstairs. When the water started boiling, she added soap and the sheets and stirred them with a giant wooden paddle. The second kettle boiled next to the first, waiting for the soapy sheets to be added for a rinse. Maddy added a few drops of her mother's perfume to the rinse water then with difficulty, wrestled the wet sheets from one kettle to the next.

Drenched with sweat and wash water, she walked out to the porch and dropped, exhausted onto the swing. It was starting to get dark. Cicadas sang their chorus in the fields, frogs croaked lazily down by the creek, and the evening breeze cooled her wet body. She sighed contentedly and offered up prayers of gratitude to her Lord.

That night, she was sure she heard someone walking across her porch. She grabbed the shotgun, which she now kept in her closet, and tried to remember if she'd locked both the front and back doors. It grew quiet and she couldn't see anything in the yard. From the top of the stairs, she had a good view of the front door. She waited for several minutes sitting with the gun across her knees then went back to bed, after locking her bedroom door and propping the shotgun close by.

At breakfast the next morning, she shared the good news of Jon and Eliza's upcoming visit, leaving out the part about them reclaiming their gold. Then she brought up the subject of a dog again.

"Tomorrow's Sunday," Silas said, wiping crumbs from his mouth. "Let's all go to church together again and we can ask around."

Ollie's eyes grew big. "A dog for us, too, Pa?" he asked, jumping out of his chair.

"Yes, son. For us, too."

Maddy's heart warmed at the tenderness in Silas's eyes.

When they all went out to do the chores, Maddy scanned the area around her house for footprints or anything out of place. She saw nothing and decided it was only her worked-up imagination. Still, though, she wanted the security of a dog. A big dog, she decided.

When the five of them walked into church the following morning, both Reverend Richards and Sister Martha greeted them with hugs and backslaps. "Welcome back, folks. We haven't seen you in a couple of weeks. Hope yer all doin' fine!" the good reverend said.

Martha hugged Maddy warmly and asked quietly how she was doing. Other dear neighbors gathered around and greeted them just before the old organ started playing "Amazing Grace." People filed into the wooden pews. Silas led his troupe into one long pew, with Maddy taking the last seat next to the aisle, Anabel tucked closely by her side.

"Let's all stand and join in singing my favorite hymn," Reverend Richards invited from the front in his deep booming voice.

Amazing grace how sweet the sound, that saved a wretch like me.

I once was lost, but now I'm saved; was blind, but now I see.

They had just started the second verse when a commotion was heard at the back as latecomers entered. Soon, Maddy heard whispering and from the corner of her eye saw movement. To her chagrin, she saw Bonnie Adams motion for Silas to move over. He did as much as he could, which sent every person in the crowded pew scooting over as well. She managed to squeezed her ample bottom into the space next to Silas.

Maddy had to ask God for forgiveness throughout the long service. If anyone had asked what the sermon was about, she couldn't have answered.

After the service, Bonnie slipped her arm into Silas's

and hung on. At one point, he removed her hand and leaned over to greet old friends. He maneuvered away from her and started asking if anyone knew of any available puppies or dogs. Ollie quickly joined him. Bonnie and Maddy reached the door at the same time, and Maddy tried with every ounce of grace she could muster to be kind. She truly wanted to be. After all, Bonnie was also God's child and if she wasn't yet saved, then all the more reason to extend her friendship.

"Good morning, Bonnie," she said with genuine warmth. Bonnie simply gave her an icy stare and turned to Sister Martha with a gushing greeting. Hurt, but determined, she waited in line to greet the reverend's sweet wife. Bonnie talked on and on as other ladies gathered. Finally, Sister Martha kindly and expertly ended the flow of words and extended her hand to Maddy.

"Maddy, how are you, dear?" She pulled her into an embrace which further served to dismiss Bonnie.

"I am fine. And how are you, Sister Martha?"

Martha put her hands on either side of Maddy's face. "I am fabulous, dear girl. I think it's time for the reverend and me to drop by your place for a good long visit. How does this evening sound? We'll bring food."

Maddy blushed with the pleasure of the idea. "Oh, I would absolutely love that! I'll make a pie!"

"Can you arrange for it to be just you?" she quietly asked.

"I'll do my best, but Anabel might be there."

"That will be fine. We can talk around Anabel, if need be," she said with a delightful twinkle in her blue eyes.

When Maddy descended the steps, she noticed that Bonnie had again attached herself to Silas. She decided to let that drama play out without her. There were more neighbors to greet and more inquiries to make about dogs. Although, she couldn't help but watch when she saw Silas repeatedly shake his head no then reach out and grab Luke by the arm. Luke smiled and shook his head yes. Bonnie looked angry then stalked off with Luke trailing behind.

In the wagon on the way home, she asked what had happened. Silas merely scowled.

"You don't have to answer me if you don't want to. After all, it's really none of my business."

"Let's look at it this way," Silas began. "I think I took a big step in discouraging her."

"Oh?"

"She packed a picnic lunch just for the two of us. I told her I had other plans. She insisted, as only Bonnie can, so I grabbed Luke, who happened to be walking by and said he would love to join her for a picnic." Silas laughed at the ridiculous moment. "It sounds mean, but Luke will jump at every chance he gets to eat her food."

"I can't imagine she was very happy about that. Luke is probably a decade or more younger than her."

"No. She was pretty irate. Hopefully their meal is pleasant."

They looked at each other with somber faces then burst into laughter.

"Oh, by the way," Silas said after he composed himself. "I found a dog for you. A puppy, actually. One for you and one for us: both from the same litter."

Ollie heard from the back. "Really, Pa? Really?"

"A puppy? A tiny baby puppy?" Anabel squealed from the back.

"Well," Silas answered, "they're puppies, but they're certainly not tiny."

"Oh good!" Maddy said. "I wanted a big one. Big enough to be a good guard dog."

"They're ready to go, about ten weeks old in fact. Donald Wright's going to deliver them sometime next week. There's one male and one female left. Which one do you want?" he asked Maddy.

"Ollie can choose first," she said.

"The boy! I want the boy!"

"Alright then, the female is mine and Anabel's, since we're girls. What do you think, Anabel?"

"Yes, yes, yes!" the little girl answered. "Can I name her, Ma?"

"Yes, sweetheart. You may name her."

"And I'll name the boy!" Ollie declared.

The two of them discussed names for the remainder of the day, neither of them able to settle on their favorite.

Maddy managed to get alone for her evening with the Richards. She quickly made an apple pie and put it in the oven just as they drove into her yard. Martha came laden with a basket of fried chicken, biscuits, dandelion greens, and sweet pickles.

They prayed and dug in, to both the food and the conversation.

"Now, Maddy, you know I won't apologize for being a meddling old woman, so…"

"Oh Lord." Reverend Richards lifted his eyes to heaven. "Here we go. Lord, please help little Maddy, as she's about to partake in an onslaught of unsolicited advice."

"Oh, Richard!" Martha gently slapped his shoulder. "Admit it. Yer as bad as I am, old man."

He shook his head sadly. "I'm sorry. But she's right, Maddy. I can't help myself sometimes. I guess that's why the good Lord has us in the ministry. That way, we can use that as an excuse for our meddlin' ways." He shook his head again in mock shame.

Maddy laughed at these dear people. "I don't mind at all. If my memory serves me well, and it does, your advice, solicited or not, has pointed a lot of people in the right direction."

"Thank you, dear," Martha said and squeezed her hand. "I need to hear that now and then."

"And, before you go any further," Maddy said, "let me make it perfectly clear that I am, at this moment, soliciting your advice. All of it that you can give me. I need it."

"Bless you dear. What kind of advice are you seeking?"

"What kind of advice do you think I need?" Maddy answered with a serious tone. "I somehow trust that you will give me the exact words I need to hear. I trust in your wisdom and I trust that God will use you."

Reverend Richards took his wife's hand and asked, "Is it any wonder why we love this child so much?"

Tears came unbidden to Maddy's eyes as she encouraged them to proceed. "Start meddling," she said.

And meddle they did.

Martha started. "The first question I have for you is, how do you feel about Silas MacGregor?"

"Silas is the finest man I know," she easily answered.

"Are you in love with him?" Martha asked with glee and a twinkle.

Maddy laughed in embarrassment and covered her face. "I don't know." She looked at them. "What exactly does that mean? I admire him greatly. I…I even love him. But I love you two and I'm not *in love* with you."

"Let me put it this way, would you like to be Silas's wife?"

Maddy's face burned and she looked away. She started weeping and covered her face to hide her tears. The Richards looked knowingly at each other.

"Is 'yes' your answer, dear?" Martha asked softly as she stroked Maddy's arm.

Maddy, face still covered by both hands, nodded yes then sobbed, "Please don't tell anyone. I'm so ashamed. It's hard to even admit it to myself."

"Oh, Maddy dear. There's no reason to be ashamed."

"At first, I thought I felt this way because of Ollie and

Anabel, but now I know it's more than that. If I lost Silas, I think I'd die!" She tried to compose herself. "But I can never have him."

This time the reverend jumped in. "Why, in God's name would you say such a thing?"

"Because it's true. He's handsome, brilliant, and amazing in every way. I'm small, mousy, and weak."

Neither of the Richards tried to hide their laughter. "You, dear one, are one of the most beautiful young women to ever grace this planet!" Reverend Richards declared.

"Beautiful inside and out," his wife added. "Can't you see what we see?"

"I look in the mirror every day. I know what I see."

"Your problem is that you're so used to seeing that beautiful little face that you've grown used to her."

The reverend added, "I'm a man and I think I know what Silas sees when he looks at you."

Maddy looked at him with a questioning gaze.

"He sees the prettiest little girl he's ever laid eyes on. And he adores you. I see it in his eyes whenever he looks at you. He would die for you, Maddy."

Maddy sniffed and dabbed at her tears.

"You see the problem, don't you?" Richards asked.

"I…I think so. He only sees me as a girl? Not a woman?"

"Exactly. He even said as much when we asked him about you."

Maddy sat up straight. "What? Surely you didn't…"

Reverend Richards held up a hand to stop her. "Don't worry. We didn't get very far. We were just trying to plant the seed of a thought in his thick skull. How old are you anyway?"

"Twenty."

"Ah, just as we guessed," Martha said. "That Silas persists in keeping you the age you were at the beginning of the war. He has no clue."

"There's still enough of an age gap that he might not consider me," Maddy said. "Argh! I can't believe we're having this conversation. When I asked for your advice, I certainly didn't expect it to go this direction." She paused and added, "At least not this quickly."

"It's a matter that we will both continue taking before the Lord. And we promise. This conversation is only between the three of us," Martha said. "Although, I can almost guarantee we'll bring it up again in the future."

CHAPTER FOURTEEN

The following morning when Maddy woke up and looked
out her bedroom window, she saw a man. Quickly she
moved behind her curtain and watched. It was Sam Potter
and he didn't seem to care if he was seen. He ambled over
to the pigpen then back to the center of the yard. Slowly,
but deliberately, he turned and looked up at her window.
Gasping, she pulled back a fraction of an inch. Surely, he
couldn't see her. She didn't move a muscle. After about
two full minutes he raised his hat, nodded toward her, and
walked down the path to his place.

When the others arrived for breakfast, Silas studied her
carefully. It was obvious that he knew something wasn't
right and she was sure that he intended to find out what it
was. Between seeing Sam Potter and having the Richards
grill her the previous evening, Maddy was having a
difficult time concentrating on the meal. And she couldn't
seem to make eye contact with him.

When everyone else left to do the chores, Silas stayed
behind. "What's bothering you, Maddy?"

She stopped her work to look at him. "Sam Potter was here this morning."

Silas's entire body stiffened at those words. "What did he do?"

"He wandered around my yard then stared at my bedroom window. That's all."

"That's all?"

"Well, he looked at the pigs for a while and when he was looking up at the window, he nodded as if he was greeting me. But I'm certain he couldn't see me."

Silas clenched his fists and breathed hard. "I think it's time for me to pay that man a visit."

"Oh, Silas. I wish you wouldn't. I'm afraid of him and his brother. No telling what they would do to you."

"No telling what they might do to you, Maddy. Those Potter boys made a name for themselves in this war and no one around here trusts them. I'll take a few men with me. Mounted and armed. That should make an impression. In the meantime, I don't want you here alone."

"I've managed for several months. I...I think if they intended to harm me, they would have done it by now," she said, not very convincingly. "And besides, where would I go? And if I stay here, who would stay with me? Ollie and Anabel can't offer much protection."

"I'll have Luke sleep in your barn."

"And how will that look to our neighbors?"

"Our neighbors won't have to know. And if by chance, someone finds out, I think they'll understand when we tell them the reason." He walked over to her and held her by her shoulders. "Maddy, cooperate with me, please. This can't continue. I'm worried about you."

The warmth from his touch and the tenderness in his eyes moved her so deeply that she gasped and stepped away.

Silas raised his voice. "What's gotten into you, Madeline? I never realized you were so stubborn. I'm sorry, but I have to insist."

Maddy kept her gaze averted and mumbled, "Fine. Go ahead."

Maddy heard a frustrated sigh just before Silas stomped out of the house.

Silas impatiently flicked the reins across his horse's back. For some reason, she had refused to go with them. Rarely did he get frustrated with Maddy, but his feelings had escalated to anger as he had watched her defy him. But anger wasn't the only emotion he had to fight.

After she had stepped away from him, he had stood there a moment longer watching her, her head down, strands of wheat-blonde hair covering her tiny freckled face, fingers fiddling with her apron. Her waiflike beauty and vulnerability stirred in him a deep longing. He shook his head in confusion then left to join the others.

When he got home, he splashed cold water over his face to clear the cobwebs. Whatever feelings he had for Maddy had to be squashed. She was a child.

That evening he, Luke, and the children ventured back and joined Maddy for supper. To everyone's delight, as soon as they finished eating, the puppies were delivered. It was as exciting as Christmas to the two little ones. They had finally settled on the names Hansel and Gretel.

Later that night, Silas accompanied Luke as he showed up at Maddy's with a rifle and a bedroll. The relief he saw on Maddy's face spoke volumes. She obviously trusted Luke.

"I'll train the little pups, if you want me to," Luke announced before he headed to the barn. "I might as well, since it looks we'll be barn mates."

Maddy chuckled as she stood next to Silas on the porch

watching the puppies scamper after Luke. They were sleeping in the barn while they were still so young. They were happy as long as they had each other.

Silas sighed and ran his fingers through his hair. "Are you fine with this arrangement, Maddy?" He wanted to look at her but he was afraid to. Her vulnerability begged him to do more than look.

"Yes. I'm very fine with it. Thank you, Silas." She turned to go.

Todd trotted into Silas's yard Tuesday morning with another note from Eliza asking if they could come the following morning and stay one or two nights. Maddy was overjoyed and clutched the note to her chest. "Yes! Please tell them, yes," she said to Todd.

"Will do, ma'am." He raised his hat in a farewell and took off.

At the noon meal, she announced to the others that her visitors would be arriving tomorrow and she needed to go home and make preparations. "Bonnie didn't come yesterday, did she? Do you think she finally got the hint?"

Silas shook his head. "I'm not sure. I guess we'll see tomorrow."

"I won't be coming over here tomorrow or Thursday. I would love it if Ollie and Anabel could come and stay with me so they can see Eliza again. And you and Luke are still welcome for breakfast and supper. The noon meal, too, for that matter."

"Thank you. I look forward to seeing them again. They're good people. Do you have enough food for everyone?"

"Yes, thanks to you and that last trip you took to Springfield, my larder is full. Although I need to get home so I can start on some pies."

"Make a lot. Luke and I can't get enough of your pies."

True to their word, the Monroe's pulled into the drive in the middle of the morning. Maddy, Ollie, and Anabel ran down the steps to greet them. The puppies barked and ran circles around them all. Little Daniel wiggled to get out of his father's arms and took off after the puppies with Ollie and Anabel close behind.

After hugs and time around the table catching up on news, Eliza asked if Maddy could watch Daniel for them that afternoon while they went to the caves to find the gold Eliza had stashed there at the beginning of the war.

"I still find this whole story almost unbelievable," Maddy said. "A banker friend of your father sends you and his slave out of Springfield driving his wagon with gold hidden under the floorboards."

Jonathan chuckled. "I was with her that day and she never breathed a word of it to me."

"That's because I'd been given strict instructions to keep it quiet. Actually, Abe Goodman, the banker, had just told me about the gold about an hour before you and your men came riding up. He gave me strict instructions to hide it and to tell absolutely no one."

"I think you and I were just pawns in this crazy drama, Maddy," Jon said, smirking at his lovely wife.

"Pawns that came in might handy, I'd say," Eliza laughed at the memory. "Without a doubt, God provided the two of you on that very difficult day. I had just found out my pa was wounded. The whole city of Springfield was in a panic after the Union lost the battle at Wilson's Creek. They were all trying to leave before the whole place was taken over by the enemy. I planned to stay and wait for Pa, but Abe insisted that I leave. He actually had several wagons with hidden gold. All the banks were sending their gold out of town because they were certain the

Confederates would get their hands on it and use it to fund their war effort."

Eliza continued, "I had to find a place to hide it close to Springfield so I could return and find Pa, so I thought of your farm, Maddy. I can't tell you how tough it was for Jim and me to get it hidden without telling you what we were up to."

"You almost told me," Maddy giggled.

"No, I didn't! Admit it. Did you have any idea what we were hiding?"

"Not a clue! But to think it's been here all these years!"

"We hope it has," Jonathan said. "There's been a lot of men hiding in caves throughout the hills during the war. Someone could easily have found it."

"When you see how narrow those caves are, you'll see that wouldn't have been likely. I'm not sure I can squeeze in there now, not since I've had a baby. I'm sure I'm bigger."

"Well we'll soon find out. We might need to come back here and get Ollie to do the job for us."

"How many bags?" Maddy asked.

"If I remember correctly, there are seven. I hid four in the first cave and three in the next one."

"And it's all yours?" Maddy asked in amazement.

"I think so. There were other wagonloads of gold hidden other places that same time but we're letting Abe's lawyer sort that out."

"And where did all this gold come from?" Maddy asked.

"I'm not sure about all of it, but Abe, Abe's brother, and my pa went to the goldfields sometime in the late 40s, early 50s. They did well." Eliza's eyes twinkled. "Pa only mentioned it to me once and being the naïve girl I was at the time, I didn't give it much attention."

Jonathan added, "We'll have to take whatever we find to the bank so they'll have a record of all the recovered gold. They'll also see to it that everyone that had gold in Abe's bank gets at least a fair portion of whatever can be found."

All talk of gold ceased when Silas and Luke arrived for the noon meal. As soon as the meal was over and Silas and Luke left, Jonathan and Eliza took off in their wagon to the cave-filled bluffs along the northwest edge of Maddy's property. When they came back, Eliza was filthy and they didn't look at all happy. Eliza used the outside pump to clean most of the dirt off then went inside to change.

"When we got there, we saw some gold coin at the entrance," she whispered to Maddy who was helping her at the pump. "About five feet in, I found a bag that had been opened and gold scattered around it. We figured it must have been an animal because no person in their right mind would have left the gold behind."

"What about the other bags? Were they there?"

"I found two more in that cave. Counting the opened bag, that's only three. One bag is missing."

Eliza headed to the house to change.

Maddy found Jonathan on the porch so she joined him. "What about the other cave?" she asked him.

He chuckled. "Well she tried. It was quite the sight, I'll tell you. Looks like we might need Ollie."

Maddy shook her head. "He's small enough and tough enough to do the job, but are you sure you want a seven-year-old knowing about this? He's pretty talkative."

"I figure once we get it all out of there, it won't matter much who knows about it. By then, it'll be safe in the bank."

"Do you really want people knowing your wife is wealthy? And this nephew of Abe's, what's his name?"

"Henry Goodman." Maddy felt Jonathan's eyes on her as she paced.

"Is this Henry really gone? Might he threaten Eliza? Or worse, threaten Daniel to get at the gold he thinks is his by birth?"

Jonathan stared at Maddy for a moment. "I have

nightmares about that very thing happening. No, I guess you're right. The less people know, the better for our family. I wouldn't put anything past Henry Goodman. He's always thought he ought to be the heir and I've seen what he'll do to get at that gold."

"Where is he now?"

"Supposedly he ran off to Mexico when he heard he might hang for desertion and for his war crimes. But he's a sneaky one. For all I know, he's watching us right now."

Maddy shuddered. "I know how that feels; being watched by someone, that is." She told him about the Potters. "You know the trail you followed to get to the caves?" she asked.

"Yeah."

"Did you notice the path that kept going to the west from the end of that trail?"

"I did actually. I was a little curious about it because it's obviously well-traveled yet it's so far from your house."

"It goes straight to the Potter farm. And believe me, I never use it. They do. A lot. There's two of them. Their land is to the west of mine. They've suggested to me a couple of times that it would be to my advantage to marry Sam, the oldest, so we could combine the two farms."

Jonathan stared at her. "I am amazed that such a tiny lady such as you managed to survive through the last part of the war on this farm with no other adults to help you. Add to that, you have two pesky, possibly dangerous neighbors making unwanted advances. And you say they come here often?"

"More often than I like," she answered quietly.

"You know, Maddy, when Eliza was struggling to crawl into the second cave, I could have sworn we were being watched. Might it have been one of the Potters?"

Eliza walked in just then, toweling her curly hair. "What? You never mentioned that to me, Jonathan."

"I thought it was just my imagination. I never actually

saw anyone. I thought I saw movement. But out in those woods, there's lots of movement. Now, I'm wondering…"

"That second cave, the one you can't squeeze into, it's right on the border between my place and Potters. In fact"—she shrugged—"it just might be on their property."

"Hmmm… All things considered," Jonathan said, "I think we need to let Silas in on this big secret. I don't want Ollie involved. It's possible it could get dangerous." He turned and looked Maddy up and down. "Sorry, Eliza, but I think Maddy is skinnier than you."

Eliza laughed and slapped him with her towel. "I know that, you ninny! And no apology is necessary. She's always been tinier than me."

Maddy's eyes grew large. "Do you want me to go in the cave?"

"Only if you're willing," Jon answered with a smile. "And I want Silas and myself posted outside the cave with rifles."

"I'm willing!" Maddy answered almost bouncing on her seat with excitement.

"We'll need you, Eliza, to stay back here with the children, so if you don't mind, try to describe to Maddy where she'll find each of the three sacks."

The following morning, Silas, Jonathan, and Maddy set out to find treasure. Maddy wore her oldest dress and carried a box of matches and a candle in a sack that she could clamp between her teeth in the cramped space. Eliza instructed her to keep her arms stretched out in front so she could more easily maneuver the tightest spots. Silas insisted on taking rope along so he could tie them to her ankles before she crawled into the dark cave out of his sight.

When they crossed the creek at the base of the bluff, they noticed with alarm several gold coins scattered amongst the rocks. Quickly they gathered up all they could find. Repeatedly they scanned the nearby hayfield and woods for anyone that might be watching.

"How many bags did you say were missing?" Silas asked.

"So far only one. And several coins out of another."

Halfway up the bluff, Jon showed them the first cave then led them through thick brush to a tiny opening. "This is it," he said quietly.

"Wow!" Silas whispered. "Eliza chose well. No one would ever find this."

"Desperate men will hide in some ridiculous places," Jon said. "I've seen it."

"Yes, but this is way too small for any man I know. I'm not even sure Maddy can fit in there."

"Eliza managed to do it four years ago. I'm sure I can fit."

Silas gently tied a rope to each ankle and Maddy grabbed the sack.

"Here goes," she said and wiggled her way through the entrance. Eliza had explained that the skinniest section was at the beginning and was only five or six feet long. It then opened into a bigger area with lots of crevices where she had tucked the bags. And last, she had warned her that the cave was filled with bats. Maddy had grown up on this farm, so this wasn't her first time to venture into these caves. She knew what to do when the bats started swarming. Hunker down, grit her teeth, and wait.

She crawled slowly, painfully along, inch by inch, until she could tell she was in the larger section where she managed to get to her knees. It wasn't until then that she lit the candle. The bats started stirring. She held the candle high and moved it in a big circle. Suddenly the cave exploded with the flutter of what seemed to be hundreds of bats all trying to escape at once. She dropped to her stomach and laughed when she heard shouts from the two men at the entrance dealing with the sudden onslaught of bats all exiting at once.

When the bats were gone, Maddy searched the walls of the cave with her flickering candle. The bags of gold were not hard to spot. She carefully pried each of the three bags out of their different crevices and laid them near the opening of the exit tunnel. She saw two other narrow passages leading away from the area she was in. Thankfully, because of the ropes tied to her ankles, there was no question which tunnel led out.

Because the tunnel was so narrow, Maddy could only carry one bag out at a time. She had to push it ahead of her then, using her fingers and toes, crawl a few inches, move the bag, crawl a few inches more, and so on until she had exited.

She stood and stretched. "Ouch! That hurts. They're all there, but I don't think I can do that again two more times. I'm going to try carrying both bags this time." She dropped down and inched her way back in.

Soon, the men saw her emerge with the two bags. Instantly they reached down to help her to her feet. "You did an amazing job, Maddy," Jonathan said. "You are certainly tougher than you look."

She laughed. "I'm not sure if that's a compliment or not."

"Oh, it is, dear girl. You amaze me."

Maddy looked up to see Silas looking at her with obvious admiration. She quickly looked away and started down the steep slope when he said, "She amazes me, too. Every single day."

It was a relief that all three bags were found, yet out of the total, one bag was missing and that was a huge concern to all of them.

That evening, they all puzzled over it together.

"Did an animal drag it off somewhere? That's the only thing that makes sense," Eliza said. "If someone had come to the cave and stolen a bag, he would have also taken the bag and coins that were at the entrance. Is that missing bag now lying in the middle of the woods somewhere?"

"Or the hayfield or in an animal's den?" Silas added.

"Or possibly someone found it after it had been dragged away," Maddy suggested.

"I think I'd like to go back to the first cave tomorrow and look again. It's possible I missed it," Eliza said. "That's an awful lot of money. We can't just walk away without trying."

Everyone agreed, so the next day she tried with no success.

That afternoon, Silas accompanied the Monroes as they drove straight to their bank in Springfield. Silas instructed Luke to stay with Maddy and the children, with his rifle next to him at all times. He also told her to have the shotgun loaded and ready and to keep Ollie and Anabel inside unless they had to use the outhouse.

It almost seemed as if they were at war again.

As he rode, he had time to think. And again, he fought the direction his thoughts took him. When Maddy had crawled out of that cave, he had looked at her smiling eyes, her dirty freckled face, and matted hair and all he could think was what an incredible, young woman she was. Something more than admiration stirred in his gut. Again, confused and somewhat ashamed, he shook his head to clear his addled brain.

CHAPTER FIFTEEN

Silas stood up in the middle of the wheat field and stretched his aching muscles. He waved at Maddy and the kids as they headed down the driveway. A contented sigh escaped into the warm, humid air. Life had gone back to normal after the treasure hunt. With September came the beginning of harvest. Both men stayed busy throughout the hot, steamy days. He loved having Ollie work alongside him every morning. After the noon meal, he released him to help Maddy and Anabel do the afternoon chores. Then the three of them took the short walk back to Maddy's farm.

Silas sighed in frustration when he saw Bonnie's wagon turn down his drive. She continued to make an occasional appearance, but she seemed to time it when she knew Maddy had left for the day. Instead of a meal, she always packed ice-cold water and a succulent dessert, enough for only two. She'd drive her buggy into the yard, stand up, and shield her eyes from the bright sun until she discovered the field Silas was working in. No distance was too far for her to haul her heavy frame and covered basket to his side.

It would be unkind to turn her away. And besides, the

thoughts of her succulent desserts were a powerful motivator. The two of them would settle on the blanket that Bonnie had packed in her basket and hurriedly spread over the rough ground. Silas would devour the goodies, quickly wipe his hands clean, and with a quick apology, try to get back to his work.

Sometimes Bonnie followed. On those occasions, Silas would make a pretense of needing to find Luke. That didn't seem to deter her in the least.

And then of course, there were Sundays. At church, Bonnie would always make a beeline for Silas and wiggle her way into the pew next to him. He'd heard snatches of talk floating around after church that seemed to indicate some people assumed a wedding was soon to follow. *Ignorant busybodies.*

On the last Sunday of the month, Silas pulled up to Maddy's porch as he did every Sunday morning. Gretel bounded out of the barn with happy barks. He waited while Ollie and Anabel jumped down, greeted the dog then ran into the house to get Maddy. Silas again caught himself drinking in her beauty as she came down the porch steps, a child of his on either side, chattering away about anything and everything. They adored her; it was plain to see. He quickly jumped down and helped her up onto the seat then took his place beside her. She wore a shimmering brown dress with a cream-colored shawl. Her hair gleamed in the morning sun. An intoxicating fragrance teased his nose.

For some odd reason, on that particular day, he had a difficult time meeting her eyes. Both Ollie and Anabel leaned into her from behind, competing for her attention. She glowed with obvious pleasure, turning from one to the other, listening, responding, planting occasional kisses on their heads. A lump grew in his throat watching their easy, intimate exchange. No one had this kind of relationship with them, he realized, not even himself. He wondered if it was reserved for mothers only. It made him sad and happy at the same time.

Silas dropped his crew off at the door of the church then slapped the reins on Maud's back, directing her to the back of the building where everyone parked their wagons. Just as he made it to the porch, Bonnie slid up next to him and placed her hand possessively around his upper arm. This was a first. In the past, she had always arrived too late to walk in with him. Irritation rose quickly in his gut. This had to stop. What could he do without creating a scene? They were surrounded by people. He gently but firmly led her away from the building. He felt eyes following their every move. Bonnie went eagerly with him to the lawn next to Reverend. Richard's house.

Silas took her hand from his arm, but she seemed to think it was an invitation to hold hands. She gripped tightly, faced him, and stepped closer. Silas noticed that people lingered on the porch steps longer than usual. Keeping his voice low, he kindly said, "Bonnie, I'm so sorry if I've given you the wrong impression, but I'm not interested in starting a relationship with you."

Bonnie never let go of his hands. If anything, she squeezed harder. "Starting? What are you talking about?" her voice a silky purr yet laced with disbelief. "This relationship started months ago."

Silas' eyes grew large. He tried to disengage hands but she wouldn't let him. "There is no relationship between us except friendship."

She threw her head back and laughed. "Oh, Silas, dear!" Her shrill voice carried across the churchyard. Her voice lowered almost to a whisper. "You are delusional! This, my boy, is a full-blown courtship. Anyone with a brain can see that." Her voice rose. "All those meals! All of our time on a blanket in your fields!"

Silas felt his face warm as he realized her words could be heard by those lingering on the porch. What had he done? Whatever it was, it had to be undone.

"Bonnie, this has never been a courtship. At least not to me. You have been a good friend and that is all. And this idea of yours has got to end. I'm not courting you, Bonnie. I'm so sorry that I've given you the wrong impression."

At that, she quickly dropped his hands as if bitten. She stepped back and covered her face. When she finally looked at him, she screeched, "You are a brute, Silas MacGregor! A brute! I never want to see you again!"

Silas instinctively reached out to her but she pulled back as if she expected to be hurt. She turned and fled to her buggy, tears streaming down her face in full view of every person in front of the church. Silas stood rooted to the ground. If he followed her, it would only encourage her to believe a lie. Best to yank that rotten tooth out and deal with the repercussions later.

Not one to fret about the opinions of others, he made his way to the church door past curious gazes. His friend Mark Donaldson shook his hand and whispered, "Welcome to the service, you brute, you."

Silas simply shook his head in frustration. He whispered, "I might need some help disentangling myself from this one. This is harder than being in battle."

Mark laughed and slapped him on the back just before they stepped through the door. His wife, Sarah, followed behind, obviously trying to stifle a giggle.

On the way home, Silas turned to Maddy. "If you don't already have meal plans, I have a suggestion."

"Oh?"

"How about Ollie, Anabel, and I fix a picnic? We'll come pick you up when it's done and maybe we can all ride out to the river."

"The river?" Ollie asked. "Can we swim?"

"Of course. We can even take the dogs. I think they'd love that."

Anabel responded by throwing both arms around his neck. He clutched her little hands. This was a feeling he could get used to.

An hour later, he, the kids, and the dog, Hansel pulled up to Maddy's porch. When they stopped, Ollie stood up in the back of the wagon and shielding his eyes from the sun, stared toward the barn. "Ya better get the shotgun, Maddy," he hollered. "Sam Potter's hiding behind the pigpen!"

Silas jerked to see. "Where, son?"

Ollie pointed. "He slipped behind the barn. Better hurry if ya want to catch him. He's a sneaky varmint."

Silas jumped down and headed for the barn. The sight of Maddy on the porch wringing her hands only fueled his anger. Anabel ran up to hug Maddy while Ollie tagged closely behind his pa.

Silas jerked the barn door open and trotted to the back door. He was too late. There was no one in sight behind the barn. He and Ollie walked around the barn to the pigpen then went the other direction to the garden at the back of the house.

"Are you sure you saw him, Ollie?" Silas asked.

"Yep, Pa. I'm sure."

Silas got on his knees and faced the boy. "Do you see him often?"

"Yeah. Not as much as I used to, but I'm not here all the time."

Silas stood and shook his head. "This isn't right. I need to talk to Maddy about this."

"You know they have their own path, don't ya?"

Silas squinted his eyes and stared at his son. "I remember you showing it to me last spring, but I forgot about it." Just before they reached the others, Silas asked, "When we get back from the picnic, would you show it to me again?"

The river was low but clear. Everyone waded in, including Maddy, with her skirt held just high enough to not get wet, musical peals of laughter spilling out unrestrained. Oh, how he loved that about her. Silas tried to keep his eyes off her and on his children but it was work. Again, he wondered about her age. Surely, she was approaching marriageable age but still way too young for a man at his ripe age of thirty. It wouldn't be long before someone snatched her up. Possibly Luke. That thought pained him enough that he groaned and turned away. Thankfully no one noticed.

Well, Luke is certainly better than Sam Potter. Where had that thought come from? Was that why Sam kept making an appearance? Was that his uneducated, backwoods attempt at a courtship? Silas walked up onto the bank and growled again, this time certain no one could hear him. He grabbed a branch of the closest tree and snapped it off.

"Hey, Pa! Can we have crawdads for supper tonight? Ma says she knows how to cook them!"

Silas turned and forced a smile. "Sure, son. If that's what Maddy wants to do."

Maddy came laughing out of the water, her skirt wet to her knees. "We'll need something to put them in," she called back to the kids.

"Are you sure you want to do this?"

Maddy turned soft, green eyes to him in surprise. "Of course I want to. It was my idea. They're easy to cook." She laughed. "Not so easy to eat though. It will be fun."

"I've got a bucket in the back of the wagon." He turned to fetch it for her. Her smiling face was a welcome sight and one he'd never grow sick of. For a while last spring and even into mid-summer, her smiles were rare and often seemed forced.

She grabbed the bucket with a quick "thank you" and headed back into the river. Silas followed. Crawdads were in abundance. Ollie ran and grabbed the bucket.

"Hurry, Ma! I've got a whole bunch cornered in these rocks over here." He started fearlessly grabbing one after another and dropping them in the bucket. Anabel tried but screamed with every attempt. "Anabel, you gotta grab 'em behind the pinchers so they can't pinch you!"

"I'm trying but they wiggle too much!" she squealed.

"I'll help you, honey," Silas called. He joined her and tried unsuccessfully to show her how to hold them. After a while, he swooped her up in his arms and buried his face in her neck. "I think you just want an excuse to scream, you little rascal."

After a scrumptious meal of crawdads, baby potatoes, and carrots, heavily seasoned with garlic and pepper, Silas asked if the children could stay with Maddy for an hour or two while he went to talk to Reverend Richards. "Keep the doors locked and the gun ready," he whispered to Maddy just before he shut the door.

He made his way down the road to church for the second time that day, hoping the reverend would be home and wondering just what he'd say when he saw him. Knowing Frank, the way he did, he knew it wouldn't be long before he spilled his guts, saying far more than he intended.

Thankfully, both Frank and Martha were home and hadn't yet turned in for the night. Martha greeted him with her usual enthusiasm. "Come on in, dear. I just happen to have some peach cobbler that I can warm up in a jiffy. That is if you plan to sit for a spell."

"I do. Thanks, Sister Martha. You're too kind."

Frank sat at the table and watched with a huge, knowing grin on his wise, wrinkled face.

"Not at all, Silas. Something tells me that you came to see Frank and not me. So, after I serve the two of you, I'll make myself scarce. Coffee?"

"Yes, please," Silas muttered miserably as he seated himself across from Frank.

Frank merely nodded and winked as he took another sip of his coffee.

Martha set the steaming coffee down and checked the

progress of the cobbler that she had hurriedly thrown into a skillet on the hot stove. Soon, it was hot enough, so she scooped it onto a plate and set it in front of Silas. She patted his shoulder before she left.

Frank chuckled and sighed with contentment. "She's one good woman."

Silas jerked his head up to look at Frank. "Who?"

Frank stared for a moment. "Martha, of course. Who did you think I was talking about?"

Silas shook his head to clear the cobwebs then looked down with embarrassment. He shoveled another bite of cobbler in and took a sip of coffee.

Frank paused for a moment then asked, "Bonnie Adams, perhaps?"

Silas choked on his coffee, almost spitting it across the table. He shot a piercing look at Frank.

Frank laughed and shrugged. "What? She's probably a fine woman. I hear you've been seeing quite a lot of each other."

Silas' look stayed the same.

Frank laughed and held his hands up in surrender. "I'm sorry, Silas. I know you didn't come here to be teased. It's just so…so tempting."

"Well, resist temptation please. This is painful."

Frank composed himself and leaned forward across the table. "What can I help you with?"

Silas leaned back and studied Frank's face wondering if he could trust him to take this seriously. Frank looked him in the eye and gave a slight nod. That was enough to satisfy Silas. At least enough to dare entrusting Frank with a portion of his troubles.

"Well, as you've obviously guessed this is about Bonnie."

Frank nodded.

"I'm sure you got an earful about what happened before church this morning."

Frank nodded again, a little twinkle in his eyes. "I did. I'd like to hear it from you though."

"Has Bonnie talked to either of you?"

"Not to me. I haven't seen her around so I'm pretty sure she hasn't talked to Martha."

Silas took a deep breath before he started. "I'm afraid I've made a mess of things. I've given Bonnie the wrong impression and I think I've hurt her. Badly. I'd like to somehow make it up to her without giving her the impression that I'm at all interested in her. Because I'm not!" he said with added force. He lowered his voice. "Interested in her, I mean. At all."

"So, how do you think you gave her this impression?"

"I didn't stop her when she brought meals."

"She's brought us meals, too."

Silas threw an exasperated look his direction. "You know very well this is different. She brings them to me and always expects me to eat alone with her. Most of the time, I've managed to avoid that, but lately it's been desserts after Maddy and the kids leave. And she only brings enough for the two of us, never enough for Luke."

"So, what's this I hear about the two of you on a blanket in the field?"

Silas felt his face redden. "What?" he sputtered.

Frank smiled. "There are a couple of ladies from church that made it their business to let me know they heard those words come from Bonnie's mouth." Frank paused. "And if they heard it, others heard it. And if others didn't hear it directly, then I'm sure they heard it repeated from someone. I agree. This is indeed a mess."

"Yes, it's true. But to me, that blanket was merely a substitute for a table. She always brought food when I was out working in one of my fields. Before I could stop work, she'd usually make a beeline for me then quickly spread the blanket. I never dreamt that she'd see it as anything more than a convenient place to put the food."

"Was Luke around?"

"He was usually a ways off working in another field." Silas fidgeted like a schoolboy. "And it was pretty obvious that there was only enough food for the two of us."

"So, you sat on a blanket with a woman in the middle of a field eating her food when no one else was around."

"Yeah…"

"Kind of stupid on your part, don't ya think?"

Silas looked down in shame. "Yes, sir. I think I let my stomach make that decision. I was hungry and thirsty and there right before my eyes appeared food and drink. Good food, I might add. She's an amazing cook."

Frank chuckled. "Kind of reminds me of the story of Esau selling his birthright for a bowl of stew."

"Surely it's not that serious."

Frank laughed. "Thankfully, no. Without a doubt, Bonnie saw all this as something much more that feeding a hungry man. Surely you're not so naïve that you didn't see what she was up to."

"I knew she was interested in me but I thought I'd made it pretty clear that the feelings weren't mutual."

"The fact that she kept dropping in on you should have been a clue that she hadn't taken the hint."

"I thought she was just being neighborly."

Frank merely raised an eyebrow as he looked at Silas.

"And I felt sorry for her. We were pretty mean to her way back when we all went to school together. I'm ashamed." Silas looked down. "I guess in a sort of convoluted way I was trying to make it up to her."

"And, in the meantime, get to feast on her offerings."

When Silas didn't respond, Frank quietly added, "Do you realize that what you've been doing for the past few months has been far more cruel to Bonnie than what you did as a schoolboy?"

Silas merely stared. Then as the truth of those words sank in, he dropped his head in shame.

CHAPTER SIXTEEN

Silas yanked his thumb back and stuck it in his mouth, trying to ease the pain. This was the third time this morning that he'd smacked himself with the hammer. He stood and paced the floor in agitation. He could hear the children playing on the porch and Maddy banging pots around in the kitchen.

Rain had dictated that he and Luke concentrate on inside jobs. He was rebuilding the stairs to the second floor and Luke was building shelves in the barn. Silas walked out to join his kids. His mind was too muddled to enjoy the gentle autumn rain. Guilt and worry stirred deep in his gut.

Reverend Richards had been right. Silas had stupidly led Bonnie to believe there was reason to hope for a relationship with him. He needed to talk to her, but he knew it would be foolish to see her alone. The guilt of how he'd used her ate away at him. He tried to rationalize it by saying it was unintentional, but he knew he could have tried a lot harder at discouraging her. Maddy had hinted at that more than once and he'd ignored her. Soon, he would set up a meeting with Bonnie, the reverend, and Martha.

The worry that ate away at his peace of mind had nothing to do with Bonnie though. It was those Potter boys. He thought about last night and the disturbing discovery that the well-traveled path between the Potter's place and Maddy's had a side path straight to Maddy's small back porch. He and Ollie walked up the back steps without a squeak and looked in the back window into the kitchen, trying to get an idea what the Potters could see if they'd done the same. Silas then checked the locks.

A few weeks earlier he, Luke, Luke's pa, and Mark Donaldson had ridden out to pay a neighborly call on the Potters. Both Sam and Nate put on their best manners. When asked about their visits to Maddy's farm, they both expressed their concern for her safety. Being her closest neighbors, they had explained, meant they felt it was their duty to check up on her now and then. Nothing about their words had him feeling uneasy. Everything about their demeanor caused the hair to rise on his neck. He had ridden away without making the threats he was prepared to make. His companions didn't seem nearly as concerned as he was. They were all missing something. He was sure of it. Next time, he'd take Frank Richards with him. Frank had an uncanny ability to read people.

Maddy turned from Silas' new cast iron cookstove to see him duck as he stepped through the doorway. His blue cotton shirt stretched across his tall, muscular frame. Brown denim pants with patches at the knees begged to be laundered. Drying his hands with a faded green rag, his eyes swept the room then settled gently on her. She quickly turned back to the stove to remove two freshly baked loaves of bread, their fragrance quickly filling the room. Then she lifted the cover off a pot and stirred its contents.

"This stew should be ready in about ten minutes. Are you hungry yet?"

"I'm always hungry."

Maddy glanced at the window. "Looks like the rain is going to keep at it for a while."

Silas hung the damp rag on a hook near the stove. "Looks like it."

Maddy opened the cupboard and took out bowls and plates. She went to the door and called to Ollie. "Ollie, would you go get some milk please? It's almost time to eat."

When she turned around, she saw Silas still standing next to the stove. He was distractedly studying his thumb.

"Is everything alright, Silas?"

Silas looked up and chuckled. "Yeah. Everything's fine. I smacked myself on the thumb a few times though. Man, that hurts! You'd think I'd learn."

Maddy moved to his side and took his hand. "Here, let me see it." She turned it gently to get a better look. "You certainly did smack it. It's starting to swell. Maybe I should wrap it so you can protect it."

"From what? A hammer-wielding maniac named Silas MacGregor?" He laughed.

Maddy smiled. "Maybe the best thing to do is take all tools away from Silas MacGregor until he learns how to use them properly."

Silas' deep chuckle stirred her. She turned to stir the stew again. "Almost ready."

At that moment, both Ollie and Anabel bounded into the house with Hansel right behind them. Ollie handed the cold container of milk to Maddy.

"Would you two go tell Luke that the meal is ready? I think he's in the barn. No. On second thought. Ollie, you go. It's still raining. I don't need for both of you to get wet. And take this wet dog with you."

Soon, they all gathered around the hot stew and warm

bread. Silas gave thanks for all their blessings and asked God to bless the meal. He added a request for wisdom and for protection. Maddy looked at him for clues as to why. *What might be going on inside that head today?* He had seemed preoccupied since he had walked through the door.

"If the rain lets up, I need to drive down to see the reverend."

"Again?" Luke asked as he sopped up stew with a large chunk of bread. "You just went there last night, didn't you?"

Silas scowled at the younger man, who was oblivious. Maddy couldn't help but laugh at the two of them.

"I'm sorry," she quickly apologized as Silas turned his scowl on her. His eyes twinkled.

"I'm thinking someone has too much time on his hands if he's getting to the point, he pays such close attention to my comings and goings."

Luke stopped in the middle of a bite. "Who? Me? Are you talking about me?"

"I think he is, Luke," Ollie said as he gulped his milk down.

Both Silas and Maddy laughed.

"I'm sorry, boss." Luke wiped his mouth. "But it's true. You just met with the reverend last night, didn't you?"

"It doesn't matter if it is true. It doesn't matter if I go there every day. It's not your cotton-pickin' business."

Luke's face reddened slightly. "Oh! I'm sorry."

"Now, as I said, if the rain lets up, I'm heading to the Richards'. And, Maddy, I'd like to leave the kids with you."

"Of course."

"But I want you to stay here."

"If the rain lets up, I need to go home, Silas. I have a lot to do."

Silas looked around the table and started to speak but stopped himself. He smiled at Anabel. "I think I'll have those stairs finished in a few days. That means you two can start using the upstairs bedroom."

"I don't want to sleep up there, Pa," Anabel said. "Not unless you do, too."

"I'll be up there, Anabel," Ollie said. "I'll take care of you."

Anabel got down from her chair and walked over to Maddy. Maddy put an arm around her. "I want Ma to sleep up there with us."

Maddy kissed the top of her sweet head. "I can't, sweetheart. My bedroom is at my house."

"Then I'll sleep there with you, Ma."

Silas reached his hands out to his daughter. "Come here, pumpkin."

Anabel walked slowly to him. He pulled her up into his lap and hugged her. "I never said you had to sleep up there. You can stay in my room if you want. At least until you're big enough and brave enough to sleep up there."

"I'm pretty big right now, Pa. But I think I'll just say with Ma," she said in a calm, matter-of-fact voice.

Silas smiled and shook his head. "We'll see." He set her on the floor. "For now, both of you help your ma, uh, Maddy, wash dishes." He caught Maddy's eye and motioned for her to follow him out to the porch.

Luke got up as well. "Thank you, Maddy. That was fine eatin'. You're a mighty good cook. Some man's gonna be real happy to call you his wife someday." He wiped his mouth one last time and dropped his napkin on the table. "I'll see you later."

"Thank you, Luke. I can't wait to see those shelves you're building. Silas tells me you're a fine carpenter."

Luke flashed a smile at Silas. "Thanks, boss."

"It's true, Luke. But I ain't paying you to stand around here. Get back to work, boy." He grinned as he spoke.

Maddy loved the easy camaraderie between the two men. She followed them out to the porch where Luke asked a couple of questions about his next job. When he left, Silas turned to her. He was standing so close she had to crane her neck to look into his face.

"If Luke or I can't be close by, I don't feel good about you being at your house," he said quietly.

"Even during daylight?"

"I didn't want to talk about it in front of Anabel, but those Potter boys are making me nervous. Ollie and I found a path that led right to your back steps."

"Silas, I use those steps to go out to the garden almost every day. That path is probably from me."

"No. I saw a path that led directly from their path out in the field all the way to your back steps. Is that from you?"

Maddy caught her breath and looked down. "Oh. That means they come to my back door and look into my kitchen?"

"That's what it looks like to me. I checked your steps. They're very quiet. They could easily step up to your door and look into the window without being heard."

"That's a little scary."

"So that's why I prefer you stay here."

Maddy was silent for a while. "No. That's my home and I'm not going to let anyone rob me of my home. I need to be there." She looked squarely into Silas' face without flinching. Putting her hand on Silas' arm, she added, "I'm serious, Silas. I will have Ollie and Anabel in my sight at all times. And it's broad daylight. They won't dare try anything stupid."

She laughed, "Maybe Ollie and I can rig up a booby trap for our sneaky neighbors."

It was obvious that Silas wasn't at all amused. Maddy had to fight the urge to stroke his worried face and ease the scowl lines away. Suddenly the sound of rain stopped. The eaves dripped pleasantly onto the sharp pebbles surrounding the house. A rainbow peeked through the trees as the sun made an appearance. Silas stroked his raspy jaw, deep in thought.

"Well, it looks like you'll get to visit the Richards after all." Maddy studied him for a moment. "Does this have anything to do with Bonnie?"

Silas looked at her, his eyebrow raised slightly.

"I'm sorry. That's none of my 'cotton-pickin' business, is it? I'm as bad as Luke."

"Actually, I don't mind you asking," he said softly. "You've done enough for me and my kids that you've earned the right to dig into my business. And yes. This has to do with Bonnie."

"I only asked because of the talk flying around after church on Sunday. It was hard to ignore."

"The time has come to put an absolute, unquestionable end to our 'relationship.' For my sake as well as hers. I've been unfair to her. Actually, rather unkind. And frankly, I'm ashamed of myself."

Maddy grew quiet as she watched the emotions play over his face. He was serious. He was truly ashamed.

"How are you going to do it? You've tried before and she hasn't taken the hint."

"I haven't been consistent. I told her one thing and as soon as that food shows up, I happily devour it and that told her something else."

"Well to be truthful, I was even starting to wonder."

Silas jerked his head to look at her. "Seriously?"

She shrugged. "Why not? This has been going on since when? June? That's three months, Silas."

His face registered both shock and hurt.

"I'm sorry. I think I know you well enough to not believe the rumors. And yes, there were rumors," she said in response to his questioning look. "But when you let her visits continue into this month and always after I had left for the day...then I started to wonder. Even Luke was wondering."

"Maddy..." Silas turned to her. "Surely you've seen

how she treats the kids. She can barely stand to be in the same room with them. And they can't seem to get away from her fast enough. If you thought for a moment that I could marry a woman like that and let her be a mother to my kids, then you have severely misjudged me."

Tears came to his eyes. Against her better judgement she reached up and briefly cupped his face. "I'm sorry, Silas. I truly didn't believe that about you. I wasn't sure what to think. Forgive me, please. I do know you better that that."

Silas gripped her hand and held it against his face. "What they need, Maddy, is a mother like you." Their eyes locked.

"Pa! The rain stopped! Are you going to Reverend Richards? Can I go?"

Silas stepped abruptly back and turned to his boy. "Not this time, son, I need you to take care of Maddy. You're all going to her place." Without looking at Maddy, he added, "Luke's going, too. I have a job for him to do there." With that, he bounded down the steps and took long, quick strides to the barn.

CHAPTER SEVENTEEN

A quick glance around her yard and toward the barn calmed Maddy's fears that Sam or Nate Potter might be there. Luke jumped down from Silas' wagon and followed him to the chicken house where, Maddy had just learned, he was going to rebuild the rotting hen boxes and repair the door.

Maddy and the kids went to check on the pigs and Daisy. Maddy's eyes swept over every possible hiding place in the barn. They exited out the back and walked through the garden, picking a few tomatoes and green beans on the way. Her nerves were on edge ever since Silas had told her about Potters' path to her back door.

To Maddy's relief, Ollie and Anabel were happily oblivious to the possible danger. She was determined she wouldn't let the Potters destroy her peace. In all this time, they had never harmed her or the children, even though they had had many chances to do so. Surely, they wouldn't with Silas and Luke living so close and eating their meals here. She paused at the back door and looked down the path leading north, the one Silas had just discovered. She had never noticed it. Was it new? She shuddered and looked through her window, wondering if the Potters had done the same. If so, why? And just what had they seen?

"Ma! Do you want me to dig for potatoes? I think we're running low."

"Yes, Ollie. Please," she hollered back. Their potato patch was at the far end of the garden near an overgrown pasture.

"Ma! We have pumpkins! They're still babies though."

"That's great, Ollie. Pumpkin pies coming up."

Maddy could see Anabel's little head bent over the green beans. She loved to eat them while picking, which was fine with Maddy. Oh, how she loved those two. She entered the kitchen and looked around. Nothing out of place. There was a knock at the front door. Silas. He opened the door and knocked again, letting her know he was there.

"Do you ever lock these doors when you're gone?"

"No. I can't. They only lock from the inside."

"Do you ever look around in here to make sure no one's here?"

"Only when I'm feeling particularly nervous."

Silas walked over to a window to check on the kids. Then he started checking the downstairs for any possible hiding place. Maddy joined him. They worked their way upstairs. It didn't take long since there weren't that many places to hide.

When they got to the bottom of the stairs, Silas turned to her. "From now on, if you don't mind, could you do a quick check every day when you get here? And I'll see to it that either Luke or I will be in the house when you do it? No more walking home with just you and the children."

Maddy nodded.

"Also, make a list of projects for Luke or me to work on." Silas smiled and gently tweaked her chin. "Call it an early Christmas present."

She shook her head as he turned and walked out the door.

Giggles twittered through the pasture as Ollie shook the persimmon tree as vigorously as possible while perched on a branch twelve feet in the air. Maddy and Anabel tried to catch as many as they could in their outstretched aprons without getting hit on their heads. They failed miserably. At the sight of Anabel's face when several brown persimmons landed on her, Maddy bent over with uncontrollable roars of laughter. Anabel ran to her and threw herself into Maddy's arms.

"Is that enough, Ma?" Ollie hollered from up above.

Maddy looked around at all the fruit they had failed to catch. "Yes, Ollie. I think we have enough. Come on down and help us pick the rest of these up."

Ollie swung from branch to branch like a monkey and dropped to the ground beside them. "Did you say you're making bread this time, Ma?"

"Yes. I got a new recipe from Sister Martha. I have a feeling it's going to be even better than persimmon pie."

All three busied themselves gathering the soft fruit and dropping it in a basket setting in the sun. Both Ollie and Anabel stopped occasionally to sink their teeth into the mushy, ripe goodness.

"How are they?" Maddy watched with a smile.

"Really good." Brown goo dribbled down Anabel's chin.

"Perfect," Ollie said, grimacing slightly. "Only a few of them make me pucker up."

Maddy tried one. Ollie was right. Sweet with little to no puckering. Perfect.

"Can I get some walnuts for the bread?" Ollie looked at

her with pleading eyes.

"I would love that. They should be ready. But you'll have to hurry. I want to get this bread in the oven in time for supper."

Both kids took off in the direction of the giant walnut trees in the back of the pasture. Maddy picked up the basket and headed for the house. She took the persimmons out front to wash them under the pump, picking out twigs, leaf bits, and bugs. Then she hauled them inside and dumped a quarter of her load into a colander where she broke into them with a heavy wooden spoon, driving the pulp through the holes and leaving skin and seeds behind. It was exhausting work, but she was finished before Ollie and Anabel came in with a small pail of black walnuts still in their husks.

"Why don't you take those out and get Luke to help you husk them. And wear your gloves if you can find them. Your hands will get stained from those husks. Remember what happened last year?"

"Yeah." Ollie grimaced. "I think it took months for it to wear off. Soap and scrubbing didn't work."

"I know where my gloves are," Anabel hollered as she scrambled upstairs.

"Mine are in the barn, I think." Ollie headed toward the chicken house and Luke.

Maddy put all the pulp in a large bowl and mashed it finer with a fork, then she forced it through a strainer. She found Martha's recipe and gathered the rest of the ingredients; flour, sugar, baking soda, butter, and eggs. The oven was still warm but she added wood to bring the heat up. She glanced out the window. Hopefully the walnuts would be ready in time.

She sifted two cups of flour and one teaspoon of soda then creamed the sugar and butter before adding the eggs.

Anabel walked in proudly holding a handful of nuts in dark-brown hands. "Anabel! I thought I told you to wear gloves."

"I did. But they made my hands itch."

Maddy received her offering of crushed nuts mixed with a few bits of shell. She put it in a bowl and showed her how to pick the shells out then checked her work. Anabel jumped down from her chair and ran out the door. "There's more, Ma! Don't bake the bread yet!"

Maddy added the creamed mixture to the dry and mixed it gently. She then added the persimmon pulp and folded the whole mixture together several times. Just then, Ollie and Anabel walked in with two more small handfuls of nuts. Ollies hands were worse than his sister's. Maddy sighed and shook her head. After the children picked through the nuts, Maddy let them mix it into the bread batter. They filled two loaf pans and opened the oven. Maddy placed them side by side on the middle rack, closed the door, and stepped back with a happy sigh of satisfaction.

"They should be done in about an hour. In the meantime, I'm going out to milk Daisy and I want you two to sit and practice writing your letters. If you get that done before I get back, then you can read."

"Okay, Ma," both kids said at once.

Maddy could hear Luke hammering away from the direction of the henhouse. She was looking forward to seeing the finished product. Everything Luke did turned out beautifully. She chuckled. Too bad the hens couldn't fully appreciate his work.

She swung the milk pail back and forth and looked up at the deep blue of the sky to the east. A chill was in the air. A few leaves drifted down around her. The silver maples had started to turn yellowish orange and the walnut trees were yellowing. Perhaps when she got back to the house, she'd have time to sit out here with her watercolors. Painting always seemed to soothe her soul. Twirling around, she scanned for perfect scenes. Bright scarlet Virginia Creeper climbed up around the giant oaks in the front yard; oaks that stubbornly refused to join most of the other trees in accepting that it was fall. One of the last to change color and the last to drop leaves.

The acorns on the other hand were dropping in abundance. The biggest oak in Maddy's yard was a white oak that supposedly had sweet, edible acorns. Maddy had tried her hardest last winter when food was scarce to do what the experts advised her to do to prepare them for eating. It was an abysmal failure. She fed them all to the pig who was quite delighted.

Daisy mooed a gentle greeting as Maddy stepped through the barn door. She ran her hand down the cow's back and clucked softly to her before setting the pail under her udder. Grabbing the stool off a nail on the wall next to the stanchion, she tucked her skirt between her legs and sat down. The milk flowed easily with musical pings into the empty pail. Maddy rested her head against Daisy's flank and worked both hands on the warm nipples. It usually took her about twenty to thirty minutes to complete the job. Her hands had grown very strong over the years.

As usual, she hummed and prayed during this quiet time. It had become sacred to her, so much so, she coveted the evening milking. Ollie and Anabel accepted that fact and happily busied themselves with their daily writing and reading assignments.

When she finished, she moved the pail out of Daisy's reach and turned her out into the lane that led to the pasture behind the house. Luke had taken it upon himself to call her back into the barn every night.

Maddy reached down for the pail and froze. From the corner of her eye, she saw a shadow move toward her. Heart pounding, she stood and saw Sam Potter smiling from the corner next to the door. How long had he been there? Luke's hammering could still be heard, so she knew he hadn't seen the intruder. She took a calming breath to steady her nerves and deliberately bent over again to pick up the pail of milk. She mustn't show fear.

"Well hello, Mr. Potter. You gave me a little fright there." She forced a laugh. "What can I do for you?" she said as she moved to the door.

Sam merely chuckled and took a step to block her path.

"Do for me? As a matter of fact, there's a lot you can do for me, Maddy girl."

Fear sliced through her gut. She could barely take a breath. "I need to go to the house. I have bread in the oven. Would you like some?" She tried to push past him, but he grabbed her arm and roughly turned her around to face him. Milk slopped out onto her dress.

"I'd love some bread, darling. But I want a lot more than bread. And I'm sick of waiting." He backed her away from the door until she was against a post. Her heart pounded. She tried to free herself. His other hand grabbed her throat and he pushed her head against the unyielding wood.

Maddy saw a look in his eyes she had never seen before. Anger? Hatred? He had always tried to be friendly but she saw none of that today.

"If your friend Silas ever threatens me and my brother again, I promise he'll regret it. Do you hear me, girl?"

Maddy nodded.

Sam went on. "He thinks he has a claim on you. Well he doesn't. I'm your closest neighbor and you're mine." His hand tightened on her throat. Suddenly Sam released his hands from her and straightened. He awkwardly smoothed her hair.

Maddy swallowed and tried to control her breathing.

"I...I'm sorry, Maddy. What I meant to say w-was, 'will you marry me?'"

Maddy only stared wide-eyed. She couldn't speak.

"Think about it." Sam's voice had a whiney note of desperation. "It only makes sense. We could join our property and have us a good-size spread. Nate and I are both hard workers. You won't find a better catch anywhere in these parts."

Maddy stared into Sam's beady eyes and almost gagged.

"Why ain't you answering me?" Sam turned and paced. "You think yer too good for me, don't ya, girl?"

When he turned back, his eyes were full of hurt and something else. Resentment, defiance. She was frozen in place against the thick, hard post.

Sam walked back and leaned in close and whispered in her ear. "It's only a matter of time, sweetheart. I have everything set in place. And if you ever breathe a word of this visit to anyone, I promise I'll hurt someone you love." He kissed the top of her head and walked out the back door.

CHAPTER EIGHTEEN

Silas was baffled. Maddy had changed overnight from a woman who seemed to glean joy from every circumstance to a fretful, sad shell of her former self. He was tempted to ask her to spend another month with Eliza in Springfield, but when he suggested it, she adamantly refused. He then suggested she go visit Sister Martha. Again, she refused. She seemed to be overly concerned with tending to Ollie and Anabel, only letting them leave her side if she knew they were with him.

A few weeks ago, when he had gotten back to her place after visiting the Richards, she had quietly served supper along with warm persimmon bread that would have melted in his mouth if it hadn't been for a couple of hard walnut shells that almost cracked his teeth.

Both Ollie and Anabel had filled the conversation around the table with their escapades of the day, including accounts of their most recent discoveries during their reading time. He would be eternally grateful to Maddy for teaching his children to read and to love to learn. Years before, her parents had bought John Newberry's books; *A*

Little Pretty Pocket-Book and *Goody Two-Shoes*, books that had brought hours of entertainment and education to not only the Malone children but also to his.

A month had gone by since that day he had eaten Maddy's persimmon bread. That was when he had noticed a stark difference in her demeanor. And his concerns had continued to grow. Maddy wasn't snapping out of her lethargy. He suspected that one of the Potters had made an appearance but when he questioned her, she was quick to deny it. He was puzzled. He stood in his field amongst the remaining cornstalks and looked toward his house. He wondered why Maddy and the children were lingering longer than usual. She always seemed grateful that either he or Luke had projects to work on at her place and seemed to welcome his protective measures.

He had an idea, a simple thought, and walked to the house to present it to Maddy. He found her cleaning the stove. She turned abruptly when she heard him at the door. "I'm going to have the cleanest stove in the state if you keep that up."

She merely smiled. Forced, as usual, he noticed.

"It's unseasonably warm. Tomorrow's Sunday. Let's treat the Richards to a picnic."

Maddy nodded. "That sounds nice. I'll fry some chicken and make some biscuits."

"How about we go to the river again?"

"Alright." The lack of enthusiasm pained him.

He paused and watched her turn to wipe the cupboard shelves with a damp rag. "We can use some of my chickens," he offered. "I'll get Ollie to help me."

She turned. "Make sure Anabel stays inside. I…I need her to help me start some biscuits."

Silas nodded then turned to find Ollie and Anabel playing quietly in the living room. Ollie occupied with lining his toy soldiers up in neat rows poised to attack and Anabel cuddling her rag doll and stroking its yarn hair.

"Ollie and Anabel, would you like to have another picnic at the river?" Both kids jumped up and squealed their combined enthusiastic "yes," making up for Maddy's lack. "I have a big job for you, Ollie. Are you ready?"

"Yes! What is it?"

"We need to kill two chickens for the picnic."

"Yay! Can I swing the ax this time, Pa? I've watched you do it a dozen times."

Anabel shrunk back. "Not me, Pa. I'm staying inside with Ma."

Silas hugged her against his leg. "Ma...Maddy wants you to help her bake biscuits."

Anabel wiggled free from his hug and ran to join Maddy in the kitchen. "Ma, can I sift the flour?"

"Put your apron on first, sweetheart," Silas heard with some satisfaction. Hopefully the picnic would occupy Maddy's troubled thoughts and tomorrow's conversation with Sister Martha would be balm for her wounded heart. That was his main reason for a picnic with Frank and Martha. Martha had a gift for getting to the crux of an issue and then pouring on healing words. And Maddy adored the Richards.

Silas talked Ollie into watching him while he swung the axe that cut the head from the first squawking hen. Ollie argued only for a minute when Silas explained it took strength to both hold the chicken down and swing the ax at precisely the right moment. As always, the chicken's body ran free without its head for several minutes before it came to rest, blood spurting everywhere. Ollie thoroughly enjoyed this spectacle as many boys did.

When the chicken gave up its fight, they washed the blood and dirt off at the pump then took it to the giant pot hanging over the fire in the backyard. The water was perfect, not quite boiling, so Silas lifted the bird by its feet and lowered it in. In about a minute, he pulled the bird out just enough to grab some wing feathers. They came out with ease, so he threw the carcass on a board with instructions for Ollie to start plucking while he went to kill the other bird.

When both birds were mostly plucked clean, they thoroughly washed them then cut the feet off. Silas gutted the first bird while Ollie watched and mimicked his actions on the second bird. They then tried to scrape the remaining pin feathers off with a dull knife. Silas got the remaining hairs off by singeing them briefly over the flames. They washed them a third time and wrapped them in sacks for the trip to Maddy's.

Earlier, Silas had asked Luke to ride to the Richards' and give the invitation. He got back just in time for the evening meal at Maddy's. "They said yes," he announced as he sat down to a meal of ham, potatoes, and green beans. "They also said you had a good meeting with Miss Adams last month. They thought it went quite well, in fact."

Silas glared. "Do you plan to write a book about my life, Luke?"

Luke looked up, thoroughly puzzled. "What do you mean, boss?"

"I mean, you sure do seem awfully interested in my private life. As if you're gathering facts for a good story."

Luke sat back and raised his hands in defense. "Whoa! I never asked them about you and Bonnie. They just freely told me."

Silas wiped his face in agitation. "So much for private conversations with my pastor," he muttered. He turned to see Maddy staring at him.

"So, you did meet with Bonnie?" she asked quietly. "When?"

"The same day you and the kids made that persimmon bread, remember? I went there hoping to set up a meeting and Martha suggested we do it right then. She didn't want me to wait. So, the two of them drove over to her place and asked if she'd ride back with them to meet me."

"Why didn't you tell me?"

Silas was momentarily at a loss for words. "I…I'm sorry. I didn't know you were waiting to hear."

"How did it go?" Her voice was quiet.

"Uh…not well, at first. She was still angry, but after Martha talked to her, she calmed down and…uh, forgave me. At least she said she did. She never looked at me, but both Frank and Martha seemed satisfied that she got the message and that she would eventually heal." He ran his hands through his thick, dark hair. "I was a fool. I never meant to hurt her."

Maddy laid a hand on his arm. It felt good. "I'm glad it's over," she said softly.

"Me, too."

Maddy sat quietly in the wagon after church the following morning. Silas and the children were full of chatter. When they pulled into her yard, her eyes darted around looking for any signs of unwanted company. Since that horrible day that Sam had threatened her, she had only seen a Potter one time, and thankfully it was from a distance. She had gone out to gather eggs one morning with Anabel by her side and caught a glimpse of a green shirt heading back down the path. Shamefully, she had frozen to the spot, unable to grab the shotgun leaning against the outside of the chicken house. How in the world could she protect her babies if that was how she was going to react?

Silas stopped the buggy and went into the house ahead of her and the children. He did a quick check of the downstairs. He waited while Maddy and the kids ran upstairs to change out of their church clothes. Maddy took off her brown satin dress and hung it in her closet, recently built by Silas as one of the projects he and Luke were constantly doing for her. It was a simple, open structure built against the wall with a rod for her dresses. She felt blessed. She put on a green calico, one that wouldn't show grass stains. It was her favorite dress for outdoor fun.

She chuckled sadly at the thought of fun. Her days were dark and she could see no end to the darkness. She was trapped. What could she do? If it wasn't for Silas, she'd take the children and run away. Far away. She choked on a sob. What might the Potters do to Ollie and Anabel? The question kept her awake at night. Fear was her constant companion. Fear and her shotgun. At least when Silas and Luke weren't close by.

"We're ready, Ma! Let's go!" Ollie's voice came from downstairs.

After going to the springhouse to get the chilled chicken, she came back to hear Anabel bossily directing her pa and Ollie, telling them how to load the picnic basket with biscuits and tomatoes. Silas looked at her and winked. She never tired of watching him parent his two offspring. He was such a good father. In every way.

Maybe she should just disappear. That would be far better than marrying Sam, which would never happen. But what if her disappearance angered Sam to the point he'd hurt the children? She took Silas' offered hand and stepped up into the wagon. Maybe she should sneak over to the Potters' some dark night and kill both of them. That would solve everything. She'd thought about it often, but knew she would never be able to resort to murder no matter what the circumstances. Although if she caught either of them trying to hurt her babies, she wouldn't hesitate to shoot them right between their blasted eyes!

"Maddy? What's wrong?" Silas asked from the seat next to her. They had traveled quite a distance and she hadn't even noticed.

She turned wide eyes toward him and forced herself to breathe. She had just planned to murder her neighbors. If

Silas only knew. "What? I'm fine."

"Ollie asked you a question five times and you never answered."

"Five times?"

"Yep, Ma. Five times. I counted."

"I counted, too, Ma," Anabel added with pride.

"I'm so sorry, Ollie. I guess I was a little distracted. What was it?"

"Are you going in the water with us, again?"

"Sure, if you want me to."

She caught Silas looking at her. "Are you sure? It's going to be freezing cold. I'm not even sure the kids can handle it."

"Oh. Well maybe not, Ollie. We'll see."

She caught Silas staring at her again.

"What, Silas?"

His voice lowered almost to a whisper. "I wish you'd tell me what's got you so stirred up."

"I'm not stirred up. I've just got a lot on my mind, that's all."

"If you'd talk about it, maybe you wouldn't be so worried all the time."

"Worried? I'm not worried. I'm just…just trying to plan Christmas. That's all," she lied.

"Christmas is two months away!"

"Did someone say 'Christmas'?" Ollie whooped from behind them.

Maddy welcomed the distraction and turned to him. "Yes! Aren't you excited? This year you'll have your pa, and I'm going to make it the best Christmas you've ever had! We'll make presents for each other and we'll all have stockings and we'll make a huge feast. How does that sound?"

"Candy, too, Ma?" Anabel shrieked with joy.

"Of course! Candy, too! Lots and lots of candy!"

"And a new doll, Ma? I haven't gotten a new doll in

ever so long!"

As the children dreamed out loud of a magical Christmas, Maddy turned around to see Silas sadly shaking his head at her.

Her face suddenly got hot under his scrutiny. She was filled with shame and she could tell he saw right through her.

CHAPTER NINETEEN

Maddy gripped her seat as Silas turned the wagon down a rough, narrow road scarred with deep ruts. Both of them leaned to the center to avoid getting whacked by tall weeds. She could barely see ahead to where the Richards had parked their wagon. The river was low but beautifully refreshing to the ears, gurgling its way over the rocks.

Martha called out a greeting as she spread a blanket on the ground. Frank unloaded their basket and set it down. He then quickly walked around to Maddy's side of the wagon to offer his assistance. Silas lifted Anabel down then took the basket and blanket out of the back. Ollie, as usual, jumped without a look and ran to the water's edge.

"This was a great idea, Silas," Frank said. "We should do this more often."

"I agree." Martha's eyes danced as she helped Maddy overlap her blanket with theirs. "I'll vote yes on anything that gets us women out of the hot kitchen. Right, Maddy?"

Maddy forced a smile. "Right, Sister Martha."

The two women sat and started unloading the food. Martha put two pies on the blanket, along with apples, a large container of lemonade and a chunk of cheese. "Silas said you'd be bringing enough chicken for all of us and you certainly did!" she exclaimed.

"We thought Luke would be joining us. He eats enough for three men."

"After church, he told me he needed to go see his parents. He said he'd stop by on his way back."

"I guess we better save him some, then." Maddy turned to Martha. "I tried your recipe for persimmon bread."

"How was it?"

"Delicious!" Maddy smiled a genuine smile. "All except the walnut shells."

"Well now. That recipe never mentioned walnut shells. Did you get a little help from the children?"

Maddy nodded and grinned. "I could tell every time Silas bit into one. He was very kind though. Never even mentioned it."

Martha laughed. "He's a good man. The best, in fact. But I suppose you already know that."

Maddy rolled her eyes at her older friend. "I think it's time to eat, don't you?" She unpacked plates and called for Silas to get the children.

The families gathered. After Reverend Richards prayed, he helped himself to the fried chicken and passed it on to Maddy. "I brought a couple of fishing poles. If we manage to catch anything, we could build a little fire here on the bank and roast 'em."

"Could we, Pa? I haven't been fishing in a long time." Ollie jumped to his feet.

"Sit down and eat, son. First things first. Yes, you can fish. Think we might need to go downstream a bit, though, to find a decent fishing hole."

"There's a good one not too far down. I used to fish here a lot." Frank bit appreciatively into the cold chicken. "I miss it."

Maddy adjusted herself on the blanket and settled in comfortably. She wished this moment would last forever. For this little while, she could pretend all was well. Anabel, with a mouth full of buttery biscuit, moved to cuddle up against her. She sighed a little girl sigh. "I don't want to fish. I just want to stay with Ma."

The men chuckled at her sweetness. Maddy caught Silas winking at Martha. The conversation flowed easily and would have lasted hours longer if it hadn't been for a seven-year-old boy anxious to grab a rod and start digging for worms.

"How about I cover these pies and we can all gather back here after you men get your fill of fishing?" Martha leaned over and planted a kiss on Frank's whiskered cheek.

"Get our fill of fishing? I'm not sure that will ever happen." He gently cupped his wife's kind, wrinkled face then hopped up, surprisingly agile for a man of his age, grabbed a shovel, and followed Ollie to an area that looked promising for worms.

Silas stayed behind to help clean up but both women shooed him away. "Maybe a little piece of chicken will work for bait," he said, tearing off a chunk. He put some on a hook and started walking downstream.

"Well, girls. How about we go for a walk?" Martha struggled to her feet. "Heaven knows I need one." She brushed crumbs from her apron.

Maddy got to her feet and pulled Anabel behind her. "Since the boys are going downstream, let's go upstream."

The low level of the water made it easy to walk on the dried edge. Crisp leaves lined the bank and with every step, their fragrance was released. A cool breeze wafted down the river picking up the pleasant musty smell of damp earth. The warmth of the sun was perfect. Anabel ran ahead and gathered rocks, leaves, and feathers. Martha had the foresight to give the little girl a basket for her discoveries. Maddy loved this dear woman and her wisdom, borne from years of experience.

"How have you been, lately, Madeline? It seems as if it's been months since we've had a real conversation."

Maddy hesitated then answered, "I've been fine, Martha. Thanks for asking. And you?"

"Fine, just fine. Couldn't be much better, actually."

They walked on. Maddy could feel Martha's eyes on her. She turned. Sure enough. Those eyes could read volumes if Maddy wasn't careful. Sam's threat came back to her, *If you tell anyone about this visit...* Anyone included Martha. She mustn't find out! She hurried to catch up to her tiny girl. "Anabel, what have you found so far? Show me."

Anabel was delighted to share her treasures. Soon, though, she ran ahead again. Maddy's and Martha's steps crunched the dry leaves and loose pebbles.

"I sense that you are deeply troubled, Maddy. Perhaps even frightened." Martha's voice was full of compassion.

Leave it to Martha to skip past all the small talk and tunnel right in.

"Oh?" was all she could manage.

They walked in silence. "You can't talk about it, can you?"

At that question, Maddy stopped and buried her face in her hands. Sobs escaped in spite of her attempt to stifle them. She felt Martha's comforting hand on her back. "I can't, Martha. I can't talk about it. I'm suffocating, but I can't say a word."

"Is it about Silas?"

Maddy pulled away and looked at her with desperate, pleading eyes. "Don't ask, Martha! Don't ask. I can't...I won't answer you. Just pray, please! Pray!"

Martha enveloped her in a powerful hug. "I will, girl. I will. God knows and He can answer. Don't despair, Maddy."

Maddy sobbed against her for a few minutes then abruptly straightened and dried her eyes. She glanced

Anabel's direction, hoping she hadn't heard or seen her breakdown. Martha's hand rubbed small, comforting circles on her back.

Anabel took that moment to run toward them. "Look what I found!" She skidded to a stop and held up a perfectly heart-shaped rock, about an inch wide. Martha bent over and held her hand out. She took the rock and turned it from side to side.

"That's remarkable, Anabel. It's so perfect. This is a treasure to keep forever."

"I know! I love it!"

Martha turned her eyes toward Maddy and held her gaze for a significant length of time. She then turned back to Anabel. "Anabel, darling, would you do something for me?"

The little girl nodded solemnly, her eyes wide with wonder.

"I want you to keep this rock forever. Put it in a very special place. And every time you look at it, I want you to remember how very precious you are to God. I want this heart to remind you, all of your life, that God loves you very much. And that He is always taking care of you."

Martha looked at Maddy again as Anabel agreed, her little head bobbing up and down. "I will, Sister Martha. I will. Forever and ever." Her happy, shining eyes looked at Maddy. "Where can I keep it, Ma?"

"Anywhere you want, sweetie. Some place safe though. And someplace where you'll see it every day."

The two women chuckled softly as they watched Anabel walk away, clutching the stone to her chest. "Thanks, Martha. That was sweet of you."

"That reminder is for you, too, you know."

"I know. Your message was pretty clear."

Martha sighed and slipped her arm into Maddy's. They strolled that way for a while before Martha said, "I have a Bible passage for you. How long has it been since you've read the story of Ruth?"

"I remember reading it to the kids last winter, so, not so long ago. Why?"

"It's one of my favorite stories. If you remember, Ruth was a woman in dire circumstances. She and her mother-in law struggled to survive because neither had a husband to help provide for them."

"I remember. So, Ruth went to gather up grain in the field of Boaz."

"Yes. And when Boaz saw her and found out who she was, that he was actually a relative of her mother-in-law's, he took it upon himself to protect her. He told her to stay in his field close to the women there where she would be safe. He even told the men to leave her alone."

"So"—Maddy looked askance at her companion—"why do you feel compelled to share this particular story?"

Martha's eyes twinkled with mischief. "Ruth was a single woman who desperately needed a husband."

"And?"

"And she shamelessly and boldly went after what she needed."

They walked in silence, Maddy trying to decipher her older friend's meaning. Surely not what she was thinking at the moment. Ruth's boldness caused her to crawl into Boaz' bed! She shook her head in confusion. Then she laughed. "And how do you think I should apply this story to my life?"

"Go home. Read the whole story. And pray about it. God will show you what to do."

Late that night after Silas and Ollie left and Anabel was tucked into bed, Maddy opened her Bible to the Book of Ruth and read. The entire first chapter told of why Naomi and her daughter-in-law Ruth ended up in Bethlehem. She read of how, years earlier, Naomi, her husband, and two sons had left Bethlehem because of a famine and traveled to Moab. Her husband died and her two sons married Moabite women. Her sons then died, so Naomi decided to return to the land of her relatives. She urged her daughters-in-law to remain behind but Ruth refused, saying these often-quoted words, "Whither thou goest, I will go; and where thou lodgest, I will lodge: thy people shall be my people, and thy God my God."

Maddy's eyes started drooping but she pressed on. What was Martha trying to tell her? In the second chapter, she read of Ruth going into Boaz's field to glean grain after the reapers had gone through. She saw that Boaz was a kinsman of Naomi's and described as "a mighty man of wealth." Both Ruth and Naomi seemed to be certain that Boaz would show kindness. But that's all they seemed to expect, Maddy noticed. She read on to discover that Boaz went way beyond their expectations in showing kindness and protection. When Ruth asked why he did what he did, his answer was that he knew of her devotion to Naomi. He said to her, "The Lord recompense thy work, and a full reward be given thee of the Lord God of Israel, under whose wings thou art come to trust."

Was this what Martha wanted her to see? That she needed to put herself under God's wings and trust Him? Just as Ruth did as a single woman surrounded by men that might want to hurt her?

She rubbed her eyes and read on. Chapter three made her face heat. She wanted to put her Bible down and not go on. What she thought Martha might be suggesting was too bizarre to entertain. She read of how Naomi instructed Ruth to go to the threshing floor that night, watch for where Boaz would be sleeping then crawl into bed with him! Well, maybe not those exact words, but that's sure how it seemed. She read it again to be sure. "And it shall be, when he lieth down, that thou shalt mark the place where he shall lie, and thou shalt go in, and uncover his feet, and lay thee down; and he will tell thee what thou shalt do."

What else could that mean? If Martha thought for a second that those words were meant to guide Maddy, then Martha was a crazy woman and it was time to find another church! She put her Bible on her bedside table, turned the lamp down, and tried to sleep.

Her dreams were crazy that night. Downright scandalous, in fact! She woke in a sweat, threw her blankets off, and picked up her Bible. She vaguely remembered that things had turned out well for Ruth. If she would read the rest of the story, maybe, just maybe, her mind could rest.

At midnight, Boaz discovered Ruth lying at his feet. "And it came to pass at midnight, that the man was afraid, and turned himself: and, behold, a woman lay at his feet." Now wouldn't that be a shock? What must he have thought of her?

Maddy read on, "And he said, Who art thou? And she answered, I am Ruth thine handmaid: spread therefore thy skirt over thine handmaid; for thou art a near kinsman." Maddy had enough understanding of the Bible to know that a near kinsman was to protect a widow. And she strongly suspected that when Ruth asked Boaz to spread his skirt over her, it was a plea for him to protect her. But surely there were other ways of asking for protection than climbing into the man's bed.

Surprisingly, Boaz didn't get the impression that Maddy expected him to get; that Ruth was a loose woman. Instead, he praised her. He said, "Blessed be thou of the Lord, my daughter: for thou hast shewed more kindness in the latter end than at the beginning, inasmuch as thou followedst not young men, whether poor or rich."

So, Boaz thought he was too old for her? And she was showing a kindness to consider him as a possible husband?

Boaz went on to say, "And now, my daughter, fear not." At those simple words, Maddy put her head to her knees and wept. *Fear not.* If only she could somehow grasp those words to her heart. But these words were specifically meant for Ruth at that moment in history. Boaz planned to step in and care for her, not merely as a kind relative but as her husband.

Ruth's bold move was essentially a marriage proposal. And Boaz actually seemed grateful. Boaz, a man that, until that moment, seemed to think he might be too old for Ruth to consider. This wasn't helping Maddy's racing heart to calm down. As she read more, she discovered that Boaz took measures to protect her reputation. "And he said, 'Let it not be known that a woman came into the floor.'" He sent her on her way loaded down with barley to take to Naomi and with the instructions to wait until he had talked to another male relative that was first in line to marry Ruth if he so desired.

Maddy rested her head on the headboard and took a deep, calming breath. Her mind kept jumping to the similarities between Boaz and Silas. And she kept reeling those wild thoughts back under control. They were both exceptionally good men that wanted to protect a young female in their realm. They both provided for her from their abundance. Both men thought they were too old for that female. *Stop!* She stood impatiently and went to her window.

The moon offered just enough light that she could barely make out shapes below. Nothing seemed out of place. Yet, as memories stirred, she realized everything in her world was out of place. She shouldn't ever have to look down there and expect to see someone lurking about. Someone who meant her and the children harm. Life couldn't go on this way.

She crawled back into bed and read chapter four. Boaz navigated through the complicated rules and traditions of their time and won Ruth's hand in marriage. They had a son who was the grandfather of King David. So, Boaz and Ruth were David's great grandparents and direct ancestors of Jesus.

"And they all lived happily ever after," Maddy said, knowing of course, that wasn't the case. But they did live lives fulfilling God's plans. Oh, how she wished she could get a glimpse into the mind of God concerning her situation. What was His big plan for her?

With that she rested, knowing that however ominous things seemed, God did have a plan. He was still on the throne and still very present. And she belonged to Him. He had not, nor would He ever forget her.

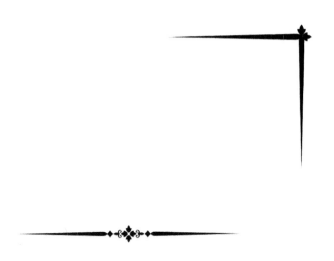

Early the next morning, Maddy looked out her window and saw Silas and Ollie trotting down the drive for breakfast. They came as always and, as always, stayed long enough to do the morning chores at the Malone farm. Maddy's heart felt lighter than it had in days. It wasn't because she had formed a plan based on the story of Ruth. She chuckled at that ridiculous thought. It was because she had been reminded that God provided for His people. No matter how unsettling the circumstances might be, God was always at work.

She quickly started frying bacon and sent Ollie out to gather eggs. Luke had already fed the pigs and milked Daisy. Always watchful, she saw Luke check on Ollie in the chicken house after he dropped the milk off at the springhouse. Anabel had yet to make an appearance, so she went to the bottom of the stairs and called for her.

"May I?" Silas said from behind her, causing her to jump. He indicated with his head that he wanted to go up and wake his sleepy daughter.

"Of course. She's your baby, Silas." The fact that she almost called him Boaz sent her scurrying to the kitchen. She received the eggs from Ollie and started cracking them into the hot pan. Chicken gravy was heating in a sauce pan and biscuits were staying warm in a bowl on top of the stove. Luke came through the door with more wood. Her extended "family" ran like a well-oiled machine, she noticed with satisfaction. For the first time in weeks, she was aware of the little things around her. The sounds. The smells. Sam Potter could not, would not, totally rob her of life's pleasures.

Silas came down the stairs holding a messy-haired child, his nose buried in her neck. She giggled and snuggled closer to him. Both tiny hands came up and framed his strong face. She planted a kiss on his cheek. The delight Maddy saw in his eyes almost made her cry. They had worked together to bring this about and they had succeeded. Silas winked at her as if he knew exactly what she was thinking.

Soon, everyone was seated and fragrant odors teased their taste buds. Silas asked the blessing and they passed food from left to right. Ollie was uncharacteristically quiet.

"What's on your mind, son?" Silas asked.

Ollie's eyebrows came together in a concerned scowl. "I was wonderin', Pa, why both you and Reverend Richards caught fish and I didn't."

Silas smiled. "Well, Ollie, maybe it was because we kept very still. Fishing requires patience, you know. Lots of it."

"I tried to be still." Ollie looked down.

Silas chuckled and ran his fingers through Ollie's hair. "It's hard when you're seven. You'll learn."

"Well I can't learn if you don't take me fishing, Pa. I want to go huntin', too. I heard you say once, Pa, that you shot your first deer when you was eight. I'm almost eight. I think it's time you took me deer huntin', Pa. Maybe even bear huntin'." His eyes gleamed with excitement.

Silas' eyebrows shot up. Maddy could tell he was stalling when he very thoroughly wiped his mouth with the back of his hand. "Uh...well. I'll give it some thought. We do need some venison for the winter, come to think of it."

Ollie sat up straight with anticipation. "I can hunt squirrels and rabbits. Killed hundreds. Ask Ma."

"Well…maybe dozens. He kept a pretty good supply of meat coming most of last winter. Between him and Matt Woodward, we had plenty of meat."

"Don't forget Boots, Ma. She brought more meat than Matt."

"Boots? Is she Matt Woodward's sister-in-law? The one that dresses like a man?" Luke asked.

"I forgot about her," Silas said. "Does she still live around here?"

"As far as I know, she does. No one ever sees her. Do you know that she came to my mother's funeral?"

Silas looked surprised. "I don't think I've ever laid eyes on her."

"Matt and Stella came, along with both of Stella's sisters, Rebecca and Naomi."

"Naomi?"

"Otherwise known as Boots." She looked at Luke and explained, "They call her Boots because of the big, man boots she always wears." Maddy smiled at the memory. "They were good neighbors after my parents died. They seemed to know when they were needed and they didn't fail to check in on me several times a week. As soon as you came back, Silas, they backed off." She stared out the window for a moment, remembering those days. "I really should drop in on them some day. Return the favor."

Silas captured her hand for a moment. "I'll join you. They helped you and my kids through a hard time. I'm afraid I haven't been very neighborly."

"They keep to themselves, that's for sure. That's their choice. I'm afraid a visit from us might scare them." She paused and smiled. "We should do it anyways. We can take one of my pies."

When everyone got up from the table and prepared to

leave for the day, Silas followed Maddy to the sink. "You seem like your old self today, Madeline." His voice was quiet, meant for her ears only.

She couldn't bring herself to look at him. He was standing too close. "I'm feeling much better." She poured hot water into the dry sink and added soap.

"I'm so happy to hear that." His kind, deep voice stirred something in her. Overly aware of the size and strength of the man next to her, she quickly moved away, back to the table to gather the coffee cups. Dunking them all in the hot water, she swallowed and started scrubbing.

"Anabel." Silas turned to his daughter. "Go upstairs and get dressed. Then come down and help your ma dry these dishes."

"Yes, Pa."

Maddy smiled with pleasure. Silas had referred to her as "your ma" and not corrected himself. This was a first. He left her to do his usual rounds of her barn and pens, checking animals and fences. Ollie's excited voice drifted briefly through the open door. Life was good, she realized. If only… She shook her head to rid it of negativity. *Trust God,* she told herself. *Trust God to do what He wants to do in His time.* She took a deep breath and bowed her head. *Oh, God! Help me, please. Help all of us.*

"Here's more corn." Silas dumped a bushel at Maddy's feet. "Let me know when it's too much."

"Keep it coming. Whatever we can't can, we'll eat or feed to the pigs." Anabel and Ollie tore the husks and silk off then washed them under the pump. Maddy finished picking the tiny silk hairs off then scraped the kernels into a big bowl. Sterilized jars lined the kitchen table and a giant pot of water was set to boil over the fire out back.

Maddy had always loved every aspect of harvest, especially harvesting the food they would eat that winter. Most of the corn would be left in the fields for the cows and pigs to forage on, filling their bellies with highly nutritious fare. The week before, she and the kids had canned and dried apples from the trees on both properties. She'd also made pies, apple sauce, and cider. The cider and canned sauce would keep through the winter.

She had given Ollie and Anabel the job of digging up the rest of the potatoes and storing them in the root cellars, along with the beets and turnips that she had already put there.

"Tomorrow, we need to can the rest of the green beans in my garden." Maddy reached out for the newly husked and washed ears of corn that Ollie handed her. "I think we already canned all of your pa's beans."

"How long until all of this is done?" Ollie complained. "We've been gathering, drying, and canning for months, Ma. I'm ready to hunt."

Maddy laughed. "You wouldn't complain if you'd just remember how little we had to eat last winter. We'll be feasting this year, children. But it doesn't come without work."

"I like working, Ma," little Anabel offered as she ran to the pump.

"Good. Because when we're done here, we'll be picking beans and squash at my place this afternoon."

And true to her word, after the noon meal, they set out for her place and immediately started work in the garden. That is, after she did the daily security check with Silas standing guard on the porch. When he was satisfied that all was well, he drove back to his place, leaving Luke to help the children in the garden.

Maddy had already sterilized her canning jars. She stoked the fire and filled two large kettles with water. Luke intercepted her when she tried to lug the heavy kettles back to the house. "Here, let me get those. You shouldn't try t' do so much by yerself, Maddy," he gently chided.

"Thank you, Luke." She gratefully handed the kettle over and directed him where to place it on the stove. "Would you and the kids pick the squash first? I need to start peeling them."

"Yes, ma'am." He turned to go out the back door.

Maddy set a chair up on the grass behind the house and started peeling as fast as they dumped squash at her feet. "Luke, grab a knife and help me. The three of you work too fast for me to keep up."

Ollie and Anabel laughed. They started working faster. Apparently, her words were a challenge to stay ahead of her. She and Luke joined in the race. "That's all, Ma. We got all the squash. We beat you!"

"I don't believe you!" Maddy winked at Luke. "You better check every corner of the garden. You know how far squash vines can travel. And while you're at it, check the field."

To her surprise, they found six more. "Well, aren't you glad I didn't let you stop?"

Ollie laughed. "Yeah. But we still beat you."

"Yes, you did. But now, I have a new job for you. And if I hear any complaining, I'll give you more work."

She and Luke cut each squash in half, and she instructed the children to scoop out all the seeds. "Save them in this bucket, along with the peelings. Food for the pigs. We've got to fatten ol' Porky up for butchering."

"So…" Luke winked at Ollie. "In a way, all those seeds and peelin's are gonna end up in our bellies. Well, some of it. Th' seeds might end up sproutin' in th' pig pen."

"I've seen that happen many times," Maddy chuckled. "After the pigs are gone of course. Nothing can survive while they're there." She picked up her knife and started cutting the seeded squash into one-inch chunks and tossing them into a bowl at her side.

The sun was peeking through the branches of a huge walnut tree whose leaves had all fallen. It helped warm her on this cool day, but still, she was grateful for her cozy wool jacket. Anabel wore an old wool dress that had been Maddy's many years before. Both children were growing and needed new clothes. Soon, when this harvesting was done, she could turn her attention to clothing them properly.

On the heels of that thought came the darkness again. What horrific events might unfold in the next few days and weeks? She shook her head and forced herself to focus on the task at hand.

Maddy cut the apple pie and served it to her happy crew. The squash had been successfully canned and was cooling in jars lined up on the floor.

Silas took one bite of pie and shut his eyes with apparent delight. He smiled and looked at her. "I'm amazed how much you can accomplish in one day."

"I had help. Lots of help. You'd be proud of your children if you could see how much they can do now."

"Yeah, Pa. But I'm ready to go huntin' now."

Silas laughed. "Soon, son, soon."

"Bear, too?" Ollie's eyes were eager.

"Well, if one happens to cross our path when we're out there, we'll be sure to shoot him."

"I saw one in our orchard last year so I know they're around," Ollie said.

Silas raised a questioning eyebrow at Maddy.

"He came running in with the news one evening so I don't doubt it." She started clearing dishes. "That's the only time recently though. We used to see them a lot when I was a girl. They got to be a nuisance, clearing out our apples and threatening the livestock." She poured hot water into the sink's basin. "Anabel, why don't you wash dishes and Ollie can dry."

Silas silenced Ollie with a look as soon as a complaint started. He rose and went outside with Luke to finish the chores for the day. Since that awful day Sam had threatened her in the barn, Maddy had reluctantly turned the job of milking over to the men. She went out to the back steps to retrieve the piles of green beans so she could snap and clean them. Tomorrow, she would can them.

After dishes and chores were done, Silas took both children back to his place. Luke bunked in her barn as usual. Maddy dared to linger for a while on her porch swing, looking at the stars in the clear sky and enjoying the night sounds. She could see a faint light coming from the barn loft. Luke was reading again. He had promised to clear a place for the lantern so there'd be no danger of fire from hay igniting. A twig snapped behind her. She got up and moved toward the door.

"Hold on there just a bit, missy." Sam's dreadful voice was unmistakable, but she couldn't quite discern the direction it was coming from. She opened her door and slipped through. Out of nowhere, a hand snaked out and held the door fast. She pulled with all of her strength to close it, but it wouldn't budge.

"I said, 'hold on.' I got something to say to you, Maddy Malone, and you better listen."

Her heart raced and breathing stopped.

"I was serious about what I said last month and I'm sick of waiting." He breathed deep and stared into her frightened eyes. "You haven't told anyone, have you? I'd hate fer a young'un to get hurt. But if that's what it takes...well it wouldn't be my fault. You were warned."

Maddy tried to think of a way she could get Luke's attention but just before she could muster up a scream, moonlight reflected off something at Sam's waist. *A revolver!* She swallowed and looked into Sam's face.

"I've found us a justice of the peace. He's happy to do the honors."

All Maddy could manage to do was shake her head no.

Sam reached into his pocket and pulled out a gold coin. Maddy gasped. "I have another reason to speed things up a little." He flipped the coin in the air twice then held it in his palm and moved it close to her face. "Did you ever see one of these out there on yer property?"

She swallowed and said nothing.

"Well, I found this in your creek and something tells me there's more. Are you hiding something from me?"

She shook her head no.

"You better not be lying. I have no patience with people that lie to me. Especially if she's my betrothed."

"I'm not your betrothed."

Sam ignored her. "Once we tie the knot, all of this property becomes mine. And all the gold hidden here becomes mine."

"Sam, I'm not marrying you."

His hand moved quickly up to squeeze her throat. "You have no say in the matter. Yer nothin' but a measly little female. Mighty purty, but still, nothin' but a female. You have no say. Yer mine, ya know. Get used to it, girl." His hand relaxed and he caressed her neck. "Everything's set in place for some time next month. Get yerself ready."

He fingered a strand of her hair. "It sure smells good in there." He raised his eyes to look longingly through the door. "Mmmm...smells like apple pie. I can't wait for you to start cookin' fer us. We need a woman's touch. I went ahead and put some curtains in fer ya, Maddy. In our bedroom. I thought ya might like that." He leaned in as if to kiss her but she jerked back. Anger flashed across his face. Then he turned and walked away.

CHAPTER TWENTY-ONE

Silas watched Maddy clear dishes from the table after breakfast. She moved methodically and seemed to avoid making eye contact with him. He couldn't figure her out. For about two weeks, she had almost seemed normal; like her old happy self. Then overnight, she seemed to have plummeted into a dark hole where no one could get through to her. Deeper than before. She still worked just as hard, but there was no happy small talk. No laughter. No spontaneous hugs for the children. She managed to get all the canning done, fix all their meals, do the laundry, and tend to Ollie's and Anabel's needs. But her sweet smile had vanished. Whenever he tried to talk to her about it, she would walk away.

So, he did what he always did when faced with a problem. He prayed. And then he invited the Richards over for a meal. Actually, he talked them into inviting themselves over for a meal on the pretext that they wanted to see all the improvements Silas had made on the farm. That way, they could bring the bulk of the food so Maddy wouldn't have a big meal to add to her already heavy load.

Both Frank and Martha had been told the real reason for the visit.

Maddy seemed to be both delighted and filled with dread at the news of their upcoming visit. Silas couldn't quite read her. On the day of their visit, halfway through the month of November, she brought cider and applesauce from her house. She then busied herself making an apple pie and a pumpkin pie. Whatever was bothering her seemed to drive her to work harder than normal. It almost broke his heart to watch her bustle around his kitchen. She was like a machine in her efficiency and in her silence.

The Richards arrived to the enthusiastic greeting of the kids and the loud barks of the two dogs. "Well hello there, children. It's good to see you again. I missed you at church last Sunday." Martha leaned down to hug Anabel and sent a scolding look Silas' direction.

He looked down quickly to hide his sheepish face. "Uh, sorry. A couple of us weren't feeling our best."

"Well I wasn't feeling my best, either, Silas, but I managed to show up."

"But you live there, Sister Martha," Ollie jumped in to defend his pa.

Martha set her basket of goodies down and gave Ollie a hug. "You're right, Oliver. Should I show a little more patience with your pa?"

"Yes, ma'am. If you could see how hard he works, you'd be kinder to him."

She hugged him even harder. "Oh, Ollie, sweet boy. I'm only funnin' with your pa! It's one of my favorite things to do."

Ollie gave his pa a quizzical look. "Is that true, Pa?"

Silas rubbed his head. "No, son. She's just mean."

Martha laughed and whacked Silas with the back of her hand. "You hush, boy."

When Silas hugged her and joined his laughter with hers, Ollie finally smiled.

"Let's quit gabbin' and haul this scrumptious feast into the house." Frank picked up the basket that Martha had set down. "After we eat, I want a tour of your farm, Silas. I can see from here that you've transformed this place."

The pleasure Silas felt at those words warmed him throughout. Approval from Frank was akin to approval from his father.

"I dropped by here a couple of times during the war. It didn't take long for the Missouri jungle to claim every square foot." Frank shook his head.

Silas reached into the wagon to grab another basket and followed Frank and Martha into the house. He saw Maddy turn from the stove to greet them with a tight smile. She received the food and set it on the table. "Thank you so much, Martha. This is kind of you. It lightens my load considerably today."

"From what I been hearin', you and these two young'uns have been workin' up a storm. Everyone needs a break now and then." She followed Maddy to the cupboard to get plates and intercepted her just before she reached up. Silas watched and was filled with gratitude when he heard words meant only for Maddy. "How are you holding up, dear?"

"I'm fine, Martha. Really I am." Maddy handed a stack of plates to Martha then turned to get the glasses. Together, they finished setting the table and sat down.

"Reverend Richards, would you please ask the blessing?" Silas nodded Frank's direction. Frank also held to the wonderful tradition of having everyone hold hands around the table. Anabel was to Silas' right and Luke to his left. The difference in the size of their hands was amazing to him. When Frank said "Amen," Silas lifted Anabel's delicate hand to his mouth for a kiss. A protective urge flooded over him as he smiled down into her happy blue eyes. Maddy sat just on the other side of Anabel and his eyes briefly met hers.

Who would take care of Maddy? Her family had either died or moved far away. He wondered if any of her brothers had any desire to come home and take over the old family farm. He doubted it because from what little he knew, they were successfully building lives of their own, one in Sedalia, one in Colorado, and one in Oregon. Between them, they had large cattle and horse ranches. Her three sisters were scattered as well, all three married and raising large families.

He was jolted out of his musings when Luke grabbed a bowl of steaming, buttery mashed potatoes and shoveled a heaping pile onto his plate. Next, Silas helped himself and then put a small plop on Anabel's plate. When he handed the bowl to Maddy, he was struck again by the deep sadness in her eyes. He looked pointedly at Martha who sat across from him. She, too, had noticed. She shook her head and pinched her lips together.

Maddy pulled her shawl tighter around her shoulders. She had invited Martha to sit with her on the porch while Silas took Frank on a tour of the farm, but as the evening wore on, the wind picked up. After forced small talk, Martha had asked her again how she was really doing. How could she answer a question like that except to lie? Again. She knew she wasn't fooling this wise woman who wouldn't stop studying her. Oh, why did Silas have to invite them?

"Madeline, dear. You know that sharing one's heart always makes the burden lighter."

Maddy stared at the boards in the porch floor and shook her head. "Not this time, Martha."

"Why?" Martha's voice was gentle yet coaxing.

"I really can't say." Maddy raised anguished eyes to the

older lady. "And if you keep prying, I'll be compelled to leave."

Martha sat back stunned. She rocked silently for several minutes. "Did you read the Book of Ruth?"

Maddy only nodded.

The wind blew dead leaves up onto the porch where they swirled for a moment before settling at Maddy's feet. She shivered. It was getting dark and she still had to tend to chores at her place. What was taking Silas so long? Maybe she should find Luke and leave.

"And?"

Maddy looked up to see Martha waiting for an answer. She couldn't think. "And? And what?"

"What did you think of Ruth?"

Hansel and Gretel both barked and bounded up onto the porch, wiggling their way against Maddy for attention. Behind them she saw Silas, Frank, and the children coming around the corner of the house. "Ruth was good," she said quickly before she stood and went to greet the touring party. "Silas. It's getting late. I need to get things done at home before I turn in for the night."

Frank answered instead, "I'm so sorry, Maddy. It's my fault. I wouldn't stop asking questions."

"Don't worry," Silas interjected. "I sent Luke on ahead to take care of all your chores. He knows what to do."

Maddy breathed a sigh of relief. But still, she'd have to go in her house when it was dark. Her unlocked house. She tried to remember if she'd loaded the shotgun yet or not.

"It is awful late." Frank took his wife's hand and helped her stand. "We should be getting home. Sorry we kept you so long."

Martha turned and captured both of Maddy's hands in hers. She whispered, "I'll be praying, dear. Remember, God knows everything and nothing is outside of His power." She pulled Maddy into a comforting hug and whispered in her ear, "I love you, Madeline. God is very present in the midst of your trials. I am going to pray for deliverance for you, my girl. Tonight! Yes, I will pray that deliverance will come tonight." She released her and turned to Silas, grabbing his shoulders. "God is good!" She released him and walked down the steps to their wagon.

Maddy, clad only in her nightgown, sat on the stairs with her loaded shotgun across her lap, staring at her front door. Surely, she was only hearing things. The wind was blowing harder than normal. Acorns were still falling and hitting the roof and the porch with sharp cracks. Dried leaves swirled around the house and against the windows. She was sure she heard Gretel whine. What good was Luke when he could sleep through anything?

There! She heard it again. Gretel's pitiful whine. Something was wrong. Shaking so hard she could barely stand, she inched her way to the dining room window and looked out. The moon peeked between clouds that moved fast across the sky. She held the gun to her shoulder and aimed at moving shadows. A floorboard creaked behind her. She turned, her heart pounding. It was too dark to see, but the faint light coming from the kitchen stove gave an outline to a few familiar objects. Nothing seemed out of place. Both doors were locked, and she and Silas had done a thorough search before he and the kids had left that evening.

Backing into the farthest corner of the dining room, she pulled a chair out from under the table and sat down, shotgun ready at her shoulder. From there, she had a good view of the kitchen door and to her left, she could see out the window onto the porch and yard. In spite of the cold, sweat beaded on her forehead and moistened her hands. She wiped each hand in turn on her nightgown and tightened her grip on the shotgun.

A noise on the porch grabbed her attention. It was Gretel! A low, mournful whine escaped from the poor dog as she limped to the door and scratched. Maddy quickly moved to the door and opened it. Crouching down to receive her wounded dog, she set the shotgun on the floor next to her. Before she could close the door, she felt a strong force slam it open, smashing it against the wall with a crash.

Maddy fell back in terror and reached for her gun. A heavy boot kicked it away.

"I can't believe you'd actually try to use that thing on your future brother-in-law." She heard Nate's whiney, sinister voice. Nate! He was worse than his brother. Maddy was paralyzed.

Nate reached down and jerked her to her feet. His breath reeked of alcohol. He pulled her close and nuzzled her neck. Maddy pushed hard against him to no avail. "I might as well get a little something for my trouble, don't ya think, darlin'? Before you and Sam get hitched, yer still fair game, right?"

She managed to spit in his face. He shoved her back and in the faint light, she saw him wipe his hand across his chin. "Oh, you're a fighter. This is gonna be fun." He reached out and grabbed her arm, tearing her nightgown at the shoulder. "Come on. Sam's waiting. Lucky guy. Man, I wish I'd claimed you first." He yanked her down the porch steps and shoved her into Sam's arms. "Here she is. She even dressed in her weddin' night clothes. Must have known you were comin' for her."

Sam held her at arm's length and gaped at her from head to toe. "What a right purty sight, you are, Miss Malone."

The stench of his body and the lust in his eyes made her want to gag. *Oh, God! Please let me die right here!* Paralyzing terror coursed through her. She looked to heaven and pleaded.

Sam pulled her close and kissed her on the forehead. "Tonight's the night, Maddy, girl. The justice of the peace will be at the house when we get there. I've got our room all set up and I'm more than ready. Do you know I've been plannin' this night for years? And it's finally here. You, the gold, this farm." He chuckled. "Well, the gold is an extra bonus. It's better than Christmas!" He picked her stiff body up in his beefy arms, twirled around with her, and whooped. "Let's go!" He grabbed her hand and started down the path.

CHAPTER TWENTY-TWO

Maddy stumbled behind Sam, weeds tearing at the thin material of her nightgown. She wanted to scream for Luke, but nothing but a squeak came from her throat. Sharp rocks cut through her thin slippers. Several times she stumbled, but Sam roughly pulled her upright. A horror, thick and black, filled her entire being. She couldn't think. Surely it was all a dream, a nightmare of the darkest sort. The blackness closed in and all of her senses dulled. She went limp. Sam tried to yank her to her feet.

"What's wrong?" An impatient snarl escaped him. "Am I gonna have to carry you?"

Maddy heard his voice as if it were coming from far away. She dropped further from reality and from his grasp, feeling her face hit the ground then press into the hard-packed soil.

"Get up!" Sam hollered. He kicked her. Then he turned her over, grabbed her arms, and pulled her up enough that he could throw her over his shoulder. He continued down the path getting closer to his destination with every labored step.

As her head bobbed back and forth against his back, unexpectedly her mind cleared and a new and fierce determination came over her. *I can't let this happen.* The thought screamed through her very soul. Whatever the price, they couldn't win. She could barely make out her immediate surroundings and saw that the path had just entered the woods at the base of the bluffs. She struggled to get down. "I...I think I can walk now, Sam."

Breathing heavy, he lowered her to the ground but held her shoulders in a vise-like grip. "Yer not gonna faint on me again, are ya? The roughest part of the path is coming up."

She nodded. "I can do it. J...just don't walk so fast. I can't keep up."

Sam rubbed his hands up and down her arms. "Alright, darlin'. I guess it's gonna take some getting' used to, me havin' a woman and all. It's easy to forget how little you are." His chuckle sent cold fear through her.

"A...and, could you please let me get a drink from the creek? And sit down just a spell? My feet are hurting bad."

"Why, sure. Just fer a minute though. We got that justice of the peace waitin."

Too quickly, he swayed from a monster to a concerned bridegroom. She shivered so violently it was difficult to take a step. Maddy looked across the creek. She could see the black mass of a thick grove of cedars at the base of the bluff, only about ten feet from where they were standing. She knew this section of her property well. Those cedar branches were thick and close to the ground. If she could somehow make a mad dash for those trees, maybe, just maybe she could get away.

She bent to the creek and dipped her cupped hand into a pool. "It's a little deeper over there." She got up and walked closer to the cedars. "It's easier to get enough water to drink." Glancing toward Sam, she saw with great relief that he hadn't followed her. He wasn't even watching her.

He seemed to be looking up at something. She took that second to lunge quietly across the creek and into the heavy, thick branches of the cedars. They seemed to welcome her into their darkness.

"Woman!" Sam bellowed. "Where are you?"

Dared she believe he hadn't seen her? She scrambled as fast as she possibly could into the heart of the deep grove, moving like a scared rabbit up the side of the steep bank. She could hear him crashing across the pebbles of the creek, screaming in rage. "You come back here! Do you hear me, girl?"

Clouds moved across the moon again, making it impossible for her to see ahead. She scrambled as fast as she was able under the low-hanging branches, moving away from Sam's curses. A dip in the rough terrain caught her by surprise and she rolled forward into a small, rocky bowl not much bigger than her body. She felt around to discover she was still completely surrounded by low-hanging cedar boughs. She could feel them pressing in on all sides. Trying to quiet her loud breathing, she grabbed handfuls of branches, twigs, dirt, anything to cover her cream-colored nightgown. Anything to camouflage herself from Sam's searching eyes. *Oh, God, keep the moon hidden.*

Several minutes of nerve-wracking quiet passed, punctuated only by the wind dancing through the trees, knocking bare branches against each other. Then she heard Sam's voice drifting away. Should she move again? Silence filled the night and with it, her fear increased, gripping her heart. Where was he? She didn't dare move. When would she again find a hiding place so perfect?

"I can see you, you know, Maddy." A jolt of terror shot through her entire body. Sam's voice was close. She tried to bury herself even deeper without making a sound. Surely it was a bluff. She couldn't see even a few inches in front of her face.

"You're a fool. I'll find you. You can't hide forever." The fury in his voice was growing. She shook uncontrollably. He was right. She couldn't hide forever. Despair again threatened to cast her into numb blackness. She pressed her fist against her mouth. Hot tears trickled down her face.

"Nate!" Sam bellowed. "Nate!" Each time he hollered he sounded farther away. "Damn it, Nate! Where are you? We got us some huntin' to do!" Much farther that time. He was going fast up the path toward his place. She forced her stiff body to wiggle out of her hiding place and move as quickly away from his voice as she could possibly go.

Far in the distance, she could hear Nate answer. Soon, they'd both be looking for her. She couldn't go home. It was no longer a safe place for her. Instinctively she moved toward Silas' place. Tearing through the rough terrain along the bluff, she felt her way, holding her hand in front, to protect her face from branches. If she kept the bluff to her left and the creek to her right, she knew she'd end up on Silas' land. The creek cut through his southeast corner.

Branches cut across her face. Blood trickled into her mouth. She held her hands up and relentlessly stumbled on. Suddenly the branches opened up and her feet stepped into cold, sticky mud. Her momentum propelled her forward before she could stop. Both slippers had been sucked from her feet. She turned and tried to dig them out but could only find one. In the distance, she heard Sam's fury. She pulled the slipper from the ooze and turned toward Silas' house. She knew she was in the swamp at the edge of his cornfield. If she could find the split-rail fence that Luke had built, she could follow it to the driveway and then from there easily find the house. Exactly what she planned to do once she got there was unclear to her terrified mind.

Certain that Sam and Nate's voices were getting closer, Maddy stumbled down the drive to the house. She snuck around to the back and slowly, quietly approached the back door. She was shocked that she hadn't wakened the dog. With dismay, she saw that the sky to the east was beginning to lighten. Silas would be waking soon. She pressed down gently on the door latch. The click it made was much too loud. She waited, breath coming in great heaves.

Finally, she dared to ease the door open. She forced her breathing to calm as she slowly shut the door behind her. Tiny, quiet footsteps took her through the kitchen to the door of Silas' bedroom. His door was slightly ajar. She moved it a fraction of an inch. Then an inch. She could see Silas' large frame under a pile of blankets. He snored a consistent snuffley sound indicating, she hoped, that he was in a deep sleep.

She slowly pushed the door all the way open then carefully shut it behind her. Silas didn't move. The soft snoring continued. With one part of her brain screaming, "No!" and the other part screaming, "Yes!" she very slowly, very carefully picked up the corner of the blankets furthest from Silas and slipped her body beneath them.

The rooster crowed. Silas rolled onto his back and stretched. He yawned and rubbed his eyes. His foot bumped something at the foot of the bed. He sat up and saw a lump. Was it Anabel again? He smiled and gently uncovered her. But what he saw certainly wasn't Anabel.

He jumped from his bed and yanked the blankets off. Curled in a pitiful, filthy ball was a tiny woman whose face was buried in mud-encrusted hands. She was covered with leaves, twigs, and bloody scratches. And dressed in a torn, flimsy nightgown.

As he stared, he was filled with confusion and an awful dread. He would know that frame and that hair anywhere. Could it truly be his Maddy? He reached down and pulled her hands away to reveal the eyes of a woman filled with fear and with shame. Pulling her to her feet, he fought a battle between anger and compassion. The anger seemed to win as he demanded of her, the only thing he could manage to say, "What in tarnation are you doing here?"

The thought that she would be seen in his bedroom wearing only a nightgown propelled him to yank her roughly to the kitchen. As an afterthought, he ran back to his room to get a blanket to cover her. Just as he threw the blanket around her shoulders, an unwelcome greeting floated in from the dining room.

"Good morning, Silas. There you are. I knew you'd be awake." Bonnie Adams walked through the kitchen door holding a basket of food. She stopped abruptly and stared. Silas and Maddy stared back. Silas still had his arms around Maddy and had only partially covered her. And to make matters worse, he stood there in his long johns.

Bonnie's mouth opened and shut several times. Neither Maddy nor Silas said a word.

The stopped-up dam finally burst. "Well!" Bonnie screeched.

"Please don't wake the children," Silas feebly muttered.

"Wake the children? Wake the children! And why not? Because they might see this...this unforgivable, immoral act of their father? With the harlot he's been keeping a secret? A secret from the entire community? I knew something like this was going on, Silas. And you!" She leveled hate-filled eyes at Maddy. "You...you shameful hussy! How many other customers do you have?"

"Enough!" Silas roared. He pulled Maddy into an embrace. "How dare you say such things to...to my wife?" He felt Maddy's head turn to look up at him.

"Your wife? Ha! Since when?"

"Since last night," he lied.

"I don't believe you! She's but a child!"

Silas released his grip on Maddy and stormed toward

Bonnie. "You better believe it. And don't you ever darken the doors of my...our house again."

Bonnie dropped her basket and backed through the dining room to the front door, sputtering all the way. "You wait until Reverend Richards hears about this."

"He already knows," he hollered as he slammed the door. Then he ran to Maddy, still standing in the middle of the kitchen.

"I'm so sorry," she stammered.

"It's too late for that." He roughly steered her back to his room. "We don't have much time. Just do as I say." He yanked clothes from a trunk on the floor. "These are Mary's old clothes. Put them on. Quick! Then go out to the pump and clean off as best as you can." He quickly yanked his pants on then grabbed a shirt on his way to the door. Looking back, he added, "There's shoes in there, too. They'll fit good enough for now. I'll be back soon. Don't go anywhere. Wait for me. Wake the children and tell them to get dressed."

Silas ran for the barn, threw a saddle on Clara, his fastest horse, then rode like the dickens down the road for the Richards'. When he saw Bonnie's buggy up ahead, he rode at an angle into the woods to an old road that paralleled the main road. His poor horse hadn't been worked that hard in weeks. He whipped his reins back and forth on her lathered neck and coaxed her into a fast gallop.

When he pulled into the churchyard, he rode to Richards' back door and tied Clara to a bush. He pounded on the door with his fist then barged in. He had no time. "Reverend! Sister Martha!"

Frank came out of the bedroom in his bedclothes holding a shotgun aimed at Silas' head. Martha was behind him, clinging to his arm.

"Goodness, Frank! It's Silas. Put your gun down."

"What in God's green earth are you doing here this early in the morning, Silas? I almost shot your head off. It's so dark, I can barely see."

"Please, Frank, Martha. There's not much time. I need you to lie for me!"

In his desperation, he crossed the room and took their hands. "It's Maddy. Her reputation is about to be ruined if you don't do what I'm asking…no…begging of you."

"I'm sorry, Silas. I make it a practice to not lie."

Martha smacked him on the shoulder. "Frank! This is Silas you're talking to. If Silas thinks Maddy's reputation hangs on this, you better sit down and listen."

Frank sat.

"Bonnie Adams will get here any minute with awful things to say about me and Maddy. Please tell her that we're married."

"Married? But you're not."

Martha stepped around him. "We'll do it!"

"No, we won't!" Frank stood.

"Pl…please. I…I'll bring Maddy by this morning. As early as possible so you can marry us. Truly marry us. So, it'll only be a lie by a few hours."

"Wonderful!" Martha clapped her hands in delight. Both men turned shocked faces toward her.

Silas gripped Frank's shoulders. "I can explain it all later. Just trust me." He heard the Richard's dog bark in the front yard signaling the arrival of a visitor. "That's Bonnie. If she has her way with you, Maddy's reputation will be ruined. And all because of a misunderstanding. Neither Maddy nor I have done anything immoral. Please believe me."

"We believe you. Don't we, Frank?" She nudged him, but he only stared after Silas as he opened the back door to leave.

CHAPTER TWENTY-THREE

When Silas walked back into his house, he found Maddy sitting in the kitchen with an arm around each of his children. All three of them looked perplexed. Without a doubt, Ollie and Anabel knew something very serious was afoot. Maddy raised her eyes to meet his for only a second before she lowered them in shame.

Silas cleared his throat. "Ah...we need to get in the wagon right away. We don't have much time."

"Where are we goin', Pa?" Ollie turned big eyes up at his father as Silas ushered them impatiently out the door.

"The church," came his quick answer.

Anabel and Maddy followed silently.

"Why? It's not Sunday."

After all four got seated and Silas guided the wagon to head down the drive, he turned to look at each of his children in turn. "Maddy and I got married last night."

Maddy yanked her head around to stare at him, but he silenced her with a stern look and a slight shake of his head.

"You got married!" Ollie's voice was full of wonder and delight. "Does that mean she'll really be our ma? Forever and ever?"

"Yes, it does, son." At least he was doing one thing right. If for no other reason than providing this kind of security to his babes. "We're going to the church to have a real wedding. To…to make it more official."

"Hooray!" Silas could feel the wagon shake as Ollie jumped up and down in the back.

Silas turned to gauge Maddy's mood. Her eyes were downcast. And for good reason. What she had done was wrong. She had thrown all of them into living a lie. A temporary one albeit, but still a lie. Something he felt forced into. But the alternative to his lie was unthinkable. She looked so tiny and vulnerable in his Mary's clothes. His desire to protect her was almost as fierce as his desire to protect his children.

He impatiently flicked the reins over Maud's back. What had possessed her to do what she'd done? He looked at her again. He'd find out soon enough.

Up ahead, he saw Luke riding their direction. Luke! He'd forgotten about Luke. He had to lie again and this time, he'd have to work harder at making it believable. He'd need Maddy's help. "Maddy," he whispered. "Luke's coming."

Maddy raised her head then turned to Silas with frightened eyes.

"Just go along with me. We have to make him believe us."

She nodded and looked down again.

"Try to look happy about it," Silas growled. "Otherwise, he'll be suspicious."

She raised her head and smiled just in time. Silas stopped the wagon.

"I was startin' to wonder where everyone was," Luke said as he pulled up next to the wagon.

"Pa and Ma got married last night, Luke!" Ollie hollered, jumping up and down.

Luke's head jerked back and his eyes got big. He stared at Silas in disbelief.

"Hi, Luke. Sorry we left you in the dark." Silas was ashamed at how easily lies slipped off his tongue. "We've been planning this for a while and decided last night was as good a time as any. Reverend Richards did the honors, of course. We're heading in now to see him again."

"We're going to the church to have a real wedding," Ollie added with a loud voice. "Why don't you come with us, Luke?"

Silas forced a laugh. "No, son. This will just be family. Besides that, I need for Luke to stay here and get all the chores done." He tipped his hat at Luke and motioned for Maud to get going. Luke only stared after them. Maddy turned to wave a good-bye.

The wagon wheels crunched on the dirt road as they continued on their way, not saying another word. Silas let the guilt and frustration wash over him. He honestly didn't know what else to do other than let this play out. The lies would settle over time and no one would remember how this day started. Except him. He would never forget.

Maddy walked woodenly up the steps into the church. She was vaguely aware that sweet little Anabel's warm hand clung to her own. She hated what she was putting Silas through yet felt compelled to move forward. It was what was best for everyone, she kept repeating to herself. When she raised her eyes to meet the stern, questioning gaze of Reverend Richards, she almost changed her mind.

She paused and looked up at Silas' scowling face. Her feet stopped moving. "Silas, no."

"What do you mean, 'no'?" He had a slight panicky look in his eyes. "There's no other option."

Just at that moment, she felt a plump arm encircle her waist from behind. "Maddy, this is a good thing. A very good thing," came Martha's quiet, soothing voice. "Don't be afraid. God will work all of this out." She squeezed her and whispered, "You're getting a good man. And," her voice lowered, "he loves you, Maddy. Oh, so much."

Maddy looked at Silas again and saw an encouraging smile. He gestured with his head to move forward. So, she did.

They stopped in front of Reverend Richards. He quietly asked them a few questions. "Are you both aware of how solemn this occasion is?"

They nodded.

"Are you both entering into this state of matrimony willingly?"

They nodded.

"Maddy, look at me."

Her eyes lifted from staring at the floor to meet the reverend's. She saw only kindness there.

"Are you being forced in some way to enter into marriage with Silas?"

She swallowed and thought for a moment. A long moment. She felt Silas turn toward her.

"Maddy?" came Reverend Richards' worried voice.

"No," came her soft answer. She heard a relieved sigh escape from Silas.

Frank paused then cleared his voice. "Under the circumstances, we will proceed as quickly as possible with your wedding vows. I hope you both know; I wouldn't do this for anyone else."

Maddy couldn't focus as he opened his Bible and walked them through their vows, ending with, "I now pronounce you man and wife."

Silas pulled her into a quick embrace and kissed the top of her head. Ollie and Martha cheered, with Anabel soon joining in. Maddy smiled in spite of her rage of mixed-up emotions. She quickly wiped away unwanted tears.

"Come on over to the house for refreshments," Martha said. "Then I'll watch the children while Frank has a little talk with you two."

Maddy let Silas take her arm and guide her down the steps and across the yard. In spite of everything, it felt good. His hand was large and strong. And…and she was his *wife*. A thrill shot through her.

Ollie and Anabel ran ahead giggling and chasing each other. Maddy could hear Frank walking slowly behind them. Although she trusted him implicitly, she still dreaded the conversation they were about to have. She had a lot of explaining to do, yet she still didn't feel safe sharing everything. After all, the Potters were still out there. And one never knew what they might do.

But…a new reality was now in place. Sam could no longer force her to marry him. Her relief was huge. She smiled as she stepped up onto the Richards' porch and into their kitchen. Martha's twinkling eyes met hers. They nodded at each other with a secret understanding. Silas guided Maddy to a chair which he quickly pulled out for her. He sat next to her. Martha served pumpkin pie and hot steaming coffee. Frank sat opposite them. His expression was inscrutable. He cut into his pie, put it in his mouth, and shut his eyes.

"As always, Martha, dear, yours is the best pie in the land."

She bent down and gave him a quick kiss on his cheek. "I'm going to take the little ones for a walk now. I'll see you all later."

Silence reigned while the three of them ate and sipped their coffee. As more time passed, Maddy's hand clenched tighter and tighter in her lap. She couldn't look at anything other than her plate. No longer able to swallow, she just studied pieces of the pie as she pushed it around with her fork.

Silas cleared his throat and shuffled his feet. "So…did Miss Adams have anything to say about us?"

As embarrassing as the question was, Maddy was relieved to have it be asked. Silence between them was so uncharacteristic. But this was a strange day and Reverend Richards deserved to have some answers.

"Yes…yes she did. I'm glad you warned me."

"And did you believe her accusations?"

"Should I have?"

Maddy saw Silas narrow his eyes. "It depends on what she said. What she saw was one thing. How she interpreted it was another."

Frank leaned back in his chair. "Why don't you tell me what she saw."

Silas looked at Maddy and struggled for words. She turned to Frank and spouted, "It was all my fault, Reverend Richards. Silas had no part at all in…in the situation I put him in this morning."

"And what was this situation, Maddy?" Frank's tone was gentle.

She looked from him to Silas then dropped her head in her hands. "I'm so sorry." She tried to compose herself and look Frank in the eye. "I don't know how I can possibly explain this to you. Either of you."

Sitting back, she took a deep breath. "I know this won't make sense but I walked to Silas' house early this morning and entered his room and…and crawled under his blankets." She quickly added, "Just at the foot of his bed. I never touched him. He slept through the whole thing."

"Why?" they both asked at once.

She looked down and answered quietly, "I was terrified and desperate for protection."

The men were silent. Finally, Silas spoke to Frank, "When I saw her, she was bloody and covered with mud. She had twigs all through her hair and stuck to her nightgown."

Maddy looked up to see a stricken look on Frank's face. "Go on," he said.

"So, I took her to the kitchen, ran back to get a blanket to throw around her. Right then, Bonnie walked in and saw me with my arms around her. She wasn't quite covered, so Bonnie saw us just outside my bedroom with both of us still in our nightclothes."

"She immediately thought the worst," Maddy added. "And made horrible, horrible accusations. Nothing we said made any difference. She refused to listen."

"So, to shut her up, I told her we were married. Of course, she didn't believe me. She seemed intent on spreading the bad news as fast as possible."

"So, you hopped on a horse and beat her here?"

"Yes. And asked you to lie. Marriage seemed the only option."

Guilt overwhelmed Maddy. He really didn't want this marriage. But it was too late.

"Well, I did lie for you, as you asked. Bonnie had a really hard time believing it, but she will adjust." Frank leaned across the table. "And now you two are truly married. You'd better make the best of it. We'll talk more about that later. What I really want to know, Maddy, is what had you so terrified that you had to resort to such extreme measures to get protection?"

Silas shifted his chair so he, too, could look at her while he waited for an answer. Maddy felt like a trapped animal. "I can't really answer that," she mumbled.

"You were being chased, weren't you?" Silas spoke slowly, as if a horrible truth was just then dawning on him. He grabbed her shoulders and turned her to him. "Maddy, it was the Potters, wasn't it?"

Maddy shook him off and stood. "No!"

Silas stood just as quickly and followed her as she paced. "Why can't you tell me, Madeline?"

Maddy turned and faced him. "I will tell you. Just not

yet. Please, please trust me to keep this quiet for now."

Silas' voice was laced with anger. "Whoever, whatever has been threatening you, are they still a threat?"

She turned to see his fists clenched. "No. At least they're less of a threat."

"One of those Potters was pressuring you into marrying him. Am I right?"

Maddy knew her face betrayed her. "I…I can't answer you. Please!" She moved to hold his arms. "Please, Silas. Don't keep asking."

"Then let me ask you this; whose house should we live in? Yours or mine?"

"Yours," came her quick answer.

He turned from her. "That says a lot." He headed for the door without her.

Maddy sent a pleading look toward Frank who was already on his feet. Maddy watched from the door as Frank approached Silas just as he was about to jump in the wagon. He laid a hand on Silas' arm. Silas yanked away and paced back and forth several times before he stopped in front of Frank, head down in defeat. Frank talked for quite a while, while Silas listened and nodded. She saw Martha and the children approach from the barn. Frank motioned for Maddy to join them.

The ride home was filled with excited chatter from two happy kids. Maddy dared to look at Silas only once. His face was etched in stone, eyes narrow, jaw clenched. He never uttered a word.

CHAPTER TWENTY-FOUR

Silas stormed into his barn to find Luke milking. He turned away and raked his hand through his hair.

"Morning, boss. Or should I say congratulations?" Luke didn't sound particularly happy for him.

"Thanks," Silas mumbled while pretending to look for something in the corner. It dawned on him all of a sudden that Luke might have heard some of the gossip from Bonnie's busy tongue. And not just Luke. Many people in the area might have heard by now. He growled under his breath. No matter. They were married. Tongue wagging would fade.

"Aren't you two gonna take some time to get away for a little wedding trip or something?" Luke carried the bucket of warm, steaming milk to the door.

Silas forced a chuckle. "Farmers and fathers rarely get to take a break, son." He continued to rummage around, keeping his head down.

"Sister Martha could watch the kids and I can keep up with most of the chores."

"We might take you up on that. Later though."

"By the way, have you seen Gretel? I thought maybe she was here, but I haven't seen her all morning. Hansel keeps running circles around the barn looking for her."

"No. I'll ask Maddy. In fact, I think I'll head over to her place and look around. We've decided we'll be living here."

Luke nodded and turned to leave.

Silas followed him. He kept his voice lowered. "Luke."

Luke stopped and turned; his eyebrows raised.

Silas caught up to him. "Did you hear or see anything strange at Maddy's last night?"

Luke slowly shook his head. "I just remember the wind being extra loud. Why?"

"Nothing…" Silas rubbed his jaw and decided to change the subject. "Did you manage to find something to eat for breakfast?"

"Actually, yeah. I found a basket on the floor of the kitchen filled with biscuits, jam, and a couple pieces of apple pie. I thought maybe Maddy left it for me." He snorted and walked away. "Don't know why she'd leave it on the floor though."

Silas stared after him then turned to the barn again. He climbed up the stout ladder that led to the loft. Alone at last, he walked over the piles of loose hay and dropped to his knees when he reached the far wall. Taking his hat off, he crushed it in his hands. He wanted to smash something. He pictured Sam Potter's face and ground his teeth. A shudder went through him. What had happened last night? Who or what had gone after an innocent girl? The thought of what could have happened filled him with such anguish he could barely breathe.

God, help us! I don't know what to do. Whatever evil led to this is still out there and I don't know how to stop it. You know, God. Please end this, whatever and whoever it is, before Maddy or…or my babies are hurt. Protect them. Show me what to do. Calm my spirit. Give me wisdom.

When he finished his prayer, he was bent with his face almost to the floor. He stood, wiped the tears from his eyes, and straightened his hat. One thing at a time. For now, he'd go with Maddy to pack her clothes and find the dog. He thought about it for a moment and realized he didn't dare leave the children, even with Luke close by.

As he walked across the yard, he was beginning to realize what a fool he'd been. All those days and weeks of Maddy closing down must be connected to what had happened last night. Her refusal to talk then and her refusal to talk now. She was under the control of something that terrified her. If it was Sam or Nate, why couldn't she simply tell him? Was she trying to protect them? Surely not.

Or was it someone else? Someone he didn't know? What was she hiding?

He stepped into the house to see her mixing something in a big bowl. Ollie was reading to Anabel in the sitting room. Maddy's tired eyes glanced his direction without a greeting or a smile. Silas was again struck by how small she looked in Mary's old dress.

He cleared his throat. "Uh, do you know where Gretel is?"

Maddy set the bowl down and whirled around. Fear filled her eyes. "I forgot about her. I think she might be in my house. Oh, Silas. We have to get her. I think she's hurt."

Silas reached out to stop her as she rushed by him. For the first time, he noticed that she was limping. His hand at her waist, he looked down into her frantic eyes. "Why do you think Gretel was hurt?"

"She whined and…and limped up to my door. I let her in." Maddy pulled her apron up to cover her mouth. "Please, we need to hurry." Silas released her and went to get the children.

Unsettling thoughts swirled around in his head as he

harnessed Maud to the wagon for the second time that morning. "I want to keep Ollie and Anabel close to my side while we're at your place," he said in a voice that could barely be heard above the clip-clop of Maud's trot. Maddy nodded. "And while we're there, you should pack up all your clothes and anything else you need."

Maddy again nodded. But this time, she touched his arm and mouthed, "thank you," when he turned to look at her. He forced a quick smile. He still fumed inside. Mostly at whatever nameless evil they were dealing with, but he was also angry at Maddy. She should have come to him openly and honestly. Her sneaking around had led to a pack of lies. And no marriage should have to start the way theirs did. He had always trusted her and now he didn't know what to think.

A dog's pitiful whine greeted them as they approached Maddy's front door. Frantic, Maddy scrambled up the steps, the children beside her, all of them calling for poor Gretel. Thankfully Gretel was able to jump into their arms as soon as she was released. Silas bent down and ran his hands over her body.

"There's quite a bit of dried blood on her back leg and she's still limping. What do you think happened?"

Maddy averted her eyes. "I'm not sure. She seems ok, though, thank God."

Silas told the kids to stop when they ran into the house. "You know the routine. Let me check first." He stepped into the house ahead of her and stopped abruptly. Bending down, he reached for her shotgun which was partially under a chair. "What's this, Maddy?"

"Uh…that's mine." Her eyes darted around the room as she tried to come up with a good answer. "I must have dropped it...or something."

Silas turned and looked down at her. She couldn't bring herself to meet his questioning gaze.

"Or something?" His eyes followed his children as they played with Gretel on the porch. Maddy swallowed. Silas checked the gun for ammunition. He sighed. "When will you tell me the truth?"

It pained her to hear those words. She longed for him to trust her, but she was still so frightened for the children. And for Silas. Who knew what Silas might do when he found out the truth?

Silas turned from her and did his search from room to room as usual, this time taking more time. Ollie followed him. Maddy stood at the door with Anabel and studied the yard. In spite of the close proximity of Silas, she caught herself trembling with fear. It had been mere hours since Sam had dragged her through that field. She jumped when Silas stepped up behind her.

He still wore his scowl. His eyes narrowed at her. "Go get your things. I'll wait here with the kids."

She couldn't remember a time before when he'd looked at her that way. They might be married, but something undefinable had changed. She swallowed and turned to the stairs. Anabel clung to her skirt. The poor child always knew when things weren't right.

Maddy grabbed an old satchel from the spare bedroom at the top of the stairs and went to her room to gather up her belongings. Not taking great care, she merely pulled dresses off hooks, wadded them up, and stuffed them in. She emptied her drawer of underclothes and barely managed to close the bag. In spite of her meager stash of clothing, the bag was full. When she handed it to Silas, he asked, "Is that all?"

Maddy looked at the bag and back at Silas. "This is a lot. It's all I need for now." Staring at the floor, she added, "I...I'd just like to leave. Now, please."

She felt his hand gently clasp her upper arm to guide her out the door. No matter how awkward things were at the moment, she felt safe with Silas. And for that reason, she had very little regret for what she'd done.

In spite of her fear, a sense of freedom began to tickle the depths of Maddy's being as she sat in the wagon next to Silas and rode away from her childhood home. To leave behind the place that would always remind her of the terror brought on by Sam and Nate Potter's presence. She knew the danger probably wasn't entirely over, but for the first time in months, she dared to believe that maybe, just maybe, she and the children were in a safe fortress where the enemy no longer had free access. Not just the fortress of Silas' home but the fortress of marriage. The horrors of being forced into a marriage to Sam were gone. The relief from that one fact overshadowed all the doubts about what she had decided to do.

She glanced at Silas. Was she being entirely selfish? Had Ruth been selfish when she tucked herself under the blanket of Boaz' bed? Had Boaz reacted in anger? She'd have to read the story again.

The wagon creaked and swayed as they made their way the short distance. Silas was silent. At some point, she hoped he'd open up. Although she knew he hoped the same of her and she wasn't ready.

When Silas stopped in front of his porch, he got down, grabbed her bag, and led the way up the steps. At the door, he paused and studied her. "You're limping, Maddy. Are you alright?"

Maddy nodded as she went through the door he held for her. "I was wearing nothing but slippers last night. I think my feet might have gotten a few cuts and bruises. But I'll be fine."

Ollie ran for the barn with Gretel right behind him, but Anabel stayed glued to Maddy's side until she got inside, then she went into the sitting room and started playing with

Tommy, her rag doll. Silas stepped in behind Maddy. She turned to him when he cleared his throat. He raised his eyes from the floor and looked at her.

"This home is now yours as well as mine, Maddy. I want you to know that. But…" His eyes dropped to the floor again. Then, with an expression she couldn't quite read, he looked into her eyes again. "For now, I think it's best that you share the upstairs room with the children."

The hurt cut like a knife but she merely nodded and reached for her bag. Silas held on for a moment then surrendered it to her.

Silas was undone. Since the day he had dropped his wee little ones off at the Malone farm so he could go to war, he had not felt such a tearing of his soul. He had deeply hurt his Maddy. But it had to be this way. The beginning of their marriage was a sham, but the consummation of their marriage didn't have to be. The time would come. But it wasn't now. Why couldn't he simply tell her that, he wondered as he made his way back to the barn.

He stopped at the doorway when he heard Luke and Ollie talking. He wasn't ready to face either of them, so he turned to his fields and continued to walk so he could sort through his conflicting thoughts.

He couldn't tell her because he couldn't trust her. As long as she continued to keep hidden the reasons why she did what she did, he wouldn't allow the intimacy that a man and woman should have. And besides that, he raked his hand through his hair in frustration at the next thought. She was still a child in his mind. Hadn't Bonnie said as much? *She's a mere child!* Bonnie was right. How old was she? He figured she was probably only twelve or thirteen at the beginning of the war, which would put her at sixteen or seventeen. That was downright shameful. The Richards had tried to tell him she was old enough, but their opinion about marriage was a little old-fashioned to his mind.

He wandered aimlessly at first. As he walked south through his wheat field, he approached the area where the spring trickled down the hillside then spread out, forming a swamp just before it joined the creek. He stopped abruptly. Maddy had been covered with mud when she came to him this morning. She must have walked through the swamp. It was the only place she could have picked up that much mud. He walked along the edge, looking for the tracks she would have made as she walked out of the muck.

He finally had something he could do. If she wouldn't tell him what happened, maybe he could figure it out on his own. Her tracks were easier to find than he'd hoped. Mud, still wet in places, clung to the weeds where she had stepped. As he followed the trail to his back door, he couldn't help but imagine what she had been thinking and feeling as she groped through the darkness, running from something. And again, his anger and frustration rose.

He opened the door to find Maddy on her hands and knees scrubbing the floor where she had walked. She turned teary eyes to him then got up and limped to the sink. He wanted to gather her in his arms and soothe away the fear and the hurt. But instead, he gruffly asked her to show him her feet.

Maddy looked thoroughly embarrassed at that request. Silas ignored her discomfort and filled a pan with water, warming it up with hot water from the kettle. He grabbed a couple of clean rags from a pile under the sink and pulled up two chairs, facing each other. Sitting in one, he motioned for her to sit in the other.

The stubborn woman only stared at him. "Maddy, come over here and let me see your feet. You're obviously injured."

"No," was all she said.

"No?" He was surprised at her refusal. He gentled his voice. "I just want to help you, Maddy." Again, he gestured for her to sit.

At this, she put her hands on her hips and stared at him. Then, "I'm not going to have Luke or the children walk in here to find me with my bare feet in your lap."

Silas considered her words and chuckled. "I'm sorry. I guess that might be awkward. How about we move into my room?"

Maddy looked at him for a moment with the saddest eyes. Then she nodded and grabbed one of the chairs.

When they got situated, she carefully removed her boots and bloodied socks. Slowly she lowered both feet into the water and groaned. Silas took one foot and raised it enough to look at her soles. What he saw shocked him. Poor girl. Cuts and scratches covered the entire surface. Some were deep.

"No wonder you've been limping. This foot looks awful." He bent down to get a better look. "It's still oozing blood and it looks like you have dirt embedded in these cuts." He gently placed her foot back in the pan and lifted the other one. "This one's just as bad." He lowered it into the warm water. "Sit here for a while. You need to soak your feet long enough to soften the skin. It'll make it easier to clean the dirt out." He sat back and studied her face. She wouldn't meet his gaze but for a fleeting second. "Stay here. I'll be back."

He knew it would be painful to clean her feet and he had an idea. Maddy had her paint supplies in a basket in the sitting room. He rummaged through it until he found a couple of soft paintbrushes. These had to be better than the rags. Then he found the honey in the cupboard. Honey was both soothing and healing. His family had used it for as long as he could remember.

When he walked back into his room, he found Maddy slumped in the chair, fast asleep. No wonder. She probably hadn't slept much the night before, if at all. Yet here she was, scrubbing his floor and, from the smells coming from the kitchen, it was obvious she was already at work fixing the noon meal. Hard work seemed to soothe her.

When he gently touched her shoulder, she jumped and lunged away from him, sloshing water from the pan. "Shh... Maddy. It's me."

She looked at him with wild eyes then pressed her hand to her chest and drew in big gulps of air. "Oh, Silas. I'm sorry."

He sat in front of her. "No. I'm sorry. I didn't mean to startle you. You fell asleep. You must be exhausted."

"Asleep? I'm so sorry." She tried to get up but he stopped her. "I need to get the meal ready."

"No, you don't. You need to sit here and let me doctor those feet. If we don't get those cuts cleaned out, infection will set in then we'll need to amputate."

Her head snapped up to stare at him.

He held up the paintbrushes. "These will be the least painful way to do this." He grabbed one foot and set it on his knee.

"Amputate?"

He winked and smiled at her worried face. "Not likely, but I suppose it's possible." He dipped the paintbrush in the water and stroked it through the dirtiest cut. She gasped and yanked her foot away from him.

"I'm sorry, Maddy, but I can't think of a better way to do this. And it has to be done."

She set her foot on his knee. "Go ahead." Clenching both hands together under her chin, she stared at the ceiling and did her best to hold still while Silas thoroughly cleaned both of her feet. They looked so tiny and delicate in his large, work-roughened hands. He followed the cleaning with a thick coating of honey then wrapped both feet in strips of cloth. "We'll have to change these dressings every day."

And while he worked, his anger smoldered. What kind of monster would try to hurt this vulnerable human being? A girl who had never hurt or threatened anyone. One whose life had been spent taking care of others. Again, he found himself wanting to hurt the perpetrator. Wanting revenge. But most of all, he wanted to do whatever was necessary to protect his family, which now included Maddy.

CHAPTER TWENTY-FIVE

Maddy cried herself to sleep that night. The silence at suppertime had been awkward. Silas had asked Luke to move into Maddy's house and keep her animals there. He made no attempt to at least pretend he was a happy newlywed. Thankfully the children seemed to be oblivious to the mood of the adults. They were simply happy that Maddy got to spend nights with them.

Nightmares kept her awake most of the night. At one point, she jerked awake to find Ollie trying to comfort her. He turned and ran downstairs, returning later with a very worried Silas behind him.

"Maddy, are you alright?" he asked as he leaned over her and felt her head.

"She keeps cryin' in her sleep, Pa."

"What?" she asked confused and realizing for the first time that she was drenched with sweat. "Crying?" Then the dreams came to her mind and she shrunk back into the bed with fear, clutching the blankets to her chest.

Silas gently smoothed hair from her face. "Shh... You're safe, here, Maddy.

She looked him square in the face and grabbed his arm. "Are…are the doors locked?"

"No. I never lock my doors."

"Could you please? At least for a while?"

He smoothed more strands of hair back. "Of course. Is there anything else I can do?"

Maddy shook her head and pulled the blankets higher. Silas sighed and left.

Finally, Maddy managed to get in a few hours of solid sleep before becoming aware of Anabel's tiny arms wrapped around her waist. She tried to get up without waking the girl, who had moved to her side in the middle of the night. Her arms were wrapped around her and one leg was over her hip. Slowly she lifted the tiny leg then tried to extract herself from the tight embrace, but every time Maddy moved, Anabel tightened her grip. In spite of herself, she giggled. Ollie sat straight up at the noise.

"Good morning, Ma." He rubbed his sleepy eyes and smiled at her.

"Good morning, Ollie," she whispered, watching vapor rise from her lips as she spoke.

"I sure do like having you here, Ma."

"Oh, Ollie, thank you. I sure like being here, waking up to you two."

Anabel grunted and clung to her. Maddy didn't mind. She reveled in the sweetness. And in doing so, a new resolve grew in her. She had to cast aside the crippling fear. As much as possible, she would force herself to think about what was good in her life. What was that verse? "Whatsoever things are trustworthy, whatsoever things are honest, whatsoever things are just, whatsoever things are pure, whatsoever things are lovely…think on these things." She could, over time and with effort change the course of her thoughts and right now, she wanted one thing. She wanted to make Silas happy that he had married her. It would take time, but she knew she could be a good wife to him and she knew the character of the man. Her husband. Oh, how she loved those words. He'd come around. She was sure of it.

She finally slipped herself out from Anabel's grasp, surprisingly not waking her then stepped quietly over to the wash basin that she had filled the day before. The cold water on her face made her gasp and felt heavenly at the same time. She ran a brush through her fine hair, twisted it into a knot, and secured it with a few hairpins. Using her finger, she rubbed a pinch of tooth powder on her teeth then rinsed with water. She stepped behind a partition to slip out of her nightclothes and into her blue calico work dress. Digging into the satchel she'd brought from home, she found warm woolen socks, stuffed her cold feet in, and followed with her favorite old boots.

The stairs creaked as she descended into the darkness below. Silas' bedroom door was to the left of the stair landing, the kitchen to the right. She stopped and waited a moment before she took the last step. Oh, how she wanted to get breakfast started before Silas stirred. She wanted him to wake up to the tantalizing smell of bacon frying in the skillet and biscuits baking in the oven. After all, it was his first morning married to her. It just had to be as perfect as she could possibly make it.

The coals were still red, she noticed with satisfaction as she added kindling from the woodbox. In no time, a blaze started, so she added several small sticks of wood and adjusted the damper. After mixing up a fresh batch of biscuits, she walked out to the springhouse to get milk and bacon. The air had chilled to almost freezing, so she pulled her shawl tighter and tied it in a knot at her waist so she'd have free hands to carry food. The dried leaves crunched under her feet sending up their fragrance. Maddy breathed in deeply and let her air come rushing out with contentment. She was happier than she'd been in months.

Soon, bacon was sputtering and biscuits were baking.

Ollie had run outside to gather eggs, and Anabel appeared at the bottom of the stairs yawning and rubbing her eyes. She had dressed herself without help as she often did, but this morning, all of her buttons were offset by one. Maddy picked her up and nuzzled her neck, whispering "Good morning, little one."

Suddenly she heard Silas' door open. Anabel turned to greet him. She reached one hand out and grabbed his neck as he moved to her. But rather than leave Maddy's arms, she pulled Silas into a hug that included all three of them. And to Maddy's surprise, Silas didn't resist. She felt his strong arm encircle her as well as his daughter. And she basked in it, brief as it was.

He released them and moved to the kitchen. "Well, this is certainly a treat to wake up to. Do I have time to milk before we eat?"

"If you hurry." Maddy bustled over to the stove and turned the bacon. It was thick and the fire was slow building up heat on this cold morning.

Silas stepped up next to her and warmed his hands. "Looks like winter is moving in. I'd better start keeping a fire going in the fireplace, too." He walked to the door, slipped his feet into his boots, and shrugged into his heaviest coat. "I'll hurry." Then he walked out.

Breakfast was on the table when Silas walked back in. He hung his coat and moved quickly to warm his hands at the stove again. "Can we wait a minute or two? I just saw Luke ride in."

"Of course." Maddy moved around the table pouring three mugs of coffee. Ollie and Anabel waited patiently at their places.

"Can I butter my biscuit while I'm waitin', Ma?"

"May I," Maddy corrected as she set a pitcher of milk on the table. "And yes. You may."

The door opened again to let Luke and a gust of wind in. "Wooee! The temperature sure has dropped some since I crawled out a bed this mornin'." He stomped his feet. "I wouldn't be surprised if it snowed later today."

"Snow?" Anabel's face lit up with glee.

Ollie jumped out of his chair and ran to the window. "I don't see no snow!"

"I don't see any snow," Maddy again corrected as she pulled her chair out and sat down. "Come on over here, Ollie. We're getting ready to pray."

Silas held his hands out to either side and captured Anabel's in one and Maddy's in the other. He waited until hands were joined around the table before he bowed his head and asked the blessing. Maddy had always loved the feeling of his strong, warm hand around hers, but this morning it took on a whole new significance for her. He was hers and she was his. How that warmed her from the roots of her hair to the tips of her toes.

As soon as Silas said, "Amen," Luke helped himself to a serving of eggs. "I heard somethin' strange at the Fair Grove Mercantile yesterday."

"What was that?" Silas, too, put a big helping of eggs on his plate.

"I took some of our eggs in to sell an' just when I was about to walk up to the counter, I heard this loud voice bragging about somethin' he found. I knew right away it was Nate Potter. Man, he's got a mouth. 'Bout makes a feller wanna gag."

Maddy cleared her throat.

Luke glanced at her. "Sorry, Maddy. He's loud but sorta whiney at the same time. Ya know what I mean?"

"I know exactly what you mean," Silas almost growled.

"Well, I stopped in m' tracks and stayed hidden. I could see the counter. Nate threw down two gold coins then started braggin' about how he found 'em and knew where he could get more."

Silas glanced at Maddy. She froze.

Luke went on, "Yep. Made me sick. Everyone in these

parts knows just what kinda character them Potter boys are. All kinds of stories circulatin' 'bout those two doing all kinds o' mischief during the war; harassin' 'n' stealing from folks around here. They always wore masks so there's no proof, but people know those voices. They're guilty alright." Luke helped himself to another biscuit.

"I heard 'em one time when they came to our place and we were hidin' in the secret room," Ollie said.

Both Silas and Maddy stared in shock. "Ollie, are you sure?" Maddy asked. "I didn't think any of us could hear a thing when we were hiding down there."

"They came in and stood right over the trap door. You and Mama had your hands over yer ears. But I listened. It was Sam and Nate and some other guy. They were arguin' about something. It scared me to death. I thought sure they were gonna find us."

All three of the adults stopped eating. They looked from one to the other.

Finally, Maddy spoke, "Ollie, I'm so sorry. I didn't know." She swallowed a lump. "I...I'm just glad it's over."

Ollie smiled. "Yeah. And Pa is home." He happily shoved another bite of buttery biscuit into his mouth, quickly forgetting the terrors of that day. "Pa, can you or Luke build a toboggan for when it snows?"

Silas turned to Maddy with raised eyebrows. She shrugged and looked away. Talk of the Potters was quickly draining her happiness. She tried to get through the rest of the meal without causing more concern.

Silas responded to his eager son. "I think maybe we can do that. What do you think, Luke? You're the better carpenter."

Luke's eyes gleamed with childish enthusiasm. "Yeah, boss. That would be fun."

"Can I help?" Ollie jumped from his chair.

"Of course. Maybe Luke can teach you a thing or two while you're at it." Silas winked at the boy.

"Can we start today?"

"After all the chores are done and only if Luke says it's okay. I'm putting him in charge of this project."

Both Luke and Ollie left the house, discussing where they'd find some scrap lumber to do the job. Anabel showed no interest. Maddy let her leave the table without helping with the cleanup. She distractedly started gathering dirty dishes then turned to find Silas helping her.

"You don't have to help. I'm sure you have enough to do."

He kept working alongside her. "You and I need to have a talk."

Anxiety clenched at her gut. She only nodded. When the last bit of food was put away and the last dish washed and dried, Silas turned to her and searched her face. She tried to meet his gaze but failed.

"Anabel is busy in the other room so no one can hear us. What I'd like to know is, do you have any idea where the Potters got that gold?"

Maddy hesitated. She thought about the implications of her answer then decided it was safe to be honest, at least about some of what she knew. She looked at Silas and nodded.

"Is it from Eliza's stash?"

Maddy hesitated again. Silas gently but firmly took her arms in his hands. "What are you hiding from me, Maddy?"

"Nothing. Uh…I mean…nothing about the gold. Sam told me they found some in the creek that runs through my place, so…so I'm assuming it must be Eliza's."

Silas released her and paced the floor. "Did they tell you how much they found?"

"No. At least I don't think they did."

Silas turned and looked at her. "Are you telling me the truth?"

Hurt to her core, she answered vehemently, "Of course, I am! I wouldn't lie to you, Silas!"

He took three big steps and grabbed her by the shoulders. "Well then, if that's the case, tell me why you crawled into bed with me yesterday morning."

She yanked away from him in anger. "I haven't lied about that. I just can't talk about it yet."

"You're withholding information from me. Information that could make a difference. Isn't that the same as lying?"

"Not to me!" She turned away and stared at the back door.

"Well, it is to me. And until you feel like you can confide in your own husband, how can I fully trust you?"

Silence and hurt filled the room. Maddy stood with her back to Silas and refused to budge. She clenched her fists and listened to his heavy breathing. Soon, she heard the front door open and close. She made her way up the stairs, flung herself across the bed, and wept.

CHAPTER TWENTY-SIX

To Silas, it seemed as if days passed with anger still lingering in the air between him and Maddy. Neither were inclined to take the first steps toward forgiveness. It was torture. The other males were oblivious. Luke and Ollie were their usual talkative selves, filling the awkward silences at mealtimes. They were fully engrossed in the building of the toboggans, having decided two would be more fun than one. Luke was a great teacher, Silas realized as he watched him working with the boy each day. He insisted on doing the job right, even if it took longer.

Anabel stuck close to Maddy's side as if she realized her ma was hurting. A hurt that he was partially to blame for. Well maybe more than partial. He had to do something to patch things up between them. Life couldn't go on this way.

Saturday morning, dawned clear and bright without a cloud in the sky. At breakfast, Ollie complained, "Why ain't there any snow yet? It's colder than a witch's…"

"Oliver!" both Silas and Maddy hollered at once.

His eyes about burst from his head. "What?" He looked

from one angry face to the other. "I was gonna say, nose. Witch's nose. Whadya think I was gonna say?"

Maddy leveled her gaze on Luke and raised an eyebrow.

He held his hands up in surrender. "Nose is correct," he said with a sheepish grin. "That's what he's heard from me anyways. Colder than a witch's *nose*."

Maddy looked back at Silas. He tried his best to not smile, but to no avail. Not only did he smile, but a full-blown chortle leaked out. Maddy's eyes widened in surprise. She clamped her mouth shut in a tight line. Then she burst forth in the most beautiful sound he'd heard in days. Pure, sweet, uncontrolled laughter. Soon everyone around the table joined in. It was delicious.

When they'd calmed down, Maddy looked at Ollie. "I'm not sure where you've been learning such poor grammar"—she glanced at Luke—"but I want you to stop. 'Ain't' isn't a word I want to hear coming out of your mouth." Again, she glanced at Luke.

"Yes, ma'am," both Ollie and Luke mumbled.

"Speaking of grammar, I'd like to see Ollie and Anabel start going to school." Silas wiped his mouth and stood.

The look of alarm on Maddy's face told him his idea wasn't being received well.

She quickly got to her feet and followed him to the sink. "Why? They're so young. And I love teaching them here at home. What's the rush?"

Her shoulder brushed his arm. He couldn't resist the urge to touch her, to somehow draw her closer without causing alarm. He turned slowly and ran his hand down her arm to capture her hand in his. A quick intake of breath from her and a tiny step back should have warned him, but he persisted.

"I couldn't ask for a better teacher for my…for our kids, Maddy."

Those words alone seemed to make a crack in the wall between them. She looked up into his face. Her questioning eyes softened him further. He hated this distance that had grown between them, yet he knew he couldn't change his thinking about his trust for her. If she was hiding something, and she was, what else would she hide from him? How could he ever know? That question deeply disturbed him. He had to ignore that question if he wanted to enjoy any semblance of friendship with her.

He drew her by the hand away from the sink and over to the table. Pulling out chairs, he motioned for her to sit. "I have an idea that I think you'll love." He turned his chair around and sat, leaning forward so his face was level with hers. "Have you seen the old school building recently?"

"The last time I passed there, it was so covered with weeds, I could barely see it."

"Well, Luke and I walked around it Thursday afternoon and even managed to pry the boards off the door so we could go in."

"And...?"

"We think, with a little hard work, we could fix it up enough that we could open school again. It's so close. You and the kids could walk there in about five or ten minutes."

Maddy started to get up, but Silas reached out to stop her. Frustration snapped from her beautiful green eyes. "That doesn't change anything. I want them here with me, Silas. I want to be their teacher."

"Hear me out, girl. I want you to be their teacher, too. Would you be willing to take on a few extras?"

She only looked more frustrated with him. He leaned in closer.

"Maddy, would you be willing to be the new school teacher at that school?"

She sat back and stared at him. "What?"

"The board has already talked about it and the job is yours if you want it."

"The board?"

"Yes. It's the same board that we had before the war.

Minus a couple of men that were killed and minus your pa, of course."

Maddy didn't say a word so Silas continued, "I'm still on the board, along with Reverend Richards and Luke's pa. We…" He shrugged. "We took it upon ourselves to meet and make a few decisions. School's been out since the beginning of the war."

"I remember," Maddy said, brushing a strand of hair out of her eye. "Megan O'Mally was the last teacher. She left for St. Louis. Along with about a dozen families in this area. I miss her so badly."

Silas reached out to take her hand. "She and Eliza were your best friends, weren't they?"

She nodded, tears forming in her eyes. "I'll probably never see her again. She left for Oregon with her sister's family last spring."

"It will be after Christmas before we can get the building ready, so you'll have some time to think about it."

"Oh, Silas. I don't think I'll need any time at all. It…it sounds wonderful! I…I can't believe it!" She stood and clasped her hands under her chin and walked to the sink. He stood and followed her. But then she stopped and turned. "Wait. Are you sure I can do this? How many children will there be? And books. We don't have any books. Do we? And…and slates. And what about all the work that needs to be done here? I'm not sure I'll have time." She wrung her hands.

Silas took her in his arms. "Shhh… It will all work out. You can take it one day at a time. And as far as we know, there will only be four other children besides Ollie and Anabel."

She looked up at him. "That's only six. I can handle that. How old are they?"

"Not sure. But the oldest are Luke's sisters, Matilda and Ila. I think they're ten and eleven."

"I'll do it!"

"Good." Silas hugged her in response. It felt so good to hold her.

Too soon, she pushed away. "No. Wait. I can't be gone from here all day! There's too much work to be done."

In frustration, he watched her pace the floor. "Maddy."

She ignored him. Wringing her hands, she started listing all the things she needed to do. "Three meals a day, laundry, making butter, mending, keeping this place clean, making new clothes for Ollie and Anabel." She turned and looked at him with alarm. "Have you noticed how much they've grown? All of their clothes are too small."

"Maddy." She ignored him again, so he snagged her arm the next time she passed him. "Maddy, listen to me."

"What?" Impatience tinged her voice.

He could get lost in those green eyes. And that rosebud mouth. How badly he wanted to capture a kiss. Just one tiny kiss. She was his wife after all. But, no. Not yet. He shook his head, trying to get back to the matter at hand.

He gently held her arms. "We'll all help you. Both Ollie and Anabel are old enough to take on more jobs in the house. I can help with meals. And, if you'd like, we can hire someone to make the kids' clothes. We can drive into Springfield, pick out some fabric, and ask Eliza for the name of a seamstress. We can do a little Christmas shopping while we're there, too."

He could feel her relax. Her eyes calmed and a tiny smile appeared. "Really? You think we can do this?"

"I know we can. How about you teach at the school for just a half day at first? You can go to full days later if you want. But only if you want to."

The delight on her face warmed him to the tips of his toes. He could be content the rest of his days simply doing things to please her, to continue to see her face light up with joy like it was at that moment.

Maddy bustled about the house trying to get work done but accomplishing nothing. Her mind whirred with excitement, ideas, plans, misgivings. All fighting for front and center of her thoughts. She hadn't been this happy in years. To think of it. She was going to be a teacher!

She managed to get food on the table for the noon meal just as Silas and Luke opened the front door letting a blast of frigid air and leaves into the house. The fire in the fireplace flared and ashes stirred into the room.

"I never get sick of the smells you welcome us with, Maddy," Luke said as he hung his coat.

"Why thank you, Luke." Maddy filled his mug with coffee.

Silas grunted and pulled his chair out. She smiled at his grumpy face. He grinned back and held out his mug.

The front door opened again, this time with a bang, as Ollie entered. Again, a blast of cold air filled the small house. He was slower than the men at shutting it. The fire flamed and ashes blew all the way to the table.

"Oliver! Shut the dag blamed door!"

Maddy was shocked. "Silas!" she reprimanded.

"I'm sorry." Silas was quick with his apology and hung his head.

"Do you have any idea how much trouble I would have been in had I used that sort of language in front of my parents?" She continued. "And if I ever hear either one of your…our children say what you said, there will be trouble."

Silas put his hands up. "I believe you. And again, I'm sorry. I'm surprised it slipped out."

Ollie closed the door and with it the sound of wind. Thankfully he'd missed her shameful scolding of his pa. "I'm sorry, too, Silas," she said quietly. "I'll try not to speak to you in such a manner again." She smiled. "At least not when your children are listening." She turned to Ollie. "Go get your sister, please. I think she's upstairs."

When she sat, Silas took her hand. His touch sent her heart skittering. She was afraid to meet his eyes, certain he'd read the desire she kept hidden.

"I welcome your correction, when I need it. I've gone four long years listening to some of the foulest talk imaginable and I'm afraid there's a lot of it still lingering in my brain. It's bound to leak out now and then." He squeezed her hand. "Just don't correct me in front of the young'uns. And especially not in front of this pup here." He indicated Luke sitting across the table. Maddy turned to see Luke trying to control his laughter.

Ollie and Anabel ran down the stairs and joined them. After the prayer, Silas turned to his son. "After the meal, I want you to sweep the leaves and ashes up. Every time we open that door, we make a mess for your ma. And the longer you leave it open, the bigger the mess."

Ollie looked at the floor and noticed for the first time the mess. "Sorry, Ma. I'll clean it up." She beamed at her son. *Her son!* Those were words she could barely get used to. And her daughter. If things never changed between her and Silas, she still had gained so much by her rash actions of this past week. She was truly their ma and nothing could snatch them away from her.

When they finished eating and rose to clear the table, she heard the dogs barking. One glance out the window told her they had company.

"It's Reverend Richards and Sister Martha!" Ollie danced with excitement and ran to the door. He flung it open and ran onto the porch to welcome them. Silas jumped up to close the door behind his forgetful son and sent a quick apology to Maddy. She was too happy to care. She dearly loved the Richards even though they often challenged her to the limit. But always with good intent and good results.

"I wonder what brings them here?" She wiped her hands on her apron and went to greet them.

Martha came in with a covered basket, set it on the table then engulfed Maddy in a long hug. "Happy Birthday, dear!"

"Birthday?" Silas mumbled.

"Birthday?" Maddy heard herself say.

"You forgot your own birthday? Why, it's today, darlin'. November twenty-fifth. I should remember. I was there the day your mama birthed you."

Maddy's hands flew to her face. "Today's the twenty-fifth? I've lost track."

"Yes. And we're here to celebrate with you."

Reverend Richards patted Silas on the back. "I figured neither of you would remember, what with the crazy week you all have had." He winked.

Martha made herself at home and gathered plates and forks. "I made yer favorite cake, dear. You jest sit yerself down and let me serve you."

"Am I invited?" Luke had his coat on, ready to get back to work.

His woebegone expression made Maddy laugh. "Of course you are, Luke. You're part of this family, too, you know." She grabbed his hand and pulled him to the table.

She sat next to Silas and let Martha take charge. Soon, they all had thick slices of cake and hot mugs of fresh coffee. "Pa, did we get Ma a birthday present?" Ollie asked. "Last year we got her a present."

"No, son. I'm sorry. I didn't even know it was her birthday."

"I remember last year; Mama made her an apron, and Anabel and I gave her some pretty rocks we found in the creek. Do you remember, Anabel?"

Anabel nodded. Her mouth was stuffed with cake. "Slow down, honey." Maddy touched her hand as she was lifting another forkful.

"How old are you, Ma?"

"I'm twenty-one today."

"Twenty-one. Imagine that." Reverend Richards looked pointedly at Silas who seemed to be stupefied. He stopped eating and stared. First at Frank then at Maddy.

Martha laughed. "Why if you hadn't just got married, people would be callin' you an old maid." She laughed again and patted Silas on the back.

CHAPTER TWENTY-SEVEN

Silas loved to be in his barn when the winter winds howled in from the north. He had already mucked out the cow stalls and moved to the horses. Earlier, he had turned both cows and horses into the cornfield to feast for the day on the old cobs and cornstalks. Steam rose from the fresh manure that he'd loaded into the wagon bed. It was a smell he'd grown up with and found comforting in a way that only a farmer could appreciate.

Twenty-one. His wife was twenty-one. Not a child of sixteen or seventeen as he'd imagined for the months since he'd returned home. For a week or more, he had tried to digest that news. Everything had somehow shifted. During that week, he'd allowed himself for the first time to look at her differently. To see her beauty. He'd always seen the beauty of her character, but now he dared to see more. Her face, her body. To allow himself to desire her. To…dare he think it? To lust after her. Was it called lust if it was your wife you longed for? He shook his head to clear his thoughts. She was still a maiden. If she knew where his thoughts traveled, she'd be appalled.

Could she possibly desire him also? Not in the same way a man longed for a woman, he was sure, but could she possibly want an intimate relationship with him? Or did she still think of him simply as her older neighbor? Maybe her only reason for wanting this marriage was to be a ma to his young'uns.

Yet…he remembered the look she gave him on their wedding night when he told her to sleep upstairs with the children. It was disappointment. Even hurt. Surely that should tell him something. But his reason for sending her away remained the same. Regardless of her age, the deception was still there.

Luke came in and hitched Maud to the wagon. He nodded a greeting at Silas, but no more. Silas was pleased at how easily he and Luke worked together. They seemed to read each other's minds. He would be eternally grateful to Reverend Richards for directing him to hire this boy. Chances were that he, just like Maddy, was a lot older than he'd imagined. After all, the two had gone to school together and had a friendship that went back for years. He caught himself growling under his breath at that thought. It shouldn't bother him because neither had done anything untoward.

Luke waved a good-bye as he drove the wagon through the big double doors and out to spread the manure on the wheat field. Sometimes Silas was hard on the young man but Luke seemed unfazed. He guessed that his pa, Pete, was a much harder taskmaster. Silas had known Pete for years. In fact, it was Pete and his wife, Lori, that had walked him through the startup of his farm. Along with Maddy's parents, of course. Frederick and Gertie, such salt-of-the-earth, good people. He wished they were still here. After his parents had passed almost a decade ago, Frederick and Gertie had stepped in to fill their place.

Thoughts of Mary sobered him considerably. She was the best of women. And he missed her. But she had been gone for over five years. He knew without a doubt she would approve of Maddy as his new wife. Nowhere could he have found a woman that loved Ollie and Anabel the way Maddy did. He smiled at the thought as he loosened up manure packed in a corner of Maud's stall. He had done right by his children in this second marriage. He snorted at the thought. As if he'd had much say in the matter. He realized if he'd continued in his blindness, this marriage might never have happened.

As frigid as it was outside, it was plenty warm in the barn. He stopped working and propped the dung fork against the wall. Pulling his handkerchief from his pants pocket, he wiped sweat that had trickled from his hair into his eyes. Luke swung the doors open letting another blast of cold in then hurried back to guide Maud into the barn. With the doors closed again, a dark, cozy calm settled once more over the interior of the barn. Luke picked up a shovel and headed to clean out the pigpens, a job Silas had gladly assigned to him. Luke never complained.

From where he stood, he could see the two toboggans Luke and Ollie were working on. If they finished the deep mucking of stalls today, they could spend time finishing the toboggans tomorrow. He also planned to take Maddy to the school. Asking her to be the new teacher was like giving her a gift of pure gold. She had been floating through her days for a week, planning lessons and drawing maps for the walls on old paper she had pieced together.

Earlier that week, he had driven her to her house so she could go in search of a big trunk full of old books that her ma had used years ago when she had taught school. Her parents had stored it somewhere in their attic. After much digging and lots of dust, she found it, along with an old, crumbling map of the world and an alphabet chart. He hauled the trunk home and after pawing through it, she found a treasure trove of books, along with the old slates she and her siblings had used when they went to school, five of them! She did a little jig when she spotted them, much to Silas' amusement.

Enough daydreaming, Silas scolded himself. He picked the dung fork up and got back to work.

The following day after breakfast, Maddy and Silas walked the short distance to the old school. When she laid eyes on it, her heart dropped. It was worse than she had imagined. She pulled her green wool cape closer around her shoulders to keep the biting wind out. It had finally snowed the night before, to Ollie and Anabel's delight. It swirled around them and piled up in a few places.

"Surely you can't have this ready by January. That's less than a month away." She stepped up onto the creaking boards of the porch and tried in vain to open the front door. All of the windows had been boarded over but most of those boards were missing. Silas stepped up beside her and gave a hard yank on the door, scraping it across the uneven, splintered boards and revealing the interior. It was far worse than the outside. She was almost afraid to step in. Silas led the way.

Rays of sunlight leaked through the boarded-up windows, lighting up floating dust particles. Leaves, rags, broken boards, and hay littered the floor. A few desks were still intact, but most had been chopped up for an easy source of firewood. What was left apparently had been used for squirrels to build their nests in. Or rats. Maddy shuddered. Wasp nests covered the rafters. Someone had even built a fire in one spot in the middle. Sure enough, when Maddy looked up, she saw charred beams directly overhead.

"It looks bad, but it's entirely salvageable." Silas rubbed his hands together for warmth.

Maddy just turned slowly, trying to take it all in. She noticed the chimney in the center of the room and the gaping hole where the stovepipe had gone, but there was no stove. "I wonder where the stove disappeared to."

"No telling. I'd actually be surprised if it was still here." Silas thumped on the chimney and looked through the hole. "This will need to be cleaned and repaired a little, but for the most part, it appears to be functional."

He turned and looked at her. "What do you think?"

She swallowed. "Well… It will be a lot of work, but if you and Luke think it can be done, I'll believe you." She smiled into his eyes. He looked relieved.

"My plan is that Luke and I will clear all this debris out of the inside, pile it up outside, and burn it. When we're done with that, you women can start cleaning and painting."

"Women?"

"Martha, and Luke's ma, Lori, want to help. You shouldn't have to do this by yourself."

All of a sudden, the job didn't seem so daunting. "That will be fun, having those two help me with this."

"Luke plans to build more desks, but he can do that in our barn then haul each one over here as it's finished." Silas looked around the room. "We'll salvage every bit of lumber we can out of here then burn the rest of this trash."

Maddy's enthusiasm grew by leaps and bounds as she listened to Silas. "Can we start today?" Silas' giant smile warmed her heart. It felt good to be working on a project together.

"Well, whatever we do, it'll be just you and me today. I gave Luke permission to work with Ollie on the toboggans."

"You're the boss. Tell me what to do and I'll do it." Maddy blew on her frozen hands. She saw Silas smother a chuckle.

"You're not dressed for this. Let's go back to the house,

sit at the table with some hot coffee, and make a list."

Maddy laughed. "That sounds wonderful! Let's get out of here! I'm freezing!" She led the way out the door and down the steps.

Silas caught up to her and grabbed her arm. "Here. Let me hold your hand. I can get at least one of them warmed up."

His big hand was so warm. She turned and put both hands in his, walking backward as she did so. He laughed at her silly antics. It was such an unexpected and merry sound to her ears. She wanted more. She stumbled. In his attempt to stop himself from running over her, he merely picked her up and carried her a few steps. When he stopped, he still had his arms around her.

Both of them froze. Their laughter stopped as they gazed into each other's eyes. Maddy saw something in his eyes she'd never seen before. A longing? She was sure she couldn't hide the longing in hers. Could he see it?

Silas grew very silent. He smoothed a strand of hair back from her eyes, sighed deeply then let her go. He took her hand firmly in his and continued walking next to her.

They stopped at the barn to check on the progress of the toboggans then walked together to the house. The teakettle was already hot, so Maddy poured scalding water through the coffee grounds in her strainer then poured the dark liquid into their mugs. Silas waited silently at the table. She sat across from him. A lot more than school repairs was on his mind.

Clearing his throat, he leaned toward her and took her hand. She waited but something seemed to stop him. He cleared his throat again and said, "I'm so glad you said yes to teaching."

Was that all? He was getting emotional about her agreeing to teach? She knew better but wasn't sure how to maneuver this new terrain. She squeezed his hand. "I'm glad, too. Thank you for asking me." With her free hand, she took a sip of the hot coffee. "Ow!" She jerked her other hand free from his grasp to soothe her burned lip.

Silas watched with concern then amusement when she smiled. Quickly she placed her hand back in his. His eyes lit up with surprise. He stared at their hands for a moment then brought his other hand up to fully enclose hers. She delighted in the moment. And waited. He stroked her hand with his thumb sending shivers through her. The coffee was forgotten. Finally, he looked at her and smiled the warmest, most loving smile she had ever seen on his handsome face. It spoke volumes and swept away weeks of doubt. *He loves me!*

Then he released his grip on her, cleared his throat, and sat up straight. "How about that list we were going to make?"

CHAPTER TWENTY-EIGHT

Maddy felt the gentle touch of Silas' hand at the small of her back as she walked up the steps to the mercantile on the corner of Springfield's massive square. Things had definitely changed between them since that day they'd made their list. Silas was much more attentive and gentler. He seemed to look for excuses to be with her. And excuses to touch her. She savored every touch.

But she still slept in the upstairs bedroom with the kids. The day would come when they would consummate their marriage. Heat rushed to her face as she walked through the doors into the well-equipped store. When? She didn't know. Why it hadn't happened yet, she was uncertain. Silas had never made it clear. She suspected it was because of her secrets. He hadn't tried to hide his disapproval of that, but could that possibly be the reason for the lack of marital intimacy? Drat it! She put a hand to her hot cheek. She tried to force herself to think of something else but it was hard. Silas wouldn't leave her side. Neither had he removed his hand from her back.

Elin and Eliza were no doubt spoiling Ollie and Anabel

rotten. They had offered to watch them so the couple could shop for Christmas gifts. Maddy wandered the aisles in wonder. Rarely had she had the luxury of buying gifts. She wasn't sure where to turn. Again, she felt the warm touch of Silas at her waist. He gently turned her to see a doll sitting on the shelf to her right. Maddy gasped. It was beautiful. Unlike the elegant doll she saw in the window, this one begged to be held and cuddled. It was entirely made of cloth, but more detailed and beautiful than any cloth doll she had ever laid eyes on. It had an intricately embroidered face with a tiny rosebud mouth. A yellow bonnet covered its head and the soft, cloth body was dressed in a long yellow gown with tiny daisies and green ribbon edging.

She picked it up and turned to Silas. He chuckled softly. "Let's check the price before we get too excited," he said.

On their way to the counter, they passed a small wooden wagon pulled by a beautifully carved horse. Silas stopped in his tracks and picked it up to study it. He looked at Maddy with a raised eyebrow. "What do you think?"

"Oh, Silas. He'll love it!" She put her hand on his arm. "Do you suppose we could get Luke to build a simple barn to go with it? And a dollhouse for Anabel?"

Silas' eyes gleamed with youthful enthusiasm. "I think he'll have time to do that. If he keeps it simple."

By the time they walked back to Elin's home, they were loaded with packages. Besides the Christmas gifts, school supplies, fabric, a couple of new kitchen gadgets, and food rounded out their purchases.

Ollie and Anabel were in the backyard with Elin when they arrived. Eliza's mouth opened in surprise when she saw the packages. "You certainly made good use of your time."

Maddy laughed. "I've never in my life walked out of a store with this much stuff."

"I don't want to stash all of this in the wagon yet. Do

you have a room where we can hide it from prying eyes until we're ready to leave?" Silas asked.

"Come this way." Eliza led them up the stairs toward a back bedroom.

"Elin's home is so big. How many bedrooms up here?" Maddy twirled around trying to take it all in. "For some reason, I barely paid attention back when we were here this past summer."

Eliza smiled. "You seemed too preoccupied all that month to pay attention to much of anything. Besides those precious children, of course." She paused to squeeze Maddy's arm before she continued. "Elin has six bedrooms on this floor, two downstairs and two tiny ones in the attic, up the stairs behind this door." Eliza pointed to a door at the end of the hallway. "Remember, she used it as a boarding house during the war. Among other things." She winked then opened the door to the back bedroom and stepped aside so they could enter with their load. "When Jon and I move to our farm, I think she'll start taking boarders in again."

Silas set his load down on the bed and turned to help Maddy. "I'm sure the extra income from boarders will help quite a bit," he said.

"And keep her from loneliness." Eliza stood at the door and watched. "Jessica and her children will continue living here. Their presence certainly livens up this place." As they made their way downstairs, Eliza asked, "Would you please stay for the meal and the night? Jonathan won't get back until fairly late and I know he wants to see you."

Silas turned to Maddy. "It's entirely up to my dear wife."

Maddy blushed. "Are you sure it wouldn't be too much trouble, Eliza?"

"No trouble at all. Elin and I have already discussed it and we were both hoping you'd say yes. Jessica is already working on the meal."

"I told Luke to be prepared. We'll head home as soon as we're finished with breakfast." Silas chuckled and turned to Eliza. "That is, if we're invited for breakfast as well."

"Of course, you are. I think Jonathan has some interesting information to share with you."

Silas lifted an eyebrow. "Oh?"

Eliza led them to the parlor and invited them to sit. "He's been quite busy since we saw you last." She left them alone for a moment then returned. "Jessica's getting some tea and cookies ready, if you'd like some."

"That sounds lovely, Eliza. Thank you." Maddy arranged her skirt to settle in more comfortably. "Speaking of Jessica, does she sew for people? I'm sure you've noticed, both Ollie and Anabel are growing like weeds and quickly outgrowing all of their clothes. We bought enough fabric to make a couple of new dresses for Anabel and shirts and trousers for Ollie. I need a seamstress."

Eliza looked surprised. "You and your ma have always sewn for your family."

Silas quickly jumped into the conversation. "Maddy won't have time for a few months. May I introduce you to our new schoolmarm?"

"Truly?" Eliza's eyes were wide. Maddy smiled and nodded. "Maddy, that's wonderful! At our old school?"

"Yes. Although it didn't fare well through the war."

Silas chuckled. "We'll get it back to its old glory in no time."

Maddy rolled her eyes. "He has a lot more confidence than I do." She smiled again. "But it doesn't matter. As long as it's warm and there are enough seats, we can have school." She felt her enthusiasm growing. "I think this is something I've always wanted to do, but didn't realize it. Did you know my ma used to be a teacher?"

"No. But I'm not surprised. She seemed to be a very educated, cultured woman. I loved your parents. I'm sorry they're gone."

Silas shifted in his chair to look directly at Eliza. "What is this information Jonathan thinks I might be interested in?"

Eliza leaned forward and lowered her voice. "I'll save it for him to share when he gets here."

"My curiosity might kill me. You said he's been busy. With what?"

Eliza kept her voice down. "I'm sure he'd like to be the one to tell you this also, but I'll say this much. He's officially out of the military now and has been since the end of the war, but his job in the last year of the war was to root out the guerrilla fighters in this area. About a month ago, he was approached by the Union military. They asked for his help in putting together lists of war crimes against certain individuals."

"Interesting." Silas sat back and rubbed his chin.

Eliza continued. "He's been working to get our farm up and running but this new job keeps him pretty busy. It requires a lot of traveling to gather evidence. I'll be happy when this is over. It's dangerous work."

Silas nodded. The look of concern on his face worried Maddy. He leaned toward Eliza again. "I imagine there are a lot of people out there that aren't happy with what he's doing."

She nodded. "He's trying to keep this job a secret. But when you travel around asking all these questions..." She spread her hands out in frustration. "People will talk and it's only a matter of time before the wrong person finds out what he's up to."

While Maddy was tucking the children into bed for the night, she heard the front door open and Eliza's voice greeting Jonathan. They had all had supper without him;

Ollie and Anabel fighting for a chair next to little Daniel. At Eliza's insistence, Jessica and her children had joined them. When Jonathan didn't show up, Eliza, looking quite worried, had covered his dish and asked Jessica to keep it warm.

After praying with her children and answering way too many questions, Maddy finally made her way downstairs. She found Eliza and Silas at the dining room table watching a ravenous Jon devour his meal. Between bites, he managed to look at her, smile, and nod a greeting. Settling in next to Silas, she looked expectantly at Jon for information.

Eliza smiled and winked. "When he's done with his meal, we can all gather in the parlor for dessert. And talk."

Silas slid his hand over and grasped hers. She could sense his anticipation.

Soon, they all made their way into the next room and settled into chairs, with Jonathan obviously savoring the fact that they were all waiting anxiously to hear his news. He sat back, stretched, and smiled at his wife. "I wonder what delightful dessert Jessica plans to surprise us with today." He made a show of licking his lips. "She's the best pastry chef I've ever known."

"I think she learned from Sally." Eliza turned to Maddy to explain. "Sally is Jon's aunt Mildred's former slave. They live just down the alley. That's where I spent the first two years of the war."

"That was before she married me. I believe Jessica has far surpassed Sally's skills."

Eliza smiled. "I think you're right. She's starting to sell her desserts to our neighbors."

"Is she able to do that while cooking and cleaning for you and taking on seamstress duties?" Maddy was impressed.

"She is one industrious young lady." Eliza shrugged. "I'm not sure how she does it, but she manages."

Just then, Jessica walked in with a platter filled with apple turnovers. Elin followed with a pitcher of milk. When they left, Silas leaned forward. "Alright, Jonathan. Out with it."

"Out with what?" Jon looked at Eliza with a raised eyebrow.

She laughed. "You know. Quit torturing them."

Jonathan laughed and sat back in his chair. "I'm sorry." He rubbed his chin thoughtfully for a moment. "Actually, I'm very sorry. What I have to tell you is nothing to laugh at."

Silas and Maddy leaned in.

Jonathan shook his head. "And I learned new information today that has me quite worried." He paused and looked at his wife. "Worried for you, Eliza."

"For me?" Her hand went to her throat. "What could it possibly be?"

Jonathan turned to his friends. "As you might already know, I've been at work in the past few weeks investigating war crimes, primarily of the renegade confederate troops north of Springfield. Most have disbanded but there are many individuals still out there doing mischief. The Union forces in this area are posed to strike." He looked pointedly at Silas. "A large amount of evidence has been gathered against some people that I believe you know, Silas and Maddy."

Maddy sat back in shock. "Who?"

"Your neighbors to the west. Sam and Nate Potter."

Maddy covered her mouth with both hands. *Dare I believe?* She lowered her hands. "Evidence? What kind of evidence?"

"Enough to have them put away for a long time. Maybe even executed."

Maddy surged to her feet, covered her face, and walked blindly across the room. The relief was so powerful it almost paralyzed her. Finally, against her will, she bent at the waist, her body convulsing with great heaving sobs. She groped to hold onto something solid before she collapsed. All three of them stood and moved toward her. Silas was next to her in an instant, gathering her limpness into his strong frame. He stroked her back and her hair while gently shushing her. After a moment, he led her to sit next to him on the settee, never letting her out of his arms.

Eliza pressed a handkerchief into her hand. Maddy wiped her eyes then her nose and glanced up to see her friends studying her. She hid her face in shame. *What came over me? Such a lack of control.* She could feel the strong hand of Silas gripping her shoulder. What must he be thinking? What must they all be thinking? She cleared her throat, trying to gain some composure.

Eliza's quiet voice broke in after a long silence. "Maddy?"

Maddy dabbed at her eyes again and dared to look up. "Yes?"

"This news must be a huge relief to you." Eliza's voice was barely audible.

Maddy merely nodded.

"They've been somewhat of a threat to her for some time now," Silas interjected. "I just haven't been sure…" His voice choked. "Maddy, the Potters are the reason you came to me, aren't they?"

Maddy turned abruptly to stop him. "Not now, Silas." She hoped the pleading in her eyes would be enough to silence him. His look penetrated through her soul, but he nodded slightly and quit asking questions.

Thankfully, Eliza seemed to sense the need for a shift in their focus. "Uh…Jonathan, you said you had news that concerned me?"

"Yes." He leaned over and took her hand. "There are reports that Henry Goodman has been seen in the area."

Eliza's eyes filled with fear. "He's back?"

"Not in Springfield, but north of here. He will be

arrested on sight for desertion. He's also been connected to the Potters."

"Well that's interesting," Silas muttered, rubbing his chin.

"It's just a matter of time before both Henry and the Potters are taken into custody. In the meantime"—Jonathan leaned toward his wife—"I'm not letting you and Daniel out of my sight. We already know the lengths Henry will go to get his hands on your gold."

CHAPTER TWENTY-NINE

Maddy dipped a paintbrush into the white paint. Before wiping the excess onto the edge of the bucket, she looked around the room. Both Ollie and Anabel were happily drawing on the new chalkboard. Luke's ma, Lori, was sanding the last of eight desks, and Sister Martha was hard at work painting the south wall. A surge of excitement coursed through her. This was her classroom and soon, very soon, it would be ready. She couldn't believe the changes that had happened in the last two weeks.

True to his word, Silas and Luke had cleared out the debris and burned it. Then the other board members had joined them to repair broken doors and windows, making the space airtight. A few days later, the wives joined in to scrub the place from top to bottom. The women decided to scrub it a second time. Way too many mice and other unnamed vermin had taken up residence and left their droppings behind.

The week before, Silas had found a stove and stovepipe in an abandoned house just outside of Fair Grove. A fire was blazing away as they worked, and the room was cozy and warm, except next to the windows. Maddy looked across the room at the three big windows on the south side. She loved the light that streamed in on most days. Today, though, the windows rattled from a storm that had blown in after they had walked back from their noon meal. The smell of snow was in the air.

"There! I believe that does it on this wall." Martha stood and stretched, rubbing the small of her back. She turned to Lori. "We better git on outa here before this storm gets worse. I need ta git home and start peelin' taters for supper."

"If we don't get snowed in, I suppose we can come back tomorrow to finish, Maddy." Lori smiled at her young friend. "I think another day will be all it takes."

"I can't make it tomorrow. Frank and I are going to make the rounds to the south of us. It's our visitin' day." She put her brush in a can of turpentine to soak overnight. "My, my. Would you look at this art work." Martha wiped her hands with a rag as she walked to the front of the room. Ollie and Anabel beamed under her praise.

Ollie wiped his chalk-coated hands on his overalls and started explaining the picture to her. "This is our barn and in front are Hansel and Gretel. The cows are in the field over there." He pointed to the far right of the board.

Anabel joined in. "This here is me, Ollie, Pa, and Ma. And that's our house." She pointed proudly to a lopsided rectangle with a triangle roof on top.

"She's planning to add windows and doors later, right, Anabel?" Ollie said.

"Yep," she muttered as she stuffed her finger in her mouth and continued drawing with her other hand.

Martha turned to Maddy. "What a blessing to have a chalkboard this big."

"That was Luke's doing. He found those wide boards, sanded them, and gave them several coats of black paint."

"He's a treasure, that boy."

Lori blushed slightly, listening to her son receive praise from Sister Martha.

"She's right, you know, Lori," Maddy added. "You should be proud."

Both women gathered up their tools, left them next to the paint cans, and bundled up for the ride home. Maddy followed them to the door and closed it behind them as a gust of wind and a few snowflakes forced their way in. She turned to the children. "I've got some more painting to do on this wall. Do you want to help me?"

They gave her the answer she hoped for. "Naw. If it's alright with you, we'll keep working on our picture. We want Pa to see it when he comes."

She chuckled and got back to work. Painting with a clumsy five-year-old girl and an overly enthusiastic, very distractable, seven-year-old boy was something she hadn't looked forward to. She had escaped.

She made good use of her time, stopping intermittently to comment on the ongoing masterpiece taking shape on the board. With her final swipe of the paintbrush, she stood and announced, "Finished! I hope we don't have to paint these walls again for years. This is hard work." As she walked across the room to clean the brushes, she stopped abruptly. A man on horseback rode slowly by within view of the windows. A man she didn't recognize. She put the brush down and snuck over to peer out of the corner of the window. He slowly dismounted and tied the horse to the fence in front. When he turned and looked toward the building, her knees buckled under her. *Sam Potter!*

She had to move fast. Very fast. There was no way she could escape. But the children... Her eyes searched frantically for a hiding place for them. She ran to the front, whispering loudly, "Ollie! Anabel! Quick! You need to hide!"

Both kids turned to her with wide, confused eyes. "It's Sam Potter. He's here." Anabel started whimpering. "No,

Anabel! I need you to be brave. Very, very brave. And very, very quiet! Under here. Quick! Not a sound!" She practically shoved them under her desk. The space was tiny but big enough for two tiny bodies. "Not a peep, do you understand? When we leave, count silently to 100 then go get your pa."

She heard footsteps stomping up the front steps to the porch. "Shhh…" She pressed her finger to her lips. "Not a sound." She rushed to the door hoping to open it and slip outside before Sam could enter. She grabbed her coat on the way. But she was too slow. The door slammed open, crashing into the wall.

Trying her best to be nonchalant, she buttoned her coat and exclaimed, "Sam! What brings you here?"

His expression did away with any hope she had. His eyes were smoldering. He advanced on her with no greeting. Her only desire at the moment was to keep distance between him and the children. *He mustn't discover them!* So, she slipped quickly out of his path and headed to the door.

"Where do ya think yer goin', missy?" he roared as one beefy hand snaked out and grabbed her roughly by the arm.

Pain shot through her arm but she struggled to be as cordial as possible. She stopped and looked up at him. "I'm done with my work here so I'm heading home, now."

He yanked her against his chest. "Home? Where's home?"

"Uh, with my husband, Silas." Hopefully Sam knew that she was married, but she wasn't entirely sure.

"Silas, huh?" He pushed her backward toward the door. Then with a roar, "Silas?" He shoved her out the door. She tripped on the doorway and rolled down the steps, ending in a heap at the bottom. She prayed that Ollie and Anabel would stay put. She needed to get him away from the schoolhouse. Whatever that would take.

He pulled her to her feet and for the first time, she

smelled alcohol on his breath. "You thought you could pull a fast one on me didn't ya? Getting that fool man to marry you?" He dragged her to his horse and demanded she mount. Then he loosened the reins from the fence and swung up behind her, wrapping one arm tightly around her waist. Vicious words whispered in her ear. "If you thought you could get away with this tomfoolery, then you are mistaken, woman. We'll have our way with you yet."

Terror coursed through her but she refused to struggle. Getting as far from the children as possible was the only thing that mattered at the moment. She hoped they would count slowly, very slowly. If they left the building, Sam might see them. *God help them! Put blinders over his eyes.*

Just as he turned the horse into the woods, she saw Ollie's face at the window. Branches slapped at them as Sam kicked his horse into a canter. Snow fell in big, fat flakes and began to cover the ground. Maddy shivered with cold but mostly from fear as she tried to form a plan for escape. Or at least a plan to slow him down. From the school, the path Sam had chosen would take them to the north of Silas' property to an old road that would pass to the west side of Potter's land. Maddy couldn't think straight. There was nothing she could do unless he stopped, which wasn't likely since they didn't have far to go.

The scenario that she had feared the most was playing out before her. Silas would come to her rescue and risk his life and possibly his children's. She had hung all her hopes on Sam leaving her alone once he'd found out she and Silas were married. But that hope was dashed. Why would she have believed Sam or Nate would be decent enough to honor a marriage? She prayed with desperation that Silas would have enough sense to go get help before he attempted a rescue.

The jostling of the horse jarred her bones. She had no place to put her feet to unweight her body and lessen the impact of every step. She tried gripping with her legs but her muscles started cramping, so she gave in to the bumpy ride, trying her best to not lean into Sam. His heavy breathing was revolting. Every few minutes, he lowered his mouth to her ear and whispered words she wished she could block out, followed by soft chuckles of the most sinister kind.

"Soon, my precious..." He nuzzled her neck. "You're softer than I remember. You must've put on some weight. I like that." Chuckles followed that curdled her blood. When he nibbled her ear, she yanked away.

"Oh, yes!" He laughed. "You still have some fight in you. We were both hoping you did." He howled in delight. "This will be fun!"

Maddy almost fainted from fear. What could she possibly do? Soon, she'd be in their home, completely in their power. Even if Silas came with Luke, what could they do? Prayer was her only hope. She couldn't even form the words in her terror-stricken mind. *Oh, God! Oh, God! Oh, God!* No other words came to her as he reined his horse into their corral and dismounted. He yanked her from her perch with such force, she fell to the manure-covered ground. Then he grabbed her by her hair and dragged her through the excrement to the gate.

"Well, looky there. The pretty lady got herself all dirty." He laughed as if he were hilarious and drew her to her feet. "We'll have to give you a bath, won't we?"

Maddy kept calling out to God while her brain threatened to give way to complete numbness. As if it came from far away, Sam's voice called to his brother, "Nate! Get out here! You don't want to miss the fun!"

As Sam led her stumbling forward, she felt another set of hands grab her from the other side. "Woo-ee! Look what the cat drug in!" Nate's nasally voice joined his brother's. "She stinks to high heaven! What did you do to her?"

Sam laughed uproariously. "Let's just say she took a stroll through the barnyard."

"Looks more like a roll through the barnyard than a stroll through the barnyard."

At this, the two of them doubled over with their mirth, never loosening their grip on Maddy's arms.

"Oh, that's a good one, Nate! Should we roll her through the barnyard again, just for good measure?"

"Why not," Nate answered. "I'm a thinkin' she's got some serious lessons ta learn."

"First, though, let's git this fool coat off." Sam unbuttoned her coat and yanked it off. He smiled. "That way, she'll have less cushion. She needs to *feel* this luxurious experience, don't ya think, brother?"

Nate's lecherous gaze traveled from her face to her feet and back again.

They turned and dragged her back to the gate and shoved her backward onto the muck. "I did the honors last time." A cruel laugh escaped from Sam. "It's your turn, brother. Have at 'er."

All Maddy could do was surrender to their evil and be grateful that the worst was being postponed. She clung to a glimmer of hope.

Nate kicked her hard in her side, sending piercing pain through her rib cage. She rolled over to her front from the force of the kick. He wasted no time in grabbing her by an arm and dragging her again through the filth all the way to the opposite side. She almost blacked out from the pain. When he flipped her over, she spit dung from her mouth and freed her hand to wipe it from her eyes.

Nate leaned in close. "Aw...poor baby. We missed a few places, Sam." With that, he picked up fresh cow manure and wiped it into her hair and over every square inch of her face and neck. He then proceeded to unfasten her bodice, with his manure-filled hand poised to continue his work. Just then, Nate fell to the ground with a roar.

A third man stood over Nate with fury in his face. "Not now, you idiot!" He yanked Maddy to her feet and marched back to the barnyard gate. He hollered over his shoulder at the brothers, "We need to get information from her first. Remember?"

"Don't worry, Henry. We'll get the information." Sam moved in and pulled Maddy away from the other man.

Maddy's rattled brain tried to make sense of the words she heard. *Henry?* Could this possibly be the same Henry that was after Eliza's gold?

Nate caught up to them by the time Sam had dragged her to the watering trough. "Bath time, Maddy, girl," Sam announced as he easily lifted her and dropped her into the frigid water of the trough.

As the water closed over her, she gasped and choked. Laughter surrounded her. Cruel hands shoved her under the water over and over and over again. Then they pulled her out and examined her with rough hands. "Is she clean yet?"

"Nope?" Then she was roughly lifted but before they could drop her into the trough again, a harsh voice interrupted them. "Stop!"

"Aw, Henry. Can't you stay out of this. We ain't gonna kill her," Nate's voice whined.

"We need information first. She's shivering so hard she can barely speak." Henry stepped in front of her and grabbed her chin. "Tell us where Eliza's gold is and we'll let you go," he hissed.

She tried to form words through her chattering teeth but couldn't.

Henry's fingers squeezed tighter. "Do you know where it is?"

Maddy managed to shake her head no. Henry backed away and nodded at the brothers. They grinned with pleasure just before they picked her up and slammed her into the trough.

Somehow, at that moment, peace rained down on her and filled her entire being with an unexplainable warmth.

Then, everything went black.

CHAPTER THIRTY

Silas heard the screams of Ollie and Anabel before they reached the barn door. Both he and Luke rushed outside to intercept the terrified children. They rushed into his outstretched arms, bawling so hard he could barely make out a syllable. The fact that Maddy wasn't with them sent a rush of panic through him.

"Shhh… What is it? Where's your ma?"

Ollie choked on his words trying to get them out. "H…he took her! S…Sam Potter! He took her, Pa! He took her!" Ollie wailed.

Silas shot to his feet. "We need to move fast!" He covered his eyes for a moment trying to come up with a plan. Then he groped for Luke, grabbed him by the collar, and lowered his voice. "I've got to get to her as fast as I can." He turned to pull his children into his arms. "Listen to me, Ollie and Anabel. I'm going to help your ma. But I'm sending you two to Sister Martha. You stay with her until we come back. Do you understand?"

They both nodded their agreement amidst their sobs.

Silas continued, "Luke will drive you to the Richards',

then he and some others will come out to help me." He glanced up at Luke who nodded in answer. Then he held Ollie's face in one hand and Anabel's in the other as he went on. "You will probably have to spend the night. Don't worry about me. This won't be the first time I've dealt with scoundrels like the Potters."

He stood, moving his hands to his kids' heads. "Luke, take them to Martha and explain as fast as possible. Get Frank and your pa to come out and join me. I'll be in the woods on the south side of the Potter house. But before you come, find someone with a fast horse to ride to Springfield to get Jonathan Monroe. He'll gather a posse to head to Potters'. Hopefully we can take care of them once and for all."

Silas turned to head to the house, dragging the kids with him. "I'll give you a note with Jon's address. This is extremely important." He ran into the house and started writing. He thrust the note into Luke's hand. "Do you know who you'll send?"

Luke stuffed the note in his pocket. "Yeah. If our neighbors the Donaldsons, are home, I'll send one of them. They have a couple of really fast horses." He paused at the door. "Silas, this will take time. By the time I drop the kids off, get this message to the Donaldsons, get my pa and Frank and head out to join you, it'll probably be dark."

Silas was out the door with Luke on his heels when he answered, "I know. Just hurry as fast as you can."

Silas saddled his horse then went back into the house to get his Remington six-shot revolver and his Spencer rifle and ammo. The Spencer held seven cartridges, so between the two, he could get off thirteen quick shots without having to reload.

Luke was still harnessing Maud to the wagon when Silas flew into the saddle and rode fast to Maddy's place. He knew the path that cut through her property was the fastest and probably the safest way to get there. His gut clenched with dread at what the Potters had planned for his Maddy. What they might have already done. He just had to get there in time. In time to save her from who knows what abuse. Or death.

The little bit of snow that had fallen actually made the path easier to see as it wound through the field and up through the woods scattered with ledges and loose rock. All the way he prayed, begging God to protect Maddy and to guide his every step. He approached the house and barn from the east then curved into the mature woods to the south. Here, there were big, thick trees he could hide behind while still able to see the house.

It was quiet. Eerily quiet. Silas tied his horse to a tree and snuck from tree to tree, trying to get as close as possible. If he had a chance to shoot one of them, he'd do it in a heartbeat. But not until he knew Maddy was away from the second brother. He would need the cover of darkness to get closer to the house. In the meantime, he had to deal with the torture of not knowing what was happening.

Two saddled horses were still in the barnyard. Someone had left them there in a hurry. He crept closer to the house, stopping every few seconds to listen. Finally, he heard the low rumble of men's voices. Lanterns were on in what appeared to be the kitchen. He prayed for darkness to fall. He could barely make out the shadows of people moving in the kitchen, but he couldn't see how many or what they were doing. Thank God there were no dogs prowling about.

Sweat rolled down his back in spite of the cold temperature. Snow continued to fall in fat, lazy flakes, barely covering the ground. He would prefer no snow. He could stay hidden against a dark background far easier than a snowy-white ground.

He cocked his rifle and aimed it at the window, trying desperately to beat down the regret that filled him. The regret of pushing Maddy away. The regret of not trusting her. The regret of not expressing his love. He raked his hand over his face. Later he'd deal with it. Now was not the time. He had to be fully focused.

A large form moved in front of the window. What careless fools! Surely, they'd know he'd be coming. He pulled his rifle up and took careful aim. Darkness slowly settled around him. The man moved from the window. What was happening in there? And where was Maddy? The suspense threatened to undo him. Wiping his brow, he stared and listened. He saw a lantern move into the next room and heard angry voices. This was as good a time as any to move in closer. Step by careful step, he moved from behind a thick tree and made his way to a bush very close to the kitchen window. The voices grew louder. And angrier. Then he almost fell backward with the unexpected shot of a gun.

What in blue blazes was happening in there? Had they shot Maddy? Fear almost paralyzed him. He took in great gulps of cold air. Quickly he moved to the window of the kitchen and raised his head just enough to peer through a corner. There lay his Maddy on the floor. Her clothes were soaked and caked with mud. No one else seemed to be in the room. How he desperately longed to rush to her side, but he knew that would be a foolish, possibly deadly move. She was completely limp. Was she alive?

Then he clearly heard angry, explosive words coming from the next room. "What have you done?" Nate's voice screeched.

Sam's response was too low for Silas to understand. He shuffled to the next window, careful to stay in a low crouch. Angry, loud voices reached his ears.

"He was gettin' far too pushy, in case ya hadn't noticed." That was clearly Sam's voice.

Who in tarnation were they talking about?

"But did ya haf ta kill him?"

"No one comes into my house and starts givin' me orders. He was treatin' both of us like his slaves and I'm not takin' that from no one. Ya hear?"

Silas raised his head in time to see Nate kick a man's body. "Well, we better get his carcass out a here before someone comes lookin' fer him."

"No one's gonna be lookin' fer this piece a trash unless it's the law. Drag him out to the south woods and dump him in the ravine. Then put his horse in the barn," Sam ordered. "In the meantime, I'll see what I can do to doctor Miss Malone back to health." He chuckled and rubbed his hands together.

In spite of the dire circumstances, relief flooded through him. Maddy was alive! Thank God!

Silas had to work fast. He knew he could sneak up on Nate and take care of him with a blow to the head while he was preoccupied with dragging a dead body. Then he could quickly get back to the kitchen window and shoot Sam. He had to do it in that order. As much as he hated leaving Maddy alone with Sam for even one more second.

He squeezed between the bush and the house and watched for Nate to exit through the front door. Agony for Maddy's safety ate at his gut. He had to focus. This was no time for a careless move. He planned to use the butt of his rifle. He'd be more than happy to shoot Nate instead, but he had to be as silent as possible. If Sam was alerted to any trouble, he would undoubtedly use Maddy as a hostage.

What was taking Nate so long? Silas heard Sam talking to someone in the kitchen. He didn't want to know what Sam was doing. He couldn't afford the distraction. Four years of war had taught him many things and this was one of them.

Finally, Nate backed through the door, dragging the body by its feet. Down the porch steps he went letting the heavy head bang on every step. Across the yard to the corner of the corral, huffing and puffing with the effort. As soon as he rounded the corner and made his way to the back side of the barn, Silas moved to the nearest tree. Then the next and the next, always aware of his visibility from both the barn and the house. Shadows were his friends. Again, he thanked God there were no dogs on the property. When he got to the barnyard fence, he used it for cover, no longer worried about Sam spotting him. Nate was easy to find from the groaning of every hard yank of the heavy body across the soft muddy ground. Snow was still drifting down and slowly accumulating on the grass and bushes but not on the wet areas.

Silas moved from tree to tree every time he saw Nate look away. He veered around a thicket of bushes, raised his rifle to strike, and moved in fast. The crack of rifle butt to Nate's head was satisfyingly loud. Nate went down like a dead man. Silas ran his hands over Nate's clothes looking for weapons. He pulled a revolver and a knife from his trouser pockets and threw them into the middle of the thicket. Then he turned and sprinted to the house, rifle cocked and ready.

Aware that Sam might have his guard up, Silas was careful to keep out of sight of the windows. Especially the kitchen window which was the only one with a lantern burning. Clouds covered the moon and the darkness was deep. From tree to tree to bush, as before, and soon he was pressed up against the side of the house. He listened. Sam was humming and moving around, clattering a dish or two as if he were preparing food. Silas dared to raise himself up enough to get a look. Maddy hadn't moved. Sam was picking a kettle up off the stove with his back to the window.

Silas decided now was as good a time as any to make a move. He would be taking a risk, but he realized anything he did in his rescue attempts would be risky. With one lightning-quick motion, he rammed the barrel of his rifle into the glass to break it then shot at Sam. Sam dropped with a roar, clutching his chest. Silas kept his gun trained on Sam's head, waiting. When he saw Sam's hand inching toward his holster, he shot his hand.

Sam writhed in agony. "Stop! No more! I give up!" A pool of blood started to form where he lay.

Not willing to take his eyes off the scoundrel, Silas used his rifle to break all the glass out of the window. He picked the shards out of the bottom of the frame then hoisted himself up and over the sill. With his gun still trained on Sam, he moved to Maddy's side. Thank God she was breathing. But her skin was as cold as ice and her lips were blue. Her hair was spread out across the floor, framing her delicate face.

Silas reached down and gently cupped her head. "Oh, Maddy. What have they done to you?" He bent and kissed her blue lips. "I'm here, honey. You're safe now. It's over. We're gonna go home." Then he quickly withdrew his hand from her hair. Hot sticky blood covered his fingers. He touched her head again and found a gash, swollen and still bleeding.

He jumped to his feet and studied Sam who lay panting in a pool of blood. He wouldn't put it past him to find some way to attack. Pulling his revolver out, he stepped over to the man and nudged him with the toe of his boot. "Get up!"

Sam pushed with his good hand against the floor and managed to sit with his back against a heavy table. He cradled his wounded hand and stared at Silas with hatred. Silas looked around the room for a rope or anything he could use to bind Sam's hands. He yanked an old dirty curtain from the window then used it to tie Sam's arms behind him. Another curtain was enough to tie him to the table. Finally, Silas was free to tend to Maddy.

First, he had to get her out of her wet clothes. What had they done to her? He fumed inside. Although she was his wife, he hesitated before he removed her dress. He'd never seen her undressed. That thought shamed him. He quickly unbuttoned the bodice and slipped it off one shoulder. Then from the corner of his eye, he saw Sam watching them. He wished he'd killed him. He grabbed his revolver, marched over to him, and knocked him out cold.

A quick search through the upstairs produced a couple of blankets. He quickly stripped Maddy's wet clothing off and wrapped her in the blankets. Then he added wood to the fire, picked her up, and sat next to the heat, holding her tight in his arms.

The front door opened. Soon Frank, Pete, and Luke stood in the living room doorway. The relief Silas felt at that moment almost brought him to tears. Frank spoke first. "We found a couple of varmints in the woods. One was dead and the other was out cold. We tied him up and brought him here."

Luke's eyes shone with excitement. "He's out there on my horse."

"Is everything alright here?" Pete walked over and nudged Sam with his foot.

Frank rushed over to Silas. "Maddy? Is she…?"

"She's alive but unconscious. We need to get a doctor. Pronto."

Frank looked over at her dress lying in a heap on the floor. Fear filled his face as he looked at Silas.

"I think I got here in time, Frank. I had to get her out of her wet clothes. She was freezing. Poor girl."

Pete moved to the door. I'll see if they have a wagon we can use to move Maddy out of here. She doesn't look like she's in any shape to ride a horse."

Soon, the four of them carried Maddy to an old but serviceable wagon. Silas insisted on riding in the back with her while Frank drove. They made a beeline for Richards' house. Luke and his pa stayed to keep watch over the two Potters until Jonathan arrived to arrest them.

Silas cradled Maddy's head and spoke softly to her all the way. Snow continued to drift down. Silas kept brushing it off his bride. She seemed to rouse enough to start shivering, which was a good sign. A few times she groaned, but she never seemed to break into consciousness. Silas prayed aloud. Oh, how he prayed. Frank soon joined him.

When they finally reached their destination, Martha swooped down the steps. "Thank you, Lord!" Tears sprang to her eyes as soon as she saw Maddy. "Shhhh…. Don't wake the children. They've been through enough. They don't need to see her like this. Take her into our room."

Silas happily surrendered his Maddy to Martha. She worked her magic on the girl while her husband rode to Fair Grove to get the doctor.

CHAPTER THIRTY-ONE

Silas pitched a forkful of hay into the sheep pen then stabbed the tines into the dirt of the barn floor. Using a sleeve, he wiped sweat out of his eyes and looked heavenward for the umpteenth time that morning. It had been three days. When would his Maddy wake up? Would she ever? And if she did wake up, would she ever fully recover from her injuries? The gash on her head was deep and wide. Her shoulder had been dislocated and several ribs broken in addition to cuts and bruises all over her body. Doc Jensen said she looked like she'd been dragged as well as beaten. Perhaps she could tell them what happened after she woke. But to ask her to relive those memories would be cruel. The waiting and the unknowing was agony. He had so much to say to her. Would he ever get the chance?

When he stepped out to greet the rising sun, a fine mist coated his face. The drone of Luke's deep voice continued in the barn as he sweet-talked the cows he was milking. Silas turned to walk to the house through the deep muck in the driveway. In spite of the light coating of snow that had fallen a few days ago, the ground was still soft. It had been like this for weeks. He longed for a hard freeze. He did his best to scrape the dense mud off his boots before he went up the steps to the porch. Stepping inside the house, he was reminded again that Christmas was only two days away. Besides the gifts they'd bought for the kids, he wasn't prepared. He wanted to buy something special for Maddy and they needed to put some thought into their Christmas meal, if he wanted to make it special for Ollie and Anabel. But what would Christmas be without Maddy?

In the corner of the living room stood a tree that Jonathan and Eliza had brought for them. The day after Maddy was rescued, they both paid him a visit. The information they brought with them had been a huge relief. Both Sam and Nate were locked up and awaiting trial. Based on evidence gathered over the past year, they would either be hanged or put behind bars for a very long time. The most surprising piece of information was the identity of the man that the Potters had murdered. It was Henry Goodman, the same man that was after Eliza's gold. Never again would he pose a threat to her or her loved ones.

Silas walked over to the tree and ran his hands over the needles, releasing their fragrance into the air. He shut his eyes and begged God again to heal his wife. A strange stillness filled the room. Silas' begging stopped.

Be still...and know that I am God... For a long moment, Silas stood in awe. He basked in the Presence of The Holy One. After a few minutes, he turned and looked around. Without a doubt, Jesus was there. Peace covered him like a warm quilt.

And then he knew. He knew with complete certainty that no matter what happened, all would be well.

Maddy opened her eyes and looked around an

unfamiliar room. Where was she? Matching ruffled curtains hung in two windows. The bed she lay on was luxuriously soft and smelled of something vaguely familiar. A smell she loved but wasn't sure why. She was clad in a soft, blue flannel nightgown. But her head pounded with unrelenting pain. And not just her head. She lay still and took stock of her body. Things weren't right. Her shoulder throbbed. And every breath sent a searing pain through her side. In fact, every square inch of her body hurt. *What is going on?*

The door creaked open. Big eyes in a tiny face peered around the edge. *Anabel! Dear sweet Anabel.* Maddy smiled past the pain and reached her hand out to greet her girl.

"Ma?" came a quiet, timid voice.

"Yes, sweetheart?"

Anabel took two more steps into the room. "Are you awake?"

"Yes, I am. Come on over here so I can give you a hug." Maddy threw the blankets aside and tried to sit up. She fell back with a groan. Everything in her body hurt, but the pain in her side almost made her pass out. She lay panting on her back. Reaching up to her throbbing head, she discovered it was wrapped in bandages.

"She's awake! She's awake!" Anabel exited, leaving the bedroom door wide open and ran with pounding steps down a short hallway. Maddy began to recognize where she was and she hoped she was right. Soon, her suspicions were confirmed when Martha rounded a corner and almost ran toward her.

"Oh my, dear girl! You can't get up!" Martha clucked and scolded as she raised Maddy's legs back onto the bed and covered her. "Doctor's orders, you know. We have to do what he says or he'll skin us alive."

Martha's cool hand on Maddy's forehead felt heavenly. She groaned. "Martha, why am I here?"

Martha sat on the edge of the bed and dipped a cloth into

a wash basin of cold water. "You've been injured, my poor lamb." She proceeded to dab at Maddy's cheeks and neck with the cold cloth. "Do you remember anything, Maddy?"

The bed creaked and sunk a little lower as Anabel climbed up on Maddy's other side. Maddy wrapped an arm around her and squeezed. All of a sudden, she stiffened and tried to sit up. "Anabel, did you and Ollie…" She looked frantically around the room. "Ollie! Where's Ollie?"

Martha pressed her back against the pillow. "Ollie is fine. He's out doing chores with Frank."

Maddy pressed her hand against her chest and breathed heaving breaths. Panic threatened to choke her.

"Shhh…. It's all over, Maddy. The Potters are in jail. They can't hurt you."

Confusion clouded her brain. "In jail?"

Maddy looked from side to side as she clung to her daughter. Her breathing slowed. "Anabel, did you and Ollie get away?"

Big tears formed in Anabel's eyes. "Yeah, Ma. We ran down the road to Pa."

Maddy shut her eyes in relief. "Oh, thank God," she breathed.

"And Luke brung us here to Sister Martha." Anabel's tears slipped out as she clenched Maddy's hand with more force. "And…and we waited and waited fer Pa to get you."

Maddy pulled Anabel forward and pressed the girl's tiny, warm hand to her cheek. "It's alright now, baby. I'm here and those bad men are gone." A choking sob escaped in spite of her efforts to sound confident. She reached a hand up to brush Anabel's wispy, soft hair out of her face. "And I never have to worry again about what they might do."

Martha turned at the sound of the front door opening. "That must be Frank. We need to get word to Silas that you're awake. He's been beside himself."

Ollie's usual happy chatter drifted down the hallway.

Anabel scooted off the bed and ran out of the room. "Ollie! Ollie! Ma woke up!" Soon, both kids raced around the corner and down the short hall.

Martha and Frank rushed in behind them, Martha scolding all the way. "Don't jostle yer ma! She's still hurtin' all over her poor body. It'll probly take days o' healin' before she can even get up."

Maddy winced as she reached both arms out to greet her boy. "Come here, Ollie."

He stepped into her embrace and broke down. "Ma!" was all he could say.

Frank stepped up beside them, and soon, all five of them were wrapped up in each other's arms. Frank's gentle eyes studied her, silently assessing her pain. Her eyes locked with his and they exchanged smiles. He stepped back, wiped his eyes, and said, "Well, I think I better skedaddle on to your place, Maddy. There's a lovesick man there that's just about to go crazy worrying about you."

Silas flicked the reins over Maud's back, breaking her into a trot. The wagon veered from side to side as it was pulled through the wet ruts. A light rain continued to fall, coating trees, bushes and fences. Silas shivered. He should have grabbed his heavier coat. The temperature seemed to be plummeting. Soon, in the midst of the mist, he saw a few giant flakes of snow float slowly to the ground. It was beautiful. He never tired of the variety of God's creation. The sky. The weather. The trees and fields. All were constantly changing and all of it was beautiful.

Silas chuckled. He realized that Maddy's love of life was rubbing off on him. He'd never met anyone that paid such close attention to nature. Everything seemed to delight her, and she had a wonderful habit of turning that delight into praise. Into worship. He caught himself doing the same.

Bring her back to us, Lord. I want my children to be raised by that woman. What life, what wisdom she will impart to them. I want...I want to be her husband, Lord. Please, give me that chance.

He looked up and saw a man approaching on horseback. Approaching fast. Through the thickening snowfall, he recognized Frank. Fear clutched at his chest.

Frank waved as he drew near. When he reined in his horse, he announced loudly, "Maddy's awake, Silas! She's awake!"

Silas stopped Maud and stood up in the wagon. "Is she...? Does she seem okay?"

"Yes." Frank laughed. "She's all there, if that's what you mean. Still in a lot of pain though. It'll take time to heal."

Silas sat down in relief.

"I'd give you my horse so you could get there faster, but I need to ride out to get the doc. He told me to get him as soon as she woke up."

Silas slapped the reins down on Maud. "Get up!" Off he went as fast as the horse was willing to go.

Maddy tried to console a weeping little boy, repeatedly brushing his hair back from his forehead. She was surprised at the depth of his relief. What a frightening experience the whole ordeal had been for him. Ollie refused to leave her bedside; his skinny arm thrown around her neck. Apparently, he had put on a brave front since the day he saw Sam Potter ride off with her. At least, that's what Martha had managed to communicate with her over the sounds of his sobs.

Twice, Martha had tried to get the children to leave the room so Maddy could rest, but both times Ollie clung more tightly. Through his choking sobs, he tried to talk. "Ma. D…did they…?" More sobs. He lifted his head to look at her, tears running down both cheeks and dripping off his chin. "Did they hurt you?"

Maddy wiped his little face and answered, "Only a little, son. But I'll be fine."

He pressed his face into her neck and wept some more. She stroked his back and cooed. "Shhh...Ollie, boy. It's all over. The Potters are gone and they're never coming back."

He raised his head to peer into her eyes. "Honest?"

"Honest." She took his face in her hands. "They hurt a lot of people and now they're in jail. And guess what?"

Ollie sniffed loudly. "What?"

"You helped put them there."

"Huh?"

"You ran to get your pa at just the right time. Your pa got there in time to stop them."

Ollie stared at her, blinking rapidly. Then he burst into tears again and threw himself against her.

Maddy heard a commotion in the kitchen but held tight to her boy. Soon, heavy footsteps pounded down the hallway. She looked up to see a most precious sight. Her Silas' big frame filled the doorway. He looked terrible. "Silas," she whispered and reached out her hand. He was beside her in an instant.

"Maddy," he gushed, tears forming in his eyes.

Ollie turned and threw his arms around his pa. "Pa!" he wailed.

Silas grabbed a chair from the corner of the room and pulled it over next to the bed, never letting go of his boy. He wrapped his arms tightly around him as he sat. Ollie buried his face in his father's chest. Anabel sat on the other side of Maddy, clinging to her hand.

"I'm sorry, Pa," Ollie choked the words out.

"Sorry? Why are you sorry?"

Ollie held fistfuls of his pa's shirt as he pressed his face harder into his chest. "Fer cryin'. Fer bein' a big baby." He hiccupped between words. "And...and fer not stopping Sam."

Silas took the boy's face in his hands and set him back just enough to look him square in the face. "Crying doesn't make you a baby, Ollie. I cried, too. A lot, actually."

Ollie stared. "Really?"

"Really?" He sniffed and wiped his nose on his sleeve.

"Absolutely. And as far as Sam goes. There's no way you could have stopped him. If you had tried, he would have hurt you and maybe hurt Anabel, too. Then who would have come to get me?" Ollie just stared. "You did stop him, you know. It took you and me and Luke and Frank to stop those two."

"I...I did?" Ollie asked, wide-eyed and unbelieving.

"Yes. You are the one that started the whole rescue plan."

"Me, too, Pa?" Anabel asked.

Silas chuckled. "Yes. You, too, little sweet pea."

Ollie scooted down from Silas' lap and turned to Maddy. Tears still flowed freely down his face. "Ma, please don't ever go away again. I was so scared I'd never see you again."

Maddy used her free arm and pulled him in as close as her pain would allow. "Ollie, they're gone. They can't hurt me or take me away ever again. And I never have to worry again about what they might do to you or Anabel." She looked at Silas, hoping he'd get her message.

Silas nodded and took her hand in his. "I have so much I want to say to you, Maddy."

She swallowed, not at all sure what that might be. She didn't dare hope for too much. After all, she had been deceiving the man for months; ever since that day back in September that Sam had threatened to hurt the children.

Martha appeared in the doorway. "Breakfast is ready. I'm going to guess that you haven't eaten, Silas. Come on out and join us. I'll serve Maddy in bed."

Silas stood. "Children, go with Sister Martha. I need to talk to your ma." He turned to Martha. "Thank you for breakfast, Martha. If you don't mind, I'll take mine in here with Maddy." He followed her to the kitchen.

Soon, he reappeared with plates piled high with fried eggs, potatoes, and biscuits. Maddy tried to scoot back in a sitting position but gasped in pain. Silas set the dishes down and rushed to her side.

"Where do you hurt?"

She smiled. "Where do I not hurt would be the better question."

He put his arm around her shoulders and gently helped her sit. Then he propped every pillow he could find behind her back. "How's that?" he whispered near her ear, sending shivers down her spine.

In spite of the pain, she felt fine. Better than fine. The best she'd felt in a really long time. She smiled into his serious, hazel eyes. "That's good. Thank you, Silas."

He kissed her forehead before he rose. That was enough to give her hope that the words to come need not be dreaded. Perhaps she could even hope they'd be the words she had longed to hear.

CHAPTER THIRTY-TWO

Maddy was ravenous. Apparently, she hadn't eaten much during the three days she was unconscious. After scarfing down several bites, she looked up to see Silas laughing silently. "What?" she asked.

"You."

She looked at him with unchewed potatoes still on her tongue. "Me?"

He stabbed a forkful of eggs. "I've never seen you eat like this before."

"Oh." She felt her face warm. Dabbing her mouth with her napkin, she muttered, "Sorry."

"Don't apologize. I love it. It means you're feeling good." He smiled warmly at her. "Keep eating. It'll help you heal." He leaned in close. "And I want you to heal, Maddy."

She smiled into his loving eyes and continued shoveling food in. "If this will bring healing, then who am I to resist?"

Martha's cooking was indescribably good. She finished all the eggs and crispy fried potatoes then started in on the buttery biscuits, followed by hot coffee laced with generous amounts of cream and sugar.

When she was finished, Silas took her plate and set it aside with his. He leaned forward and took her hands in his.

Maddy put her hand up. "Silas, before you say anything, please let me explain a few things."

He sat back and folded his arms.

Maddy looked down at her hands fidgeting with the quilt. She wasn't sure what to say first but she was very worried that she might lose this chance to explain. And it had to be brought to the light as soon as possible. She looked at him with pleading eyes. "First of all, I need for you to know how sorry I am. I kept telling you that I couldn't tell you yet why I came to you that night and…and why I acted so strangely at times. But now I can. Now that the Potters are gone. I've kept things hidden from you and I'm so, so sorry." She looked down again. "Although, if I had it to do over again, I'm not sure I'd do things any different."

Again, her eyes met his, hoping desperately that he'd understand. "Sam Potter was trying to force me marry him and he threatened to hurt Ollie and Anabel if I ever breathed a word to anyone. H…he wanted to add my land to his and he knew about the gold hidden on my property." She paused to drop her head into her hands. "As much as I knew marriage to him would be a living hell, I also knew I'd cooperate with him if it meant protecting my babies."

"You should have told me. They're my babies, too, you know." His voice sounded stern to her hurting soul. But then he leaned forward and took her hand. "If I had known, I would have protected you, Maddy. Didn't you know that?"

"Oh, Silas! I couldn't tell you. Don't you get it? If I had leaked a word to you, Silas, they would have found a way to hurt them. And, given half a chance, they would have killed you. Then Ollie and Anabel wouldn't have a pa."

Then she looked down and added, "Or a ma."

In spite of trying to remain under control, she felt a tear escape. Silas gently cupped her cheek and wiped the tear away. "Maddy…" His voice was husky.

She glanced up at him then down again. "I need to tell you more. That night I came to you was not planned." She chuckled and shrugged. "There was a seed of an idea planted in my head from a Bible story." She looked at him again to gauge his mood. "You know the story of Ruth?"

Silas smiled and nodded.

"Every time I read it, you became my Boaz." She hid her face in her hands. "I'm so ashamed. I acted like a lovesick schoolgirl."

Silas squeezed her hand. "Go on."

"Sam came to me that night. Actually, Nate came first." She lowered her head. "He's more vile than his brother, if that's possible."

"Maddy, did they hurt you?" Silas' voice was soft but tense.

Maddy clenched her eyes shut for a long moment before she answered. "Yes, but not seriously. They shoved me around then…then Sam dragged me down the path. He said we were getting married that night. He had someone waiting at his house that could officiate." Maddy paused to shake her head. She looked at Silas, hoping he would understand what she was about to say next. "Silas, I was terrified. Terrified to the point that I blacked out. When I came to, Sam was carrying me. I knew it was only a matter of time before my life would become an unbearable, irreversible hell. I wanted to die."

"After he put me down, I pretended to cooperate then managed to escape into some thick cedars." She chuckled weakly. "That had to have been the hand of God. It was as if He covered me with His hand so Sam couldn't see me." She let out one big, tired sigh before she continued. "From there, I ran to your place. I didn't know where else to run,

Silas. If I'd gone to my place, they would have found me. I ran to you without thinking. It wasn't until I walked through your back door that I made the decision to copy Ruth's plan." At this point, she couldn't bear to look at him. Her next words came in a whisper. "I was sneaky and deceptive on a colossal level. If you never want to see me again, I will understand."

Silas voice was full of emotion when he finally answered. "Maddy. All I can say is that I am sorry for all that you had to bear alone. I understand that you couldn't tell me, but…"

Just then, there was a knock at the door. Martha peeked her head in. "Sorry to interrupt, but the doctor is here."

Silas stood and pulled the chair back. "Send him in."

Doc Jensen entered with his bag and a smile. "Mrs. MacGregor, I can't tell you how good it is to see your wide-open eyes!"

Maddy made a weak attempt at a smile. Fatigue cloaked her like a heavy blanket. Her explanation to Silas left her emotionally and physically drained. The doctor checked her pulse, listened to her heart, her lungs then pulled her eyelids up to look in her eyes. He changed the dressing on her head. That's when she realized for the first time that a huge section of her head had been shaved. She gasped when her hand explored the area.

"I'm sorry," the doctor said. "It was necessary. You have a sizeable gash here. That's why you were out for so long. It's healing nicely though." He sat down on the chair and looked at her. "At least the surface is healing. I can't be sure about your brain."

He looked up at Silas. "I don't want her leaving this bed for another two days, except to get up to use the chamber pot. Her pupils look normal so I'm hopeful, but…" He turned to look at Maddy again. "Three days is a long time to be unconscious. Without a doubt, there was trauma to the brain. That's why rest is so important."

When he left, Maddy wanted to cry. "Martha told me Christmas is only two days away. I don't want to miss Christmas with you and the children."

"You won't." He looked around the room. "If you can't come home for Christmas, then we'll bring Christmas here to you."

She sank back into her pillows and yawned. "Oh, that would be lovely." In spite of her best efforts, she couldn't keep her eyes focused on Silas. Her eyes drifted shut. He smiled and leaned down to kiss her head. Then she heard him walk out and shut the door.

Throughout that day and the next, she drifted in and out of sleep. Silas was by her side whenever he could get away from the farm. Both Ollie and Anabel would have stayed next to her all day if Martha hadn't ushered them out several times so she could get her rest. "Doctor's orders," Martha said over and over. "If you want yer ma to get well, ya need to let her sleep."

On Christmas Eve, Silas and the children walked in with a small tree. "I told you we'd bring Christmas to you, Maddy. This is just the beginning." He set the tree in a big pot in the corner and told Ollie to go get some water for it. Then he went to Maddy's side and put his big, warm hand on her forehead. "How are you feeling? Have you been resting?"

"That's about all I've been doing. I'm getting a little sick of it."

"Are you up for wrapping some gifts?"

Anabel jumped up at those words. "Gifts? Can I help? Who are they for?"

Ollie walked in and watered the tree.

"Ollie, Pa and Ma are gonna wrap gifts!" Ollie turned around with anticipation written all over his face.

Silas laughed. "Slow down, you two. Your ma and I have gifts to wrap. And you're not allowed to see them. But you rascals are going out to the kitchen to help Martha wrap some gifts for your ma. Remember?"

Silas left and returned with a large cloth sack. Maddy was thrilled when, one by one, he pulled out the gifts they had bought in Springfield. He also produced a roll of brown paper, red ribbon, and scissors. Maddy pushed back and sat upright. He'd thought of everything. This was going to be fun. Silas measured and cut a large square of paper, laid it across the bed, and placed Anabel's dollhouse in the middle. Maddy tried her best to cover the house then burst out laughing. "I think you'll need to cut a piece twice this size!"

Over the next hour, they worked together, hiding each gift in the closet as they finished. Maddy's heart was bursting with joy. Silas had heard her confession and hadn't banned her from his kingdom. And furthermore, it was obvious that he was quite happy with her. She knew he had something he wanted to say, but the perfect opportunity never seemed to come. Every once in a while, he gazed at her with a very serious look, and she was sure he was about to reveal what was on his mind, but invariably a child would crash through the door, or Martha would arrive with more food.

When the last gift was hidden away, Silas turned to her again with that look. Her heart quickened with anticipation, but just then a soft knock was heard at the door. Silas frowned and shook his head in frustration. "I need to talk with you," he said with a pointed look as he opened the door.

Delectable smells from the kitchen drifted in, including that of freshly popped popcorn. Martha stood there with a tray of steaming roast beef and mashed potatoes. "Do you suppose all of us could squeeze in here for a Christmas Eve feast?"

After a scrumptious supper and a hilarious time stringing popcorn for the tree, Martha scooted the children off to bed and left Silas alone with Maddy. Again, her exhaustion made it difficult to focus. She craved time alone with this good man, but she could barely keep her eyes open. She could easily read in his expression that he was ready to have a serious conversation. And then she read his frustration followed by a look of sweet kindness. He ran his hand down her cheek and leaned in for a kiss. It was so soft and brief she wasn't sure it really happened. Then against her deepest desires, her eyes slid shut. She heard a happy sigh come from her man just before the sound of the closing door. *Is that our first kiss?* She wondered happily as she felt herself slip away.

Silas watched Luke ride away early Christmas morning after the two of them had finished their chores. Farms never took a day off, but if a farmer planned carefully, he could manage a few breaks in the middle of special days. Like today. He chose to saddle and ride Clara rather than take the wagon. Soon enough, he'd need the wagon to haul Maddy and the children back home, but today wouldn't be that day.

He put his hand down to check the small package he had shoved deep into the pocket of his coat. It was still there. Just as it had been the last dozen times he had checked. He smiled with anticipation as he trotted south toward the Richards'. He had wanted to do something special for Maddy for Christmas and thanks to Luke and a fast horse, he'd managed to pull it off. Last night while he was enjoying Christmas Eve with his family, Luke had happily fulfilled his mission. Silas knew that Eliza would be happy to help and when he saw Luke just before he went to bed last night, he found that he was right. The tiny gift that Luke put in his hands was better than he'd dared hope for.

Again, he patted his pocket to make sure it hadn't somehow hopped out.

When he walked into the Richards' kitchen, he was greeted by two ecstatic children. "He's here! Pa's here!" They dragged him down the hall to Maddy's bedside before he could remove his coat. "Now we can do Christmas!" Both kids shrieked with excitement. Maddy's eyes were dancing. Warmth flooded his soul. What could possibly be better than this?

He glanced at the tree to see that the only gifts were those wrapped by the children. "Wait just a second there, Ollie and Anabel. Something's not quite right with our tree."

Ollie laughed. "I thought something might be missing."

Silas ruffled his hair and swooped Anabel up into his arms. "What makes you think so?"

"Well," Ollie said slowly. "You and Ma did wrap some presents yesterday and I don't see them anywhere."

Anabel yanked her head around to look. "Yeah, Pa! Where are they?"

Silas set her on the floor. "I want you two to go out to the kitchen and count together to one hundred. Then come back."

They squealed and headed for the door. Silas hollered after them, "Slowly. Count very, very slowly."

Then he got to work unloading gifts and sacks of candy from the closet and placing them under the tree. When he was done, he was rewarded with the precious sight of Maddy sitting on the bed, hands clasped under her chin, and beaming with excitement and joy. Silas opened the door to the sound of, "Thirty, thirty-one, thirty-two..." Rather than tell them they were ready, he pulled the chair up to the bed, took Maddy's hands in his, and said, "Merry Christmas, Mrs. MacGregor."

Those words coming from Silas' mouth warmed Maddy to the depths of her being. *Mrs. MacGregor, indeed.* They spoke a world of meaning to her wounded heart. It could only mean one thing.

Soon, the children burst through the door. Silas stopped them and insisted they listen to the Christmas story from the Gospel of Luke before they opened gifts. He read with his deep voice, sending shivers through her. Then he had them join hands for a prayer.

"God, we give you thanks for the gift of your Son. Let us never take for granted what you did for us with this very special gift. Thank you for your unsearchable love, a love that sent Jesus to die in our place. And thank you for…" At this, Silas squeezed her hand. His voice grew husky and he struggled to complete his prayer. "Thank you for this precious family you've blessed me with. And thank you for bringing Maddy to us. Amen."

Tears streamed down her face on hearing those words. She wiped them away to see three pairs of eyes on her. She laughed and reached out to caress the faces of her children. "These are happy tears, my little ones. I don't think I've ever had a Christmas as happy as this one." She gazed into each of their faces and then at Silas. "And it's because of you three. I love you all so much."

After hugs and more declarations of love, they opened gifts. The delightful hollers and squeals of the children told Maddy that she and Silas had chosen wisely. Then they placed two crudely but beautifully wrapped gifts in Maddy's lap, one from each child. Her heart melted even before she knew what was in them. Ollie's was a heart carved from wood.

"Ollie! This is amazing! Where did you find something so beautiful?"

"I carved it myself, Ma! Luke taught me!"

Maddy gathered him to her side and nuzzled his neck. "Thank you so much, sweetheart. I will treasure this forever."

Then she opened Anabel's gift. It was the heart-shaped stone that she had picked up at the river. Someone had wrapped it in wire and hung it from a silver chain. Anabel cuddled up against Maddy's side and wiggled with pleasure. "Pa helped me make it, Ma. But I found the stone all by myself. Remember? You were with me."

"Oh, Anabel. Yes, I remember. What a special day that was. I'll never forget." She glanced at Silas and laughed. After kissing the little girl's forehead, she unclasped the necklace and fastened it around her neck. Oh, how good that simple stone heart felt against her chest. "I'll wear this forever, honey." She smoothed Anabel's unruly hair out of her face.

Then she looked at Silas. "The day Anabel found this stone, I was at one of my lowest points and Martha, in her infinite wisdom, suggested I read the Book of Ruth. I had no idea why at the time. But now...now, I'm pretty sure I know what she was up to." Holding the stone out so she could see it, she smiled. "This will always remind me of the unexpected and often strange ways God will intervene when things seem hopeless."

A soft knock at the door interrupted Anabel's story of how she and Silas wrapped the stone carefully in wire. Martha peeked her head in. "I'm so sorry to barge in on your Christmas, but I have your breakfast ready."

"Martha, come in. You have been so patient and so kind to me. Thank you." Maddy beckoned her to enter.

Silas stood. "She's right, Martha. We owe Maddy's healing to you, your home, and your food. I don't think we can ever repay you."

Martha's hand flew to her ample bosom. "Repay me? That's ridiculous. This is what family does for their own.

And, in case you haven't realized it yet, we consider you our own."

At that moment, Silas surprised her with a giant hug and a kiss on her cheek. "It's an honor," he said.

Smiling and shaking her head, she asked if they wanted breakfast in the kitchen or in the bedroom. Before Silas could answer, both children were giggling down the hallway, each carrying one of their gifts.

"Serve the children in the kitchen." Silas started down the hall behind them. "I'll get our food and eat it in the bedroom with Maddy. I have a lot I want to say to her and somehow, I haven't been able to squeeze a word in since she woke up."

In a few minutes, he came back to her with another scrumptious breakfast, this time with fat, steaming cinnamon rolls added to the tray. Maddy drooled at the smell. Silas had a grin a mile wide as he set the food down just out of her reach. He walked over to his coat hanging in the corner and plunged his hand deep into the pocket. Then he turned and walked toward her holding a tiny package.

"This is my gift to you, Maddy." He handed it to her then stepped back. She studied his face for a clue. What was going on? He was blushing! Never had she seen him look so uncomfortable, so uncertain.

"Silas? Are you alright?" she asked in a whisper.

"Just open it."

So, she did. The box inside the wrapping was tiny and lidded. When she opened the lid, she gasped. Inside was an intricately beautiful ring with a tiny topaz in the center of a silver heart. Silas had dropped to his knees next to her bed. He reached for her hand and the box. Carefully he removed the ring. "Maddy, would you do me the honor of becoming my wife? To truly be Mrs. Silas MacGregor?"

She couldn't speak. She merely stared at the face of the man she had loved for so long.

"Maddy?" His expression threatened to undo her. "I will

understand if you say no. I've been unbearable." He swallowed and looked at their clasped hands. "But, Maddy, I love you." He looked up at her, tears in his eyes. "So very much, Maddy. I've loved you for a very long time, long before you crawled into my bed." He chuckled weakly. "I am so grateful to God that you came to me that night. I can't imagine my life without you. You…you…"

"Yes!" Maddy almost shouted. "Yes, I'll marry you, Silas MacGregor!" With that, she reached out with both hands, grabbed his neck, and pulled him in for a kiss. A long slow kiss that he gladly returned.

ABOUT THE AUTHOR

Ava MacKinney formerly taught American history and Art. She is a lover of the outdoors, artist, history buff, blogger (thecrazycrookedpath.com), mother to five, grandmother to nine and wife to her amazing husband, Steve. They enjoy life on their small farm in the Ozarks, surrounded by dogs, cats and endless wildlife. Raised on a sheep farm in the mountains of Vermont, her parents gave her free reign to explore and to dream. Today she delights in dreaming up stories filled with adventure, romance, and spiritual growth.

If you'd like to follow Ava on Instagram, go to @avamackinney

On Facebook, go to her page, The Crazy Crooked Path.

Website: thecrazycrookedpath.com

If you enjoyed Maddy Malone...

You will also enjoy the other two books in this series. Two of Maddy's childhood friends, Eliza and Megan, experienced their own adventures during and after The Civil War.
I can't begin to tell you what a fun adventure it was for me to get their stories out of my brain and into print. Dig in and enjoy.

Eliza Long (Book 1)
Available now through Amazon, Barnes and Noble and other book distributers

The War Between the States hits southwest Missouri in August, 1861, with all the ugliness and horrors of war in the homeland.

Eliza is consumed by the need to avenge her father's death. Presented with the opportunity to be involved in espionage, she foolishly says yes and is catapulted into a world of lies, play-acting and danger.

Lieutenant Jonathan Monroe is furious when he discovers her occupation. Before Eliza's father went to battle, he charged Jonathan with the job of protecting his daughter. It was an easy job to accept, since Jonathan had known and loved little Eliza since she was a baby. Against his better judgement, his feelings for her evolve from his guardian role to one of strong romantic attraction.

Will Eliza listen to reason when Jonathan begs her to stop spying? Will she be able to overcome the driving force of her anger and hatred? Anger that also extends toward God. In a pivotal moment she is faced with an unexpected choice. What will her answer be?

Megan O'Mally (Book 3)

To be released in late 2023

Megan, desperate to flee scandalous rumors, leaves her teaching job in St. Louis and joins her sister's family on a wagon train headed to Oregon. Her encounters with fellow travelers challenge her and help her receive God's forgiveness.

The wagon master, Nick Webster, is the biggest challenge of all. Will they resolve their continuous conflicts and grow to trust each other? Especially when the rumors catch up to her?

What Readers are Saying About **Eliza Long**
(Amazon reviews and personal comments to the author)

-A great work of historical fiction! It had me from beginning to end. Now I'm anxiously anticipating the next book!

-What a fun read! I read it all in one night and stayed up way too late. Engaging storyline and I loved all the history about Springfield, Missouri, where I used to live. There was so much I didn't know. Nice to read a good fiction book for adults and not feel nervous about the content... Super clean but still engaging and real. I am excited for the next books to come out!

-If you enjoy an adventurous story, that's difficult to put down, then the book "Eliza Long" is for you. From the first to last page, it holds your attention. This historical fiction book, that is set during the "War Between the States" has characters that are full of emotions, faith & suspense. Ava MacKinney is an excellent writer & I can't want for her second book to be released.

-I'm really enjoying this book! I'm halfway through and only received it yesterday! I like Eliza's personality and the fire in her, also really enjoyed the portrayal of the time period! Makes me travel back in time every time I open the book. Good job Author!

-Loved it - the characters, the story, the history, and the romance. I was able to get a pre-publication copy of Maddy Malone as a beta reader and I love it even more than this one. I also was a beta reader of the third book in the series (Megan O'Mally) and love it as well - more humor and more variety in the story.

-I JUST finished this book! Read it in less than 24hrs! I loved it!! Excellent story! Deeply engaging! Fun read! Since I live in the area it was even more intriguing. Can't wait for the next one!!!!!

-Well written, great story, and historically accurate!

-This book has a great storyline and is well written. You can tell the author studied the history and area. Buy this book!

-Loved, loved your book! I read it in 2 days! Couldn't put it down!

-I read your book this week and LOVED it! Excellent writing, gripping story, history of Springfield that I didn't know - what's not to love? THANKS!

-Your first book was super engaging... I read it all in one night! I'm excited to read the next one. Way to go!

-I am reading your book!! Wow and wow!!! I am impressed. The book starts out with a bang. There is no good place to stop. So much going on. I can't put it down. I love the historical setting. You are an amazing writer and I do read mostly historical novels.

-It was so enjoyable to read your book, **Eliza Long.** You truly wrote a great book and I didn't want to put it down to get something else done. I am looking forward to your next book and next book and next book!!

Printed in Great Britain
by Amazon

44231064R00162